"I'm a very good driver," she'd said.

"I won't hurt your

He didn't suppose
might be concerned
could have refused her, but Steen knew enough
about stubborn women to realize she'd probably
have started out on foot if he'd denied her his car.
Wordlessly, he'd handed her the keys and watched
her leave.

Beautiful, determined, unyielding. Maybe he
shouldn't have let her go. What if she lost control of
the Jeep and got hurt? What if...

Something was clumping onto his wooden porch. Or
someone.

Jumping up, trying to hide a know-it-all grin, Steen
went to the door and pulled it open.

Wet and bedraggled, Frankie looked up at him.
"Don't say a word, not one. I *hate* smug men."

Dear Reader,

Welcome to the Silhouette **Special Edition** experience! With your search for consistently satisfying reading in mind, every month the authors and editors of Silhouette **Special Edition** aim to offer you a stimulating blend of deep emotions and high romance.

The name Silhouette **Special Edition** and the distinctive arch on the cover represent a commitment—a commitment to bring you six sensitive, substantial novels each month. In the pages of a Silhouette **Special Edition**, compelling true-to-life characters face riveting emotional issues—and come out winners. All the authors in the series strive for depth, vividness and warmth in writing these stories of living and loving in today's world.

The result, we hope, is romance you can believe in. Deeply emotional, richly romantic, infinitely rewarding—that's the Silhouette **Special Edition** experience. Come share it with us—six times a month!

From all the authors and editors of Silhouette **Special Edition**,

Best wishes,

Leslie Kazanjian,
Senior Editor

PAT WARREN
Winter Wishes

Silhouette Special Edition
Published by Silhouette Books New York
America's Publisher of Contemporary Romance

To Mary Lou Peres,
a fellow Gemini survivor,
for a very special friendship

SILHOUETTE BOOKS
300 East 42nd St., New York, N.Y. 10017

ISBN: 0-373-09632-1

First Silhouette Books printing November 1990

Printed in the U.S.A.

Books by Pat Warren

Silhouette Special Edition

With This Ring #375
Final Verdict #410
Look Homeward, Love #442
Summer Shadows #458
The Evolution of Adam #480
Build Me a Dream #514
The Long Road Home #548
The Lyon and the Lamb #582
My First Love, My Last #610
Winter Wishes #632

Silhouette Romance

Season of the Heart #553

Silhouette Intimate Moments

Perfect Strangers #288

PAT WARREN,

the mother of four, lives in Arizona with her travel-agent husband and a lazy white cat. She's a former newspaper columnist whose lifetime dream was to become a novelist. A strong romantic streak, a sense of humor and a keen interest in developing relationships led her to try romance novels, with which she feels very much at home.

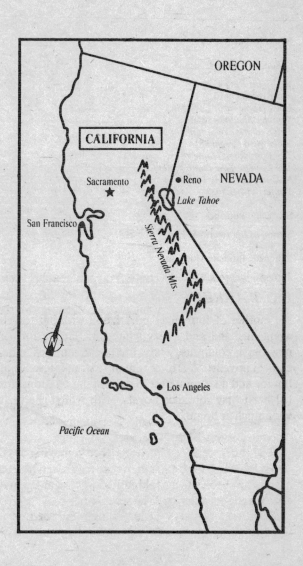

Chapter One

The snow was really coming down. Frankie Taelor peered through the front window of the big bus as it crept along the slippery highway. Clutching the armrest of the front seat behind the driver, she frowned as she watched the sluggish windshield blades try to keep up with the heavy snowfall. If only the storm would let up just a little. She simply had to get to Lake Tahoe today.

Frankie leaned toward the driver. "How we doing?" She hadn't meant to sound impatient and worried, though she was both.

The burly, red-faced driver risked removing a hand from the wheel long enough to take a quick swipe at his damp forehead, never taking his eyes from the road. "Not bad, considering," he ventured.

That told her very little. Frankie frowned as she studied the gray sky. At this point Highway 50 was down to two lanes with very few cars sharing the road with them. Most people were safe and warm inside somewhere. Frankie fervently wished she were. "How far are we from Tahoe?"

"Miles or hours?" he asked.

"Hours, I guess."

The driver shook his balding head. "Can't rightly tell."

When she'd flown out of San Francisco this morning, it had been cool but sunny, a typical December day for the City by the Bay. But the pilot had warned them when they'd touched down in Sacramento where it was already snowing that a winter storm could be seen on the radar screen just north of them. She knew that northern California winter storms could arrive quickly and be fierce in their intensity. Hurrying off the flight, Frankie had hoped this one wouldn't hit until after she'd caught her connection to the Tahoe area. But it wasn't to be. Within half an hour, the snow was falling rapidly and visibility was near zero. The airport closed down and no flights were taking off until further notice.

Feeling a bit desperate, Frankie had dragged her suitcase and joined several other disgruntled passengers in the bus information line. She hadn't been on a bus in years, but she couldn't afford to sit around an airport indefinitely. She had a job to do, people depending on her. Though she'd had to run to make it, she'd gotten one of the last available seats heading north, leaving her with not even enough time to phone ahead. She'd be much later than she'd promised, but at least she was once more under way.

The bus from Sacramento to Lake Tahoe had turned out to be a local, like a milk train run, stopping every twenty minutes at some small junction to let out passengers eagerly rushing home for the holidays. Despite the delay and the questionable weather, the people on board were in a festive mood, chattering with anticipation as they clutched shopping bags filled with colorful packages. The endless Christmas carols playing throughout the bus had gotten on Frankie's nerves as she'd gazed out the foggy window and watched the snowfall mount. With a pang of envy she seldom gave in to, Frankie listened to her seatmates sing along.

On a normal day, the express bus would take no more than two hours to make this run, the girl at the counter had said. And yet, well into the third hour, they were scarcely halfway there. But the week before Christmas could hardly be considered normal.

Bah humbug! Frankie had thought. She'd almost said it aloud.

For another hour, she'd watched the passengers, giddy with relief at their safe arrival, cautiously climb down the slippery bus steps and go their way. Now she and the man stretched out in the double seat across the aisle were the only two left. He'd been asleep almost from the moment they'd pulled away from the terminal. He was either exhausted or possessed that enviable ability of being able to sleep wherever and whenever.

Frankie felt the bus begin to slide to the right on the slick road, then ease back into the lane as the driver got it under control again. How could the man across the aisle sleep through this? she wondered. Another lurch of the bus and he slowly straightened in his seat. She thought it was about time he woke and helped her co-navigate. Obviously the driver needed all the help he could get.

Clearing his throat, the man sat up and ran a hand through his hair as he squinted toward the driver. "Feels like she's pulling to the right," he commented calmly.

"Yeah. Soon's I can, I'm going to stop and have a look."

Oh, no! That was all they needed right now, Frankie thought. A mechanical problem. She heard the brakes wheeze as the driver tapped them.

"Think you got a problem with the steering column?" the man asked.

"Don't know," the driver answered as he aimed the bus toward a wide easement up ahead.

Frankie wished they'd quit conjecturing aloud—it only deepened her fears. She turned to study the man across the aisle. Her first impression was that he looked like a gunfighter who might have lived on a Texas ranch back in the days of cowboys and Indians. He had a ruddy outdoors complexion and a square chin. His eyes as he sent her a quick glance were clear gray and quietly assessing. His hair was thick and curly, as if he hadn't bothered to visit his barber in a while. He was long limbed and rangy, his voice carrying a hint of a drawl. Sturdy, hand-tooled leather boots were on his feet and he wore faded jeans, topped by a heavy sheepskin jacket over a plaid flannel shirt. Only the broadbrimmed western hat was missing.

At least he was dressed for the weather, Frankie thought as she tightened the belt of her raincoat. As a concession to the probability of colder weather at her destination city, she'd zipped in the lining this morning, but realized how otherwise ill-prepared she was to be out in a snowstorm.

Just then, a heavy metal sound ripped through the air and the bus gave a serious lurch. The driver touched the air brakes and they all felt the dragging and scraping of something underneath. Letting out a deep breath, he shifted into park and put on the emergency brake. Turning to face his two passengers, he shook his head. "It don't sound good."

She had to agree. With a sinking heart, Frankie watched the driver shrug into his heavy coat.

Across the aisle, Steen Olson stood, ducking to keep from bumping his head on the overhead storage rack. "I'll go with you," he told the driver as he bent to look out the side window. Fortunately he'd never had trouble waking from a sound sleep and immediately orienting himself. Even now, he recognized the juncture where they'd stopped. They were already in Deer Valley and his cabin was only about two miles up the road.

The driver opened the door, letting in a cold blast of air and a swirl of snowflakes. Steen heard the woman across the aisle make a small, hopeless sound as she sank back in her seat and pulled her coat lapels close around her throat. Her hands in thin leather gloves were none too steady.

He wondered if she was worried that she'd miss meeting up with a husband or boyfriend for the upcoming holiday. She just might, at that. Steen felt sorry for her and gave her an encouraging smile. "Don't worry. It might be fixable." He waited as she raised her anxious gaze to his face. She attempted a smile but didn't quite make it. He followed the driver down the steep stairs. Green eyes. He couldn't remember ever meeting a woman with such green eyes before. Hunching into his collar, he leaned into the wind.

Why couldn't the storm have waited just another day? Frankie moaned to herself. Eric Hanley would be furious. He was counting on her. A few hours late would be bad enough, but now she seriously doubted if she'd get to Tahoe before nightfall, even with extraordinary luck, which so far hadn't been with her. Her delay could cost him a great deal. She simply had to get to Tahoe. She hated disappointing people.

His frantic call had come late yesterday, but then most of her clients knew she seldom stuck to normal work hours. Frankie had dealt with Eric before and knew him to be tough, demanding and impatient. As manager of the casino at Lake Tahoe's Diamond Nugget, she knew he had a great deal riding on this upcoming holiday week and the money that would be gambled in his place. When the security code had somehow gotten jumbled and then jammed, he had to do two things quickly. The first was to close the doors to his casino until the problem was taken care of and the second was to call in an expert computer consultant.

Frankie Taelor was one of three such consultants on the West Coast experienced enough to solve his problem. The other two, Eric had admitted to her, hadn't wanted to be away from their families during the Christmas holidays. Frankie had no such hang-ups. For an outrageous fee, she'd promised him she'd be there by noon the next day.

Frankie didn't particularly care for Eric Hanley. He was arrogant, overconfident and had cold eyes. But he paid her well, very well. She didn't feel it necessary to like her business clients as long as they respected her ability to get the job done. But here she was, at three in the afternoon, stranded on a disabled bus in a snowstorm a mere fifty miles from his casino. Under her breath, she swore at the Fates as she heard the driver stomp back onto the bus.

"Looks like we've got a problem, miss," he said shaking the snow from his hat. "Universal joint snapped. Drive shaft's hanging down clear to the ground."

Yes, that did sound like a problem. "What do we do now?" Frankie asked as the other man came aboard and reached to close the door.

The driver eased his bulky frame into his seat and rubbed his cold hands together. "I'm going to try radioing for assistance. Sooner or later, another bus will pick up my signal and call it into the terminal. Then they'll send a truck to tow us in. Or at least another vehicle to pick us up and haul us to the nearest bus station."

"But that could take hours."

"Sure could," the driver agreed resignedly.

"Don't you have a CB?"

"Nope. Management never had them installed. Too expensive, they told us."

With each reasonable explanation, she felt her hopes die. "Can't you contact the state police somehow?"

"If a patrol car happens along, they'll stop. But don't you worry none. We'll be fine. We can keep her running for quite a while so we'll have heat." He reached alongside his seat. "And I've got a thermos of coffee I'm willing to share."

Frankie took a deep breath. Affability was not what she wanted right now. Action was what she wanted. She leaned forward, putting on her most persuasive look. "I can't wait. I *must* get to Tahoe as soon as possible."

Steen swung his bag from the overhead rack and rested it on the seat as he dug out a pair of heavy gloves from one of the side pockets. He caught the urgency in the woman's voice and turned to study her.

A lady in a big hurry and again he wondered why. Her wheat-blond hair was done up in some sort of a braid at the back of her head and she had on diamond earrings that he'd wager were real. No hat in sight and, though he supposed her coat was very fashionable, it didn't look too warm. Nervously she crossed her long, slim legs and thoughtfully chewed on a thumbnail. Suddenly she turned to stare up at him, her green eyes huge in her small face, making her look young and vulnerable. Just as suddenly, he reached a decision. "You can come with me."

"Where are you going?"

"Home. I live a little ways down the road." He glanced down at her high-heeled shoes. "You got anything else to wear besides those?"

Frankie's mind did a quick inventory of her small overnight bag and she almost groaned aloud. "Just a pair of tennis shoes," she admitted as she peered out the window at the roadbank. There had to be four or five inches' accumulation already and more piling up every minute.

High heels and tennis shoes. Expensive designer ones, no doubt, Steen decided, but pretty damn useless for walking in the snow. Rich didn't always mean smart. "You don't know much about packing for this climate, do you?" He saw quick temper flare in her eyes as she swung back to him.

"I didn't expect to be hiking in a snow storm. I expected the plane from Sacramento to take me to Tahoe, and a cab to take me to my hotel. I have work to do there and it doesn't require boots." This was all she needed, to be questioned by a superior-sounding backwoodsman who thought he had all the answers.

"Got to be prepared for the unexpected."

Frankie rubbed at the spot above her eyes, feeling the beginning of a headache. The radio, still on, sang out with still another version of "Jingle Bells." "Would you *please* turn off those interminable Christmas songs?"

"No use getting testy, miss," the driver answered as he snapped off the radio. Reaching for his thermos, he unscrewed the lid. "Maybe a little coffee will make you feel better."

She took a calming breath, realizing none of this was the driver's fault. "I'm sorry. I'm a little edgy." She saw him nod as he leaned forward to fiddle with the dials, trying to signal another bus. He was obviously settling in for the long haul. It looked like the other man was her only hope.

Again, Frankie looked him over. He looked pleasant enough. A little rough around the edges, but there was a hint of amusement in his eyes. Not the ax murderer type, she mused. "How far is your home from here?" There'd be a phone there. She'd call Eric and he'd send his limo for her. It was only midafternoon. All wasn't lost.

Steen pulled on his gloves. "Not far, about two miles."

Two miles! Could she walk two miles in this snow, even in tennis shoes? Apprehension flooded her. "I...I don't know."

He shrugged as he hefted his bag. "Suit yourself." He reached for the handle that would open the bus door.

"Wait!" Frankie coughed into her fist, buying a little time. Her mind quickly raced through the possibilities and she came back to the same conclusion. He was her only chance and she'd better make up her mind or he'd walk away and leave her here. "It'll just take me a minute to change shoes. I . . . I'd like to go with you."

He nodded as she scrambled to open her bag. Quickly she tucked her pumps inside and laced up her tennis shoes. Aside from her robe and underthings she'd packed a pair of slacks and a jogging suit, but neither would hold up too well outside, even if she could slip out of her wool dress and change into them in the narrow aisle of the bus with two men looking on. No, she'd just have to make the best of things, Frankie thought with a sigh as she tied a scarf around her head.

What was he going to do with her once he got her to his cabin? Steen wondered as he watched her prepare to face the storm. What had gotten into him asking her along and how in hell was she going to walk two miles? She was small and slender and dressed all wrong for the weather.

His cabin was comfortable but far from luxurious. He liked it that way and had been itching to get home for most of the last two days. He'd hightailed it out of L.A. as soon as he'd made his last delivery, anxious for the peaceful surroundings of his Sierra Nevada Mountains. He couldn't help but wonder how the woman zipping her bag shut with short, impatient movements was going to fare in such isolation, especially if the snow continued.

Frankie moved out into the aisle and put on her best attempt at a smile. "I'm ready."

Steen moved to the bottom step, looking back over his shoulder at the woman. "By the way, my name's Steen Olson."

"Frankie Taelor," she said as she settled the wide strap of her bag on her shoulder.

He reached to take it from her. "I think you'd better let me carry that." She hated needing his assistance, but realized it would be difficult enough for her to keep up with him even without the burden of a bag. She handed it to him.

"Frankie? What kind of a name is that for a woman?" the driver interjected.

"It's short for Francesca."

"Oh, yeah," the driver said with a forgiving smile. "My name's Hank."

Frankie felt a twinge of conscience. She'd had no right to snap at poor Hank earlier. He couldn't control the weather any more than she could. She gave him a dazzling smile. "Don't think it hasn't been fun, Hank," Frankie muttered as she moved to the steps. She saw Steen hide a surprised grin as the driver swung open the door and turned the radio back on. He undoubtedly didn't think she had it in her to be adaptable. She would prove him wrong. Bracing herself against the cold rush of air, Frankie stepped outside.

New white snow engulfed her shoes immediately, but she tried to ignore the quick chill. She watched Steen bend his dark head low and start out. Cautiously she stretched to step into the footprint he'd left. But the slippery sole of her shoe could gather no traction. Unceremoniously Frankie slid to the snowy ground with a small whoosh.

The radio sang out through the open door. "*Dashing through the snow . . .*"

Never had two miles seemed so far, Frankie thought as she trudged along, head bent, teeth chattering. She couldn't decide which was worse: the unrelenting cold compounded by wet feet or the bone-tiring fatigue that increased with each step.

She had to admit that Steen had been more than kind, considering he didn't know her. He hadn't even laughed

when she'd fallen alongside the bus, but instead had
helped her up and brushed her off. He'd also slowed,
shortening his stride so she could step into the grooves
his big boots left in the snow, and he'd insisted she keep
one hand tightly clenched in his. She'd felt herself slipping a time or two, but he'd held firm until she'd righted
herself. Despite his assistance, she was sure she'd freeze
to death before they ever reached his house.

"How...how much farther?" she asked through
trembling lips she was certain must be a bright shade of
blue by now.

"Not far." The wind lifted his words and blew them
past her.

Frankie shivered involuntarily. This was the man
who'd said two miles was *not far*, she reminded herself. She risked a glance up at the threatening sky. She
hoped Eric Hanley would appreciate all she was going
through for him. Dreaming of a warm fire and a hot
drink somewhere just ahead, she marched on, grateful
for Steen's strong grip on her numb fingers.

She was bearing up better than he'd dared hope,
Steen thought. He'd give her that. After that quick fall,
he'd figured she'd scramble back up into the bus. Or
perhaps start crying. But she'd gamely dusted herself
off and tramped along behind him. He hoped she was
adaptable. Having lived in these parts a long while, he
knew that a snowfall like this wasn't going to end for
several hours, perhaps not till morning.

A few more yards and they'd be at the turnoff that
led to his cabin, about half a mile off the main road.
He'd build a fire, fix a hot meal and hope she'd get over
missing her appointment. She had a quick tongue, but
she looked more worried than annoyed. He could empathize with her.

An unexpected change of plans, especially around the holidays, brought out the worst in people, Steen knew. Maybe she hadn't spent much time away from home and the possibility of being marooned with a stranger didn't exactly make her feel like singing. He wondered if she was used to the noise and confusion of a big family. Many people were. Once, he'd envied those who had relatives to spare, but he'd gotten used to being alone much of the time. There was always his neighbor, Hannah, and little Emily, if he craved company, and Amelia would undoubtedly make it home for part of the holiday. Not a crowd, but it was enough.

If he hadn't been able to recognize every tree, bush and winding path on his property, Steen might easily have missed the snow-covered road leading to his front door due to the heavy snowfall. He came to a halt at a tall evergreen that looked as if it had been spray-painted white.

He'd stopped so suddenly that Frankie almost plowed into him. "Oh," she said, grabbing a handful of his jacket to keep from going down.

Pitiful. She looked pitiful, Steen thought as he steadied her. The expensive scarf she'd wound around her head was plastered to her wet hair, her coat was layered with snow in every fold and her tennis shoes were gray and sodden. But the green eyes she raised to his still held that spark of determination. One gutsy lady, he decided.

"I think you've about had it," he said as he adjusted the two bag straps more comfortably on his shoulders.

"I'll be all right. Are we close?"

"Yeah, real close." Steen slid an arm around her back and bent to slide his other under her knees. She let out a small grunt of surprise as he hefted her into his arms and turned down the path.

"You don't have to carry me, really," Frankie said, relief warring with embarrassment. She'd never been carried by a man before. Though she hated to admit it, even to herself, right now it was the greatest feeling in the world to just relax against him and let him take over. Her resistance had run out along with her energy.

"You're ready to drop," he told her unnecessarily. "Hang on and I'll have you inside in no time." Despite the heavy, wet clothes and the weight of the two bags, he had no trouble carrying her. They were walking into the wind now and it was slow going. When finally she relaxed enough to lay her head on his shoulder, he tucked his face into her neck to keep the cold air from her as he lengthened his stride.

Inhaling, he caught her scent, something lightly floral and probably expensive. The breeze shifted, tossing a loose handful of snow at them as Steen pulled her closer. It had been a long time since he'd held a woman just so. He'd missed it. He became aware of her warm breath on his throat. Nice. It felt very nice.

Reaching the porch at last, he climbed the two steps carefully and stopped in front of his door. Lifting his head, he watched her open her eyes. He saw reluctance in them and something else. A surprised awareness. Then it was gone as quickly as it had come and she squirmed out of his arms, landing on her feet with a thud.

"Here we are. Home sweet home." Steen removed a glove and dug in his pocket for his keys while Frankie looked around.

She had no idea what time it was, but already the sky, barely visible through snow-covered trees, was darken-

ing. The cabin was rustic but looked quite solid with a
sturdy front porch that wrapped around the side, a
heavy door and a steeply slanted roof. As long as it had
heat and a phone, she didn't care. Stomping the snow
from his boots, Steen swung the door wide. Shivering
she followed him inside.

In the dim light from the windows, she made out a
large room dominated by a huge stone fireplace at one
end, several wooden doors and an archway leading into
a small kitchen. The furniture looked roomy and comfortable, if not right out of *House Beautiful*. The Taj
Mahal couldn't have looked better to her in her present
state. With her teeth, she tugged wet gloves from her
frigid fingers as Steen set down the two bags and bent
to turn on a table lamp.

"Damn," he muttered as he tried the wall switch.
Nothing. The power was off, not an uncommon occur-
ence in this area during storms. Sighing he turned to his
reluctant guest and watched her face fall as she absorbed the news.

Frankie blew on her red hands. "I'm not surprised.
It's the way this day's been going." She glanced around.
"Where's your phone? We can call someone to come
get us."

He avoided her eyes as he removed his damp jacket.
"I don't have a phone," he said, wondering why he
should feel apologetic. He hadn't promised her a phone
or even heat, for that matter. He'd only offered shelter
from the storm and *that* he could give her.

Frankie's eyes shot up as her voice rose two octaves.
"No phone? Who in the world doesn't have a phone in
this day and age? Good grief, man, how can you live
like this?"

Steen rolled his arms to ease the sore muscles. "I manage just fine, thank you."

Feeling like a frustrated, caged lioness, Frankie began pacing, her wet shoes leaking all over the beautiful wood plank flooring. Right now, she didn't give a damn. "This is archaic. I never heard of anyone not having a phone in their house." Her temper, always a problem, oozed out faster than the snow melting onto the floor. "Why didn't you tell me?"

"Simmer down, lady," Steen said, his voice low and none too friendly. "I didn't beg you to come. It was your choice. And if you don't like it here, there's the door." He turned and marched over to the fireplace.

Damn fool women, he grumbled to himself. He opened the flue and tossed kindling from the bin into the grate. What had she thought, that he lived in a Hilton tucked away in the woods? He should have left her to freeze on the broken-down bus with the potbellied driver. Grabbing several thick chunks of wood, he piled them atop the smaller sticks. Ungrateful, that's what she was. He rolled a section of newspaper into a funnel and struck a match to it, then held it under the woodpile. With all of her expensive clothes and good looks, she didn't have an ounce of brains or a sense of compassion or a...

"I'm sorry. I was out of line."

Her apology caught him off guard. She was close behind him, her voice soft and contrite. The fire caught. He tossed in the paper, closed the screen and stood to look at her. "Guess we're both cold, wet and tired."

Frankie swallowed. Though quick to flare, her temper usually died just as quickly. "You've been more than kind and I had no business taking my frustrations out on you."

She stood in front of him, rubbing her ringless fingers. They were slender, almost delicate and looked to be half frozen. "Forget it." He touched her arms, moving her closer to the fire. "This throws a lot of heat. Stay here and I'll light some candles."

Frankie heard him moving about the cabin as she crouched and held her hands out to the fire. What in the world was she going to do now? she wondered. She had no way to get in touch with Eric Hanley to let him know where she was so he could send a car for her. Though he used other troubleshooters occasionally, she was his favorite. Correction: *had been* his favorite.

She heard the grandfather clock by the door chime the hour. Six. If she couldn't get to him tonight, Eric might just be angry enough to never call her again. He had considerable clout with the other casino managers and, she'd long suspected, a mean streak. She'd been steadily building up her personal clientele list for two years now and had worked with several small western companies—banks, hotels, a couple of hospitals. But the Reno, Tahoe and Vegas casinos were the most lucrative. The loss of a couple of important accounts could make a significant dent in her income. She dreaded the thought of having to worry about money again.

Restless, Frankie walked to look out a side window. Was it her hopeful imagination or was the snowfall easing? Scanning the yard, she suddenly brightened as she spotted the unmistakable form of a Jeep parked under a broad overhang. The answer to her prayers, she thought with a smile. She'd bet that hunk of metal could roll over the top of the roughest roads and the steepest snow. She turned just as Steen came toward her.

He held out a big towel. "You'd better get out of those wet things before you catch a cold. Have you got anything warm to wear? If not, I have a heavy shirt that might..."

"Listen, could I borrow your Jeep? I promise I'll have it brought back to you tomorrow."

Steen took a step backward. The woman was obviously certifiable. "Look, I don't think you're familiar with winter storms up here." He nodded toward the window. "It's not going to stop tonight and we've already got seven, eight inches on the ground. We'll easily have a foot by morning, maybe more. You'd have to be crazy to go out in that."

She gave him her most agreeable smile. "I'm not asking you to come with me. Just loan me your Jeep. It's a four-wheel drive, isn't it?"

"Yes, but..."

Frankie nodded. "I grew up on a farm, drove a tractor when I was only ten. I can drive anything."

Not only stubborn but stupid, Steen thought. "What in hell is so important in Tahoe that you'd risk your neck to get to it? Or should I ask *who*?"

Building her business, she'd had to learn to be patient and persuasive. Taking a deep breath, Frankie decided she'd have to call on a reserve of both if she hoped to borrow his Jeep. "Mr. Olson, there's a man in Tahoe in charge of a large gambling casino who's had a security code foul up and I'm a computer consultant on my way to get him out of his giant jam. He's counting on me and I can't let him down."

Seeing that he was still hesitant, she had a quick thought and touched one diamond earring. "I could give you these as collateral, or I have a credit card I could leave if you're worried about..."

"I don't want collateral." He crossed his arms over his chest, studying her. Not a showgirl as he'd conjectured, but a computer whiz. A brain, but did she have common sense? "It's a hell of a way to spend the week before Christmas, hanging around a gambling casino."

He was going to give in, she could tell. Frankie sat down on the hearth and began tugging off her wet shoes. "Not everybody's into this holiday hype. There are plenty of people who don't believe in all that commercialized nonsense. Like me, for instance. Christmas is just another day."

Frankie wished it wasn't so, but the truth was, she didn't like even thinking about Christmas because it hurt too much. But she owed no further explanations to this stranger. Taking the towel he'd brought, she blotted her feet, then padded over to her overnight bag and took out her pumps. They weren't for snow, but at least they were dry.

She might get a little damp on the way to the Jeep, Frankie thought as she struggled into her shoes, but once inside she'd turn on the heater and be fine. It was less than fifty miles to Tahoe, she was certain. It would be late when she arrived, but she'd be there tonight. She glanced up and caught Steen's disapproving frown.

The man had a way of making her feel like a willful child. "Please don't look at me like that. I'm really a very good driver. I won't hurt your Jeep."

He didn't suppose it would occur to her that he might be concerned about her and not his Jeep. And he wasn't about to tell her either. He deepened his frown. "Don't say I didn't warn you that you'll probably wind up in a ditch."

"I certainly will not." Stuffing the wet scarf into her pocket, she blotted her damp hair.

He'd give it one more shot. She simply didn't know what she was getting into. "Why don't you wait awhile then, warm up by the fire first? I can heat some soup over the flames. You'll feel better if you eat. Later on, I'll throw on a yule log. Have you ever seen one of those? Blue flames and red and..."

Frankie shook her head. "I appreciate your concern and all you've done for me. I'll see that your Jeep is returned first thing tomorrow." She held out her hand for the keys.

He could refuse her, but Steen knew enough about stubborn women to realize she'd probably start out on foot if he denied her his car. Wordlessly, he handed her his keys. He watched her leave wearing a brave smile. He listened to the closing door, but didn't even go to the window to follow her progress. Maybe, as with drunks and children, angels watched over obstinate females who wouldn't listen to reason. He certainly hoped so.

Within half an hour, he had unpacked, changed into dry clothes including fur-lined slippers, and was contentedly sipping a warming brandy on the couch in front of the blazing fire. As always, it felt good to be home, Steen thought. His apartment in L.A. was his offical address, but this place was home. He stretched his legs toward the heat, his mind returning to the woman who'd marched in and out of his life in a matter of hours.

Beautiful, determined, unyielding. Maybe he shouldn't have let her go. What if she lost control of the Jeep and got hurt? What if...

Something was clumping onto his wooden porch. Or someone. Jumping up, trying to hide a know-it-all grin, Steen went to the door and pulled it open.

Wet and bedraggled, Frankie looked up at him. "Don't say a word. Not one. I *hate* smug men." She marched inside past him.

Chapter Two

She was certain she'd never be warm again. Frankie caught the sneeze in a tissue and wondered if this was what pneumonia felt like. Her face was so stiff that she thought the skin might crack if she smiled. Her hair was crusted with gobs of snow that were melting and silently sliding down her neck. Her fingers were numb and she'd long ago stopped feeling her feet. It was quite possible she'd never looked or felt this dreadful in her entire life.

To his credit, Steen hadn't commented on her state of disrepair. However, she doubted if he would be able to resist a few jabs about the way she'd managed to maneuver his Jeep into the first ditch she'd encountered. Another deep sneeze shook her. Why didn't he just go to bed and let her thaw out in peace?

At least he hadn't uttered those dreaded four little words: I told you so. If he had, she'd have mustered the energy to pop him a good one.

"You need to get out of those wet clothes," Steen said. He'd watched her stand shivering in front of the fire for long minutes now, as if rooted to the spot.

"I . . . I'm not sure I can move."

All right so she'd done a damn fool thing. He'd managed a few himself. He turned her toward him and began unbuttoning her coat. She was shaking so hard it was difficult to slip it from her shoulders. All she had on underneath was a thin, wool dress. No wonder she was half-frozen. He tried to keep his features even and nonjudgmental. If he did the wrong thing now, she just might cry and then he really wouldn't know what to do.

He eased her down until she was sitting on the warm hearth, then tugged off her ruined shoes. It was a miracle she'd been able to walk back to the cabin from where the Jeep had gotten stuck in the ditch on feet this cold and unprotected. Steen tried to rub some life back into them as he raised his eyes to hers.

"The power hasn't been off too long. I tested the water and there's still some hot in the tank. Maybe a warm bath would make you feel better."

Frankie hated the tears that sprang to her eyes. Kindness always did that to her, especially when she'd done something stupid and didn't deserve his generosity. But she'd been so certain she could make it to Tahoe. Taking a deep breath, she nodded.

"I'll help you take your dress off and hang it by the fire to dry." He touched the first button just as her hand caught his. He saw her temper, never too far from the surface, flare in her eyes.

"I can do it myself."

"Fine." He dropped his hands. "I think you should know that I'm not really into ravishing half-frozen, bad-tempered women."

Frankie tried, really tried. But her fingers felt like swollen sausages. They simply couldn't manage the buttons. Now she was truly close to tears and furious with herself. When Steen took her by the shoulders and pulled her to her feet before matter-of-factly unbuttoning her dress, she had no choice but to let him. She disliked needing him, needing anyone, but at least he seemed more like an annoyed big brother instead of a handsome stranger.

She wore silk underneath, as he should have known she would—a pale peach color, so soft in his hands. He imagined the skin it covered would be even softer. Averting his eyes, he took the dress from her and nodded toward the bathroom. "The second door. I've already put your bag inside. Call out if you need anything." He turned his back and busied himself poking at the fire to allow her some privacy. He knew how she felt. Stripping in front of strangers, even under these circumstances, was embarrassing and upsetting.

Steen heard the bathroom door close and let out a deep breath. He knew that a steady snowfall such as they were experiencing could sometimes maroon residents in their homes for days. He had grown used to such capricious winter happenings, but in his bathroom was a very reluctant, very unpredictable woman who didn't want to be here and who just might drive him up his own walls before this was over. In one swallow, he downed the rest of his brandy.

The next time he was considering opening his home to a pair of big green eyes and a defenseless smile, he'd first have his head thoroughly examined, he decided.

* * *

She took her time, leaning back in the spacious claw-footed tub in the big, old-fashioned bathroom. He was surprisingly neat and orderly for a man living alone in an isolated cabin. Now that she was warming and letting the disappointment ease out of her pores along with the chill, she stopped to consider her host.

It occurred to Frankie that she knew absolutely nothing about Steen Olson—not where he'd been returning from, what he did for a living, if he had someone he cared about. Of course, as soon as the snow stopped, she'd be on her way and probably would never see him again. But she had to admit that if she had to be stranded in a snowstorm, she could do worse for a roommate than the man by the fire.

Ducking under, she rinsed the shampoo from her hair with fingers that tingled as her blood warmed. Sitting up, she cocked her ear toward the door. The unmistakable sound of Christmas carols drifted in. Frankie almost groaned aloud. Wouldn't you know he'd have a battery-operated radio? Was she the only person in the world who became depressed with the repetitious gaiety of those songs?

Every year, she tried not to dwell on the holidays, tried to keep herself busy and her schedule full so she wouldn't have to think about them. She'd had very few really happy Christmases that she could recall. And a couple that had been filled with incredible heartbreak. Growing up on a small, heavily-mortgaged Ohio farm, living a hand-to-mouth existence, didn't lend itself to many joyful memories.

Frankie shivered as she realized the water had cooled. Reaching for the towel, she stood to dry herself. In her mind, she returned to the rural area where she'd been raised. The small frame houses had been clustered along a wide country road, their pastureland spiraling behind them like spokes on a wagon wheel. There'd been neighbors, friends of her parents, yet she'd felt a sense of isolation always.

She let herself remember the nights she'd lain listening to carolers strolling the neighborhood each Christmas, feeling left out and alone as she'd tried to fall asleep on the lumpy living room couch. There'd been little heat in her second-story bedroom so in the winter, the couch near the fireplace served as her bed. From there, she could easily hear the happy laughter of the singers as they'd pass by.

Her poor, work-worn mother had always seen that they put up a tree of sorts. But Frankie's gifts inevitably had consisted of new underwear, sensible school shoes and clothes her mother had made for her. Her father had grown quieter and more stooped with each holiday. Not being able to provide more for his family weighed heavily on him. Frankie had learned to steel herself against the sentimentality of the season, to get through the days until the holidays were finally over. It had hurt much less that way. Hanging up the towel, she acknowledged that she still felt the same.

The eyes that stared back at her from the mirror looked a shade weary, but at least the anxiety in them had washed down the drain with the bathwater. There was color in her face and she'd stopped trembling. At the moment, she couldn't do another thing about Eric Hanley's problem. She'd have to resign herself to that fact. Her father had always said: You change what you can and what you can't, you endure. Somehow she would endure. She'd had to do a lot of adapting to difficult situations in the past and she could do it again.

Slipping into her robe, Frankie was thankful that she'd packed a warm one. She hadn't brought a nightgown, disliking them. Belting the robe, she realized she'd forgotten to pack slippers. But she'd noticed several oval braided rugs covering the hardwood floor, including a large one in front of the couch where she'd undoubtedly sleep. Sleeping on a couch again, like old times she thought as she opened the bathroom door.

From the far corner of the sofa, Steen watched her place her bag against the wall and look hesitantly toward him. He gave her a smile to put her at ease. "Come join me. I made some tea. I've perked coffee over the grate a time or two, but it usually tastes like mud."

"Tea will be fine." She curled up in the opposite corner of the sofa, pulling her legs up under her. There was the tangy smell of mesquite in the air, not unpleasant. Frankie accepted the mug he offered her and took a sip. "Mmm, what's in this? It's delicious."

"Blackberry brandy. My neighbor, Hannah Kingston, makes it herself. I thought we could use a little something to warm us." Steen sipped, studying her over the rim. Quite a metamorphosis. She'd unbraided her hair and the firelight turned the blond strands golden as they fell around her slim shoulders. Her skin was rosy from the bath and without a trace of makeup, she looked softer, more approachable. The wariness had left her green eyes, replaced by a hint of shyness that drew him in. He caught the powdery scent of her and fleetingly wished he could once again bury his face in her neck. *Hold on,* he warned himself. Clearing his throat, he set his cup down as his mind searched for a neutral subject.

"How'd you ever get into computer work?" Since he knew very little about her, her job seemed a safe place to start.

She smiled as she turned to gaze into the fire. "It's a long story." After the accident, she'd needed a job and needed to keep her mind occupied. Don't major in math, she'd been warned by the balding career counselor at the college, or in computers. Women have no aptitude for numbers, or for electronic gadgetry, as he'd called it. Besides, a woman doesn't need those things, especially a beautiful woman like you, he'd added. How could he, or anyone else, have known her needs?

Obstinately, she'd taken every course he'd recommended against—and fallen in love. With numbers, equations, solving puzzles, the intricacies and endless possibilities of those tiny microchips. It was just what she'd needed in her anxiety to back away from people—the impersonal computer. And a career had been born. Frankie knew she wasn't brilliant. Just damn good at what she did.

"I've got all night," Steen said as he topped off her tea, then refilled his own cup.

As he poured, she studied his face. He'd been genuinely nice and she could think of no reason not to talk with him about her work. Though she was a little tired, she supposed she owed him at least a show of friendliness. So she told him about attending school, her first job and Corbett Lash who'd helped get her started in her own business as a computer consultant. Corbett had turned out to be friend, mentor and confidante, the only person she'd allowed herself to get close to since leaving Ohio.

"I love his name," she told Steen with a smile. "Corbett means raven in Latin and it suits him. He's dark and sleek with eyes that don't miss a thing. He's a genius when it comes to computers. There's simply nothing he doesn't know about them. A wonderful man."

He heard the warmth and affection in her voice and thought that he wouldn't mind having those green eyes light up like that when she spoke of him. He should have known she had someone waiting somewhere. She was too beautiful to spend much time alone unless by choice. He drained his cup. "Did you go to school in California?"

"Yes." The insurance money had allowed her that privilege. Frankie shoved back the accompanying memory. "I'm from Ohio, but California colleges jumped feetfirst into the computer age long before others offered extensive courses. Since that was what I wanted to study, it seemed the place to be."

"Earlier, you mentioned San Francisco. Is that where you live?"

"Yes, a beautiful city. Have you been there?"

"Several times. Do you live with Corbett?"

Frankie's mouth dropped open and her eyes widened. "Whatever gave you that impression?"

He shrugged, angry with himself that he'd probed so personally. It really wasn't like him to pry. "I just thought . . . It doesn't matter."

"I live alone. And Corbett Lash is well into his sixties." It was something new for her, that small hint of jealousy. She rarely permitted anyone to get that close.

Steen felt the heat move into his face as he bent to throw another log on, and hoped she'd think it was due to the fire. Silently he busied himself with the wood.

His remark had changed things for Frankie, making her look at him more as a man than as an impersonal rescuer. She watched him easily toss large chunks of wood into the fire. He had a broad back with wide, powerful shoulders and muscular arms. Yet when he'd held her, when he'd carried her, he couldn't have been more gentle. But it was his eyes she liked best—a serious gray and oddly sensitive for such a big man. Yes, Steen Olson was a very attractive man for someone interested in a relationship. Personally she wasn't in the market.

Feeling restless, Frankie got up and walked to the mantel. Tall, thick candles gave off a pungent vanilla aroma. In the center, a manger scene was set up consisting of unusual figures carved out of wood. She picked up a shepherd and examined it carefully, noting the intricate detailing. All the figures had been given loving attention, as well. There was something familiar about the carvings, but she couldn't think what. The piece still in her hand, she turned to him.

"These are lovely. Did you buy them locally?"

He moved alongside her, bracing one arm on the mantel. "Not exactly. I made them."

"Honestly? You do beautiful work. A hobby?"

"It started out that way, then became a livelihood. I'm just back from delivering some special pieces, much larger, that I'd done on consignment for several California department stores."

A wood-carver. Yes, it suited him. "What kind of wood is this? It's so warm, almost like it's alive."

He was oddly pleased that she understood. Not many people did. "Olive wood. It's the best for small pieces and detail work." He touched the figure she held, rubbing a finger along the shepherd's cloak. "It does seem to have a life of it's own, doesn't it?"

Frankie had always thought hands told a lot about a person. Dad's hands had been twisted and bent from years of working the farm. Her mother's were freckled and deeply bronzed from the sun, yet her touch was gentle. Her own were slender and looked pampered, yet her fingers were strong as steel from hours spent typing at her keyboard.

Steen's hand was large, strong-boned, with calluses, the hand of a man who'd done his share of hard work. She noticed that he had several small cuts barely healed and thought they must be from the tools he used to carve his figures. "You have nice hands," she told him, looking up.

Frankie saw his eyes darken. Slowly he reached up and trailed his fingers down her cheek just enough to make her pulse leap, enough to make her remember she was a woman. It was not a reminder she was comfortable with.

Steen touched one small diamond earring winking in the firelight. "Nice. A gift from a man, someone close to you?" He couldn't have said why he wanted to know.

The second time he'd inquired about a man in her life. She doubted he'd believe how few there'd been. "No. I bought them myself."

His expression didn't change, but he slid an arm around her and pulled her fractionally closer. The weariness of the long day suddenly weighed heavy on Frankie. With a grateful sigh, she lay her head on his shoulder. For a moment. A long moment to feel and absorb and enjoy simple human contact.

His hands lightly caressed her back through the thick robe, but the heat spread nonetheless. She couldn't remember the last time she'd been held so gently by a man. Years; it had been years. Independence was a goal she'd struggled to reach and she had, but it had its drawbacks. For a moment longer, she allowed the slow pleasure to seep into her, then she lifted her head.

"I wouldn't want to give the wrong impression here," she told him, her voice not quite steady.

She'd felt awfully good in his arms. But they were strangers and he wasn't a man who pushed. "There's something about Christmas that makes us all more mellow. I wasn't reading more into it than that."

She moved from him and sat back on the couch. "I'm not real crazy about Christmas."

"Against your religious beliefs?"

"No, it's not that. The whole season resurrects some painful memories for me."

He'd mentally labeled her a cynic, but perhaps she had valid reasons. "For many people, I think." He glanced toward the kitchen, remembering that he was the host, albeit unexpectedly. "Are you hungry? I could fix us something to eat." She shook her head as she leaned back, looking relaxed. "Is there anything I can get you?"

He saw her shake her head, then turn toward the radio as a sentimental Christmas song began. Her eyes were suspiciously bright, tears close to the surface. Wordlessly, he turned off the radio, then stoked the fire again before sitting down alongside her. Closer than before, but not too close. There was something about her that reminded him of a doe that often wandered onto his property. She seemed to want to be near him, yet if he didn't move very slowly with her, she quickly backed off. Like the cautious doe, Frankie seemed a bit skittish.

He watched her blink rapidly, reaching for her control, and searched his mind for a way to lighten the mood. "Are you sleepy?"

"Not especially."

"Are you a gambler?" He saw her swing those incredible green eyes to his.

"Rarely. I hate losing."

"Why don't we try some safe betting then? I guess things about you and we make a bet whether I'm right or wrong." Something had him wanting to know more and he decided she wouldn't be able to resist the challenge of a harmless game.

"Guess about what kind of things?"

"Oh, like your preferences in music. I'd guess that you like that funky little San Francisco station way on the left side of the dial. The one that plays some old Peter, Paul and Mary, a little Simon and Garfunkel and some early Kenny Rogers back when he was with the First Edition."

She angled toward him, her interest captured. "WGOF. How did you know?"

Steen stretched his legs toward the fire, feeling smug. "A lucky guess. I have an apartment in L.A., but my work takes me to San Francisco occasionally. Your turn."

Frankie took a long breath and stared up at the ceiling. "Let's see. I'd guess you're an animal lover from your detailed carvings. Wildlife, too, probably. And you most likely have a dog, a golden retriever, though I don't know where he'd stay when you travel."

He nodded, pleased at her perception. "Not bad, lady. He stays with Hannah when I'm gone, an Irish setter named Red. Right now, he's about ten miles from here at a neighbor's being bred. Okay, let's try movies.

I'd guess you're into the old stuff, Bogart and Bacall, some early Gary Cooper, the classics.''

"Mmm, and Fred Astaire. How that man could dance."

"Do you like to dance?"

Did she? Matt had liked to dance, to hold her close while the DJ played records in the high school gym. So long ago. "I'm not very good at it. Rusty, I guess you could say." Frankie heard the grandfather clock chime ten and stifled a yawn. She could hardly suggest he leave her and go to his bedroom, but her eyes were getting as heavy as the memories Steen had inadvertently revived.

What, Steen wondered, had caused that look of sadness to cross her features just then when he'd mentioned dancing? Her mood shifts came and went like a twirling kaleidoscope. She'd turned back and was staring into the fire again, lost in her thoughts. She looked tired and he knew he should let her get to sleep. But he felt unaccountably good just sitting with her by the warming fire. Which was just one reason he should probably say good-night.

The candles were burning low yet the flames in the fireplace danced brightly, enveloping the room in a glow. Frankie gazed into the fire and sought to identify what she was feeling. A pang of loneliness, undoubtedly brought on by the season and the many reminders she'd had today. Memories buried the rest of the year surfaced and brought with them the expected melancholia and its accompanying emotions. Channeling emotion was something she'd taught herself slowly, painfully. But tonight, her strict discipline wasn't working. She felt the uncharacteristic need for someone's touch.

She turned her head to find Steen quietly watching her, his eyes thoughtful, his expression unreadable. He was a man who'd caused her to flare up in anger, to soften in gratitude and to relax in his presence, all in the space of a few hours. He was as kind as he was attractive, and the combination was lethal in her present state. If he reached out to touch her now, she wondered if she'd have the strength to turn away.

A log slipped, fell through the grate and the fire crackled in response, but their look held. What was she thinking? Steen wondered. He saw her as feisty, intelligent and vulnerable, but there was something more. She seemed to have a need, one she was afraid to acknowledge much less fulfill. He wanted to touch her and he would have if he hadn't noticed that wounded look in her eyes.

Frankie turned back to the fire and wished she didn't feel caught somewhere between awareness and uncertainty with this man she scarcely knew. Her eyes were suddenly too heavy to remain open and she let herself sink into the welcoming softness of the couch.

In moments she was sound asleep.

Steen watched the flames flicker. Though his life was mainly solitary, he didn't lack for friends. After Jessica, he'd avoided the female gender for a while, but he'd learned to face a simple truth. He liked women, liked the way their minds worked, the softness they lent to a man's life, the civilization they brought to the male of the species. From time to time, he'd wondered if he'd ever run across a woman he'd want to share his life with. The aftermath of Jessica had left him cautious, but not closed-minded.

Living alone for a long while now had made him a man who trusted his own instincts more than any other single factor, a man in tune with his feelings. He tried to sort them out now and wondered where they would lead him.

Carefully he touched the golden ends of Frankie's hair, feeling the silk glide through his fingers. She was strikingly beautiful, yet there was a haunted look about her. The word fragile came to mind. Perhaps tomorrow, he would discover why.

Leaning his head back, Steen closed his eyes.

Frankie awoke wrapped in the folds of a down quilt in the middle of a four-poster bed she couldn't recall climbing into. The last thing she remembered was falling asleep on the couch with Steen's warm presence beside her. Sitting up, she looked around and found she was alone in what was obviously his bedroom. She knew she'd been exhausted, but to be so tired she couldn't even recall being put to bed was a first for her.

She was still wearing her robe, she noticed. Had he untied it, thinking she wore a gown underneath, and noticed that she wore nothing, then retied it? Rising, she realized there was precious little she could do about that after the fact. On tiptoe, she peeked out the high window and almost gasped out loud. The snow was piled to just below the sill. Across the way the wind had nearly buried a toolshed she'd noticed yesterday alongside where the Jeep had been parked. When it snowed in this part of the country, it *really* snowed.

She heard the scraping of a chair leg on the wooden floor in the other room. Steen was probably an early riser. She would have liked to have dressed before going out there, but she'd left her small bag in the other room. Belting her robe and finger combing her hair, she opened the bedroom door.

Frankie moved to the bathroom to splash cold water on her face and brush her teeth before walking out to look around the living room. The fire was flickering and a weak sunshine drifted in through the windows. He was sitting at the butcher block table tucked in the kitchen alcove sanding a piece of wood. The smell of coffee, hot and strong, hung in the air. She turned toward the kitchen, feeling that uncharacteristic flush of shyness. Understandable, she decided, since she'd never before awakened in a strange man's bed.

"Good morning," she said.

Steen had heard her come out, but had kept on working, letting her acclimate herself and approach at her own pace. Now he looked up and gave her a lazy smile of welcome. "Good morning." He wiped his hands on a rag. "I'll get you some coffee. It's strong enough to put hair on your... your toes."

She laughed at his obvious word switch as she sat down. His hair was damp and, as he leaned close to pour her coffee, she caught a hint of a subtle masculine scent. Had she imagined the light touch of his hand on her hair last night? Probably. She took a hot swallow of coffee as she heard the furnace rumble on.

"I guess the power's back on," she commented as he sat opposite her.

"Yeah. Lots of hot water again."

She didn't need hot water as much as she needed a snowplow. That closed-in, trapped feeling was taking over again. Steen's calm acceptance of their situation only aggravated her more. With great effort, she resisted the urge to jump out of her chair and pace. She curled her fingers around the warm cup and sipped her coffee as she gazed out the window.

"It's stopped snowing, but the wind's really piled it up. When do you suppose they'll have snowplows out?"

Steen shrugged as he picked up the chunk of wood. "They may get to some of the highways today, but certainly not to us this far off the main road. People around these parts kind of take their time, especially around the holidays."

The holidays again, Frankie thought, always messing things up. She might as well cross Eric Hanley off her list. Not having heard a word from her in forty-eight hours, he'd probably already crossed her off his. She felt like screaming.

Steen saw her anxious look return as he continued to rub on the wood. "You're not good at relaxing, are you?"

She sent him a fiery glance. "It's easy for you to relax. You're where you want to be, and even able to work if you wish."

With a clunk, he dropped the piece of wood. The time to stop this was now. "Hasn't anyone ever thrown you a curve before now? Haven't you ever run into a roadblock and had to take a detour? If not, you're long overdue. You might as well decide to make the best of your situation because right now, there isn't a damn thing you can do to change things. Relax. You'll get where you're going sooner or later."

Feeling chastised, Frankie stared into her coffee cup. A curve, a detour? Oh, yes. She'd had several. Make the best of things. Hadn't she taught herself to do that ages ago? He had a way of making her desire to leave seem petty. Banking her anger, she settled her gaze on the block of wood he'd returned to polishing. "What are you working on?"

Steen supposed that her softening manner meant she'd decided to try congeniality. That was fine with him. He was no stranger to a quick temper. But he'd learned to control his years ago. Frankie was in the beginning stages of learning to keep a handle on hers. "I'm not sure what it'll be yet. It's a gift so while I prepare the wood, I think about the person and I settle on what would suit them best."

She found herself interested despite her discontent. "It just sort of comes to you, what you should make?"

"Something like that. When you give something you've made yourself, you give the recipient a part of yourself." He shot her a quick glance, looking a little abashed. "At least that's how I see it."

"What a nice way to put it."

He raised his eyes to see a warm smile on her face and wondered what she was thinking.

She was thinking she'd never met a man who seemed so content with his work, with his environment. She envied that. "Is wood carving something you learned from your father?"

He nodded as he rubbed the wood with an oiled cloth. "My father was born in Sweden where wood carving is still considered one of the arts. It disappointed him that Americans don't hold people who work with their hands in high regard."

"Yet he still keeps at it?"

"No, he switched to selling farm equipment in Texas."

"I thought you were from Texas. Your folks still live there?"

Steen wrapped the wood in the oily cloth and set it aside. "No, they're dead."

Frankie watched him put away his things and wipe off the table. From his abrupt tone, she gathered he wanted to end this discussion.

"Want some breakfast?" he asked. "I'm a passable cook."

"I'm starved and I'm a good cook." She moved to the refrigerator. "You've been such a good host that the least I can do is cook you breakfast."

Steen stepped back. "Go right ahead. I rarely have the luxury of a woman cooking for me. There's bacon and eggs and all the fixings. Too bad we don't have some raspberries. They're my favorite food."

She smiled at the boyish sound of him. "They're out of season."

"I know." He watched her pad barefoot around the kitchen as if she'd been there before. Her hair was sleep tousled, hanging down past her shoulders. She tossed it back out of her way and he longed to reach up and touch the soft strands as he had last night. Wishing he had better control over his vagrant thoughts, he got up and left the room.

Frankie set bacon frying, took out the eggs and lined up the bread for toasting. Outside the window, the wind rearranged snow drifts, the white flakes shining like diamonds in the morning sun. The furnace came on, filling the small kitchen with warmth, mingling with the fragrant cooking smells. In the other room, she heard Steen adding logs to the fire.

Turning the bacon, she examined her feelings now that she'd decided to make the best of things, as she'd been instructed. Ordinarily, she didn't take instructions well, which was why she'd decided to free-lance, having to answer to no one. Being in control of her work and her life made her feel good. But only God could control the weather, she acknowledged.

Even so, she'd expected to continue to feel restless, annoyed, frustrated. It wasn't because of the sentimentality of the season that she'd calmed, she was sure. It was more likely the peculiar sense of peace that came with being stranded in an isolated cabin, locked in by the elements, and unable to make nature do her bidding. There was a necessary resignation to it, an acceptance of her circumstances which Frankie admitted that she generally struggled against.

Or was it Steen Olson whose quiet strength, gentle admonitions and laid-back life-style made no demands on her? It was literally impossible to maintain her bad temper in the face of his warm hospitality.

Returning to the kitchen, Steen noisily pulled out a chair. "Come here a minute."

She placed the last of the bacon onto paper towels before glancing up. "What for?"

"Just sit down."

Going along with him, she sat. Stooping in front of her, he reached for one bare foot, placed it on his knee, and proceeded to slide a thick wool sock onto it. "I don't want to be responsible for you catching a cold in my house." In slow motion, he ran the huge sock halfway up her calf, then shifted his attention to her other foot.

His voice was gruff, but his manner gentle. At twenty-eight, Frankie had allowed few men into her life. And of those few, only a couple had been given the freedom to touch her. A man's hands were not totally foreign to her. Why was it, she asked herself as Steen's large hands carefully arranged the coarse material along her leg, that suddenly this man's touch was a shade un-nerving?

Removing her foot from his grasp, Frankie quickly stood. "Thank you. I'll have everything ready in a minute."

Steen watched her turn back to the stove, her flushed cheeks a dead giveaway to her reactions to him. Staying out of her way, he set the table. It wasn't shyness, he decided, nor probably inexperience. Yet that frightened-doe look was back in her eyes.

She was a good cook. Reaching for more bacon, Steen told her so.

Frankie smiled her thanks, then searched her mind for some safe topic to discuss before he brought up a disturbing one. "Did you always know you wanted to work with wood, despite your father's feelings about American wood-carvers?"

Steen spread jam on his toast. "I wasn't sure what I wanted to do, but my father insisted I go to college, study business administration. He didn't want me to work hard like he had all his life and he felt that a business degree was the answer."

"And you didn't?"

"No. I hated the very idea of working at something I'd probably dislike just to stockpile money. When my folks died, I quit college."

"How did they die?" She wasn't being nosy, Frankie told herself. Just interested.

"In an auto accident."

"And then you decided to become a wood-carver?"

"Not right away. I knocked around the country for a while, trying to find where I fit in. But I had some obligations and I'm really not happy wandering. I'd always loved working with wood and I'd kept up my carving. One day someone introduced me to this guy who really liked my work and it turned out he owns a chain of stores. That got me started." He poured them each more coffee.

Frankie's gaze traveled around the cabin. It was comfortable, but far from lavish. She had to ask. "Can you make a good living selling your carvings?"

Steen hid his smile behind his coffee cup. She understood his love of working with his hands in wood. But she judged his income by this house and the things in it. Maybe it was best for now that she did. "I do all right. Funny thing. When you work at something you love, the money follows."

She thought about that a moment. "I don't know. My work doesn't necessarily give me lots of pleasure, though I like it. But, more importantly, it provides me with a very good income. And independence. It's basically a means to an end." And that end waited for her in Maui. One day.

Steen's gaze was level. "What about satisfaction in doing a good job?"

"Yes, there is that."

"Why not shoot for both, to make a good income *and* love your work?"

"That's not always possible."

He questioned her thinking, but decided to let it go for now. Finishing, he leaned back. "Do you have family nearby?"

"No."

"You mentioned you were from Ohio. Are your folks there?"

She chewed on a sliver of bacon thoughtfully. He was too easy to talk with, even for someone who rarely confided the details of her life. Raising her eyes, she saw his were honest and guileless. Like Corbett, whom she thought of as fatherly. But her reactions to Steen weren't those of a daughter. She'd have to keep that in mind. "My father died some time ago. My mother lives in Florida."

Steen could empathize. "It can be tough not having much family. Have you been on your own long?"

He was getting too close. Frankie rose to clear the table. "Yes. As I'm sure you know, being on your own early toughens you. You learn not to let yourself care too much for people. That way they can't hurt you." She carried the plates to the sink.

He'd sensed sadness in her last night. Now he heard the defensiveness. "It can also get pretty lonely."

Frankie shrugged. "*Everyone's* lonely sometimes, Steen. Aren't you?"

He followed with the cups, coming alongside her. "You don't think the pleasure of caring for someone is worth whatever pain may come along?" It was a question he'd asked himself more than once.

"No." She swung cool green eyes to him. "Have you cared for many people?"

"No, not many. Have you?"

"A few. And it's a whole lot safer not to, I assure you." She bent to load the dishwasher.

Definitely a lady who didn't like someone to probe too much, Steen thought. "I'll help you clean up. Then maybe you'd like to try beating me at something. I've got chess, Trivial Pursuit, cards." Amelia loved games and kept him well supplied.

Games. She rather felt like they'd already been playing one, and she hadn't been let in on the rules. Brushing her hair back from her face, she closed the dishwasher and rinsed her hands. "There's a couple of trade journals in my overnight case that I really ought to read."

"I thought you were beginning to relax and here, you want to work."

"You have to stay on top of your chosen field. If you don't, someone else will."

He touched her shoulder and turned her toward him. "You have to learn to play a little. A life that's all work isn't a life." He raised a hand to her face. "You have soap on your nose." He brushed it away and felt her stiffen. "You're not crazy about letting anyone take care of you, even for a day or so, are you?"

"I like to go it alone. I hate being a bother to someone."

"You're no bother to me. I'm glad you're here." Again, he let his fingers linger on the satin of her cheek. She seemed to grow softer as her eyes shifted to his mouth.

What would it be like to give in? Frankie wondered. What would that strong mouth feel like touching her own? What would his kiss taste like, smooth and practiced, or hungry and edgy with passion? She had only to raise to her tiptoes to find out.

Her eyes met his and she saw the same questions there, and the quick desire. What was wrong with her? Frankie asked herself, stepping back and away. Alone with a man less than twenty-four hours and already she was fantasizing about kissing him. Disgusted with herself, she swiveled from him.

"I . . . I think I'll get dressed." She started across the room, but the socks couldn't get a grip on the smooth wooden floor. "Oh!" she cried as she reached out to regain her balance.

He rushed to steady her, his hands grabbing hers. Suddenly, she was close, very close to his chest. Steen felt the pulse pound under the thin skin of her wrist where he held her. "Better go slowly. You wouldn't want to fall."

"Thanks." Carefully, eyes averted, she moved from his grasp and walked away. Retrieving her bag she went to the bedroom and closed the door. Leaning against it, she let out a long breath.

He'd given her some good advice, and not about a slippery floor. She had better take things much more slowly. She certainly didn't want to fall.

Gazing out the window, Frankie noticed it was snowing again. She couldn't control the weather, but she could control herself. Closing her eyes a long moment, she waited for her heart to slow down. *Please, please don't let me fall.*

Chapter Three

Something didn't add up. Frankie caught her hair back and fastened it with a gold clip at her nape. While dressing, she'd taken the time to look around the bedroom, really look, and had discovered a few surprises. Leaning closer, she studied the mirror above the heavy dresser. The glass was beveled, the frame oak with brass trim matching the huge four-poster bed and nightstand. She walked over to the antique rolltop desk by the window and ran her fingers over the polished wood. Next to it was a beautifully carved footstool with a needlepoint cushion that she could more easily have pictured in the home of a maiden aunt than in the bedroom of a rugged man.

Slipping her hands into the pockets of her jogging pants, Frankie decided that there wasn't much typical about the man she'd left in the kitchen. He was a simple man, but not unpolished. Not that it made any difference to her, she acknowledged as she applied a bit of color to her lips. She'd just been too self-absorbed last night to notice much. Perhaps she'd judged him unfairly, thinking that because he looked like he wrestled horses for a living he wouldn't appreciate antiques and such.

That had been wrong of her, she thought as she added a touch of scent to her wrists. Ordinarily, she didn't generalize about people. Certainly a man who lived in the woods and felt at home in blue jeans could also like Mozart and be aware that Charles Dickens was not a linebacker for the San Francisco Giants.

Steen Olson was a nice guy with an interesting occupation and a warm house when she needed one. He was artistic and sensitive and he had a mouth that had her fantasizing and ... Where had that come from? Frankie carefully set down the bottle of cologne and took a deep breath. Could you get cabin fever this quickly? What else could explain such an uncharacteristic thought popping into her usually controlled mind?

Straightening her shoulders, she walked to the door, determined to get a hold of herself.

The moment she stepped into the room, she smelled it. She walked to the kitchen toward the scent. The table was spread with numerous carved pieces and Steen was lining up paints in front of each, opening and closing the jars, testing for the right consistency. The pungent aroma teased her nostrils, bringing back another rush of old memories. Frankie pulled out a chair and picked up a carving of a playful tiger cub.

"Do you paint your own pieces?" she said.

"No," Steen answered as he tossed out a jar containing the dried-up remnants of a deep blue paint. "I wish I could, but it takes a different talent to paint than to carve, I guess. Or maybe just more patience than I have.''

Frankie ran her finger over the intricate folds of the cub's ear. "I'd say you must possess a lot of patience to do this kind of work. Who does your painting?''

"An artist I met some years ago. She's very good, but there's a drawback.'' He held up a jar toward the light, scanning the contents before continuing. "Carmen lives in New Mexico so that means mailing things back and forth. She also works only when the spirit moves her, taking off on trips that last for weeks just when I seem to need her the most.'' He shook his head. "One of these days I'm going to find someone closer, and more reliable.''

"Artists are often characters, I think. I took some art classes a couple of years ago, just for a change from the technical work I do. I studied with a woman named Shane who definitely marched to a different drummer. She'd paint all day and most of the night, then sleep for twenty-four hours straight.''

He took the chair next to her. "What kind of painting did you study?''

"Mostly acrylic on wood.''

"And you enjoyed that?''

"Yes, very much.''

"But you never pursued it. Why?''

She hadn't thought about her painting in some time. She'd wanted to do artwork once, but after the devastation of the accident, she hadn't the strength to try to fulfill those fragile dreams. She'd been through too much, changed too drastically. The doctor had said she needed a new path to follow and he'd been right.

Frankie looked up and found Steen's gray eyes watching her. What was it about being here that

dredged up so many memories for her? She gave a gesture of dismissal. "Oh, things happened and I decided
I was more suited to the world of computers." There
was nothing artistic about computers, not in the way she
used them. Nothing that lent itself to introspection or
dreaming. Safe, impersonal computers had all but saved
her sanity.

How easy it was to send her into that abyss of sadness, Steen thought. Though he believed in respecting
a person's privacy, he was having trouble keeping his
curiosity in check. "Would you like to try your hand
painting one of these? Might as well do something con-
structive since it looks like we're going to be stuck here
at least through today."

Hesitantly, she set down the carving. "I don't know.
I took lessons less than a year. I'd hate to mess up one
of your lovely pieces."

Though she would deny it, he caught the quick interest, the eagerness. "I don't think you'll do that. Besides, paint can always be removed." He indicated the
eight pieces lined up in front of the box. "Which one
appeals to you?"

The fawn was the most beautiful. It was about eight
inches long, carved from a lighter wood, with huge eyes
that seemed almost alive. She wanted to try, but she was
hesitant.

Steen followed her gaze and picked up the deer,
holding it out to her. "Come on. You'd be doing me a
favor."

She took it and gave him a shy smile. "If you're sure
you won't be upset if I ruin it."

"I'm not worried." He sorted through the jars.
"What colors would you like? With Carmen, I usually
write out the colors I want on each piece. Before I did

that, she got a little carried away with artistic freedom and I was getting purple dogs and striped cows.''

Frankie picked through the paints, considering.

He scowled at another near-empty jar. ''I've got to order more paints and I've got to build some shelves in here to house them. The storage shed out back gets too cold and they harden beyond use. I thought the hot water heater that's in there would keep the room warm enough, but evidently it doesn't.''

She held up three jars—a warm brown, a rust and a soft beige. ''What do you think if I make him spotted? Aren't fawns usually spotted?''

''Yes, I'd like that.'' He stood and began packing the other jars into a box. ''I'll get you one of my old shirts to wear over your sweater so you don't get full of paint.''

By the time she'd finished painting one small hoof, Steen saw that she was totally absorbed. Except to set a cup of coffee at her elbow, he'd left her alone while he gathered up his own things. Now he sat down across from her and picked up the wood he'd prepared that morning and the carver he'd brought to razor sharpness. He began to whittle, letting the not uncomfortable silence sit between them.

This was new to him—working contentedly side by side with a woman—and he didn't want to destroy the ease he felt. He also didn't particularly want to question the pleasure.

Long minutes later, Frankie held the deer up to the light, examining her progress. She smiled, pleased with the results. Glancing across the table, she noticed Steen diligently working opposite her and couldn't have said when he'd joined her. ''What did you decide to carve this time?'' she asked him.

"I'm preparing the wood, but I'm still not sure what it'll be."

"Tell me," Frankie began, needing to know the answer to a question that had been nagging at her, "how much would one of these carvings sell for?"

"It varies."

A careful answer. "All right, let's say this piece, if painted professionally, that is."

"Two hundred, possibly three, depending on which store was offering it for sale."

She looked up, stunned. That much? But how... Her eyes strayed to the shipping box he'd been packing the paints and carvings into, still on the counter. Olson Carvings. Of course. "You're *that* Olson?"

He'd watched her figure it out and wondered how she'd react. "One and the same."

"I've seen your work in resort hotel gift shops, in department stores. Why didn't you tell me?"

He shrugged. "What for?"

What for, indeed. Frankie went back to her painting. And she'd thought *she* was closemouthed. What else had the enigmatic Mr. Olson left out of his life story? she wondered.

Frankie finished painting the deer by late afternoon just as the light faded. Standing, she stretched to relieve the kinks and looked out the window. "It's actually stopped snowing," she commented.

"It ought to after two days and a night." Steen got up and wrapped his carving in the oiled rag. He saw that she'd stood the deer on newspaper to dry and leaned closer to examine it. "You're good at this, you know. If you ever get tired of computers, let me know."

Trying not to let his praise warm her, she went to the sink to wash up. "I don't think there's much money in it."

"You might be surprised." He cleared the table and put the brushes to soak. "Besides, how much money can one small woman need?"

"Perhaps not much daily, but I have to think of the future, of retiring one day."

Frowning, he stuffed newspaper into the trash can. "Aren't you a little young to think of retiring just yet? Besides, there very well could be someone in your life one day, someone who'll work with you toward that goal."

Reaching for the towel, Frankie shook her head. "I seriously doubt that. I like my life just the way it is."

Steen had always admired independence, but Frankie seemed to wave it like a red flag. Opening the cupboard, he took down a bottle. "Would you like a glass of wine?" At her nod, he brought out two glasses, poured and then handed her one. "So what are your retirement plans?"

Frankie tasted the wine. It was dark red and rich. Removing his shirt, she folded it as she answered. "I like the Hawaiian Islands. There's a house in Maui I have my eye on. I made an offer on it a few months ago, but the owner was undecided about selling and the price wasn't quite what I was hoping for. But I'd love that house. I'd planned on spending this week in Maui before Eric called about his problem."

"Do you have friends there, people you usually visit for the holidays?"

"Not really. I rent a condo on the beach and just soak up the sun. Christmas is easier to handle on a tropical island away from all the schmaltz. Who do you usually spend the holidays with?"

Steen shrugged. "No one in particular." He turned away but not before she caught the hint of sadness in his eyes.

She regarded him a long moment. "But there was someone, and quite recently." It wasn't a question.

He ran a hand through his hair. "You pick up on things easily. Most people don't."

"Maybe I recognize hurt because it's no stranger to me. What's her name?"

He leaned against the counter, gazing into his glass. "Her name's Jessica. We share a friendship now, and that's all. I wish her well." There was the merest trace of regret in his voice.

"She left you and married another man?"

"No, actually, I left her. We tried for two years to be right for each other, but it didn't work. We were a round peg and a square hole. Jess loves excitement, living in a big city, traveling." He waved his hand to indicate the cabin. "I love it here. I spend as little time as possible in my L.A. apartment. And I've done all the traveling I ever want to do. Oil and water, that's what we were. It's better to live alone than to live with someone wrong for you. I had a front row seat to a good marriage—my parents'. I won't settle for less."

It seemed too simplistic an explanation. "So you parted, just like that?"

His grey eyes were calm. "It wasn't exactly easy. Sometimes I still miss her. But love can't last if you have opposite goals in life, opposing philosophies. We wanted different things from life. I'm a simple guy. Jess is an attorney, very independent, very ambitious, like— like many women today."

Frankie was thoughtful as she sipped her wine. "Did my mentioning a house I'd like to buy one day in Maui make you think of Jessica? Or is it that you see me as someone just like her?"

He shrugged. "A little, perhaps."

Frankie set aside her unfinished wine. She needed a clear head right now. "There's nothing wrong with ambition—or independence." She shifted her gaze out the window, wanting to explain, yet reluctant to relive her pain.

"I cared about someone once, and I let myself become very dependent on him. When he went out of my life, it took me a very long time to find my way back. I never want to hurt like that again. So I don't get involved—not in friendships that are too deep or in relationships that are too significant. I need to feel safe. My work and the income give me the independence to live my life my way. If I want a house in Maui, I'll pay for it myself and live there alone if it pleases me. If it's lonely once in a while, well, lonely beats hurting. If you don't care, you can't get hurt."

Perhaps, Steen thought. He raised his glass in a toast. "Here's to friendship and no entanglements."

Frankie touched her glass to his. "I'll drink to that."

Steen swallowed, wondering if the warmth he felt was from the wine or the nearness of the woman next to him, hoping for the former.

"Oh, look!" Frankie leaned closer to the window. "It's a deer and she's coming closer."

Steen moved behind her. "She lives in the woods, but she ventures over fairly often. Poor thing, she's having a hard time in that deep snow."

"She's beautiful," Frankie whispered, unwilling to move so as not to frighten the doe. "She's looking right at us. Do you think she's searching for food?"

"There's a big buck I've seen her with. He's probably the breadwinner."

"Listen, chauvinist," she teased, "maybe she's the breadwinner and he just sits around admiring his gorgeous horns in a nearby pond."

He smiled. "That could be, too. I put out a big salt lick for them in among the trees, but it's probably snow-covered right now."

The deer cocked her head at the same time Frankie became aware of Steen's warm breath on the back of her neck. She fought a shiver as she watched the deer move away from the window. "Are there any fawns?" she asked, trying to keep her voice steady.

"I haven't seen any. Maybe they'll venture out in the spring." He felt the breath flutter from her and knew they'd reached a crossroad. It was one he could have predicted yesterday when he'd picked her up into his arms and buried his face in her throat. Hands on her shoulders, he turned her until she faced him. Her eyes had gone jade-green and shiny, filled with the same curiosity and awareness that he knew had darkened his.

Frankie had known this was building. He was too masculine, too attractive for her to ignore, despite her best efforts. Perhaps becoming aware of his thoughts on uninvolvement had her unconsciously giving her body permission to respond. The thud of her heart against her rib cage told her it was doing just that. "It seems we have a problem here," she said, her hands touching his chest as if to control his nearness.

"I don't see a problem. I see a solution." His hand cupped the back of her neck as he rubbed his lips over

hers, nibbling at the corners. Her mouth was so soft and
his was patient. He felt her fingers curl into his shirt as
she let out an unsteady breath.

He smelled of soap and nothing more—a clean,
masculine scent that drew her in. Somehow her arms
found their way around his neck and suddenly her body
was straining against his, eager, searching. Frankie
tasted a pleasure she could only think of as mindless as
he took her up the roller coaster. He was alternately
gentle and demanding, stealing the breath from her.

His tongue entered her mouth, then withdrew, teasing her, tempting her. Feeling uncharacteristically
reckless, she followed, tangling with him, learning his
dark flavors. She felt his large hands mold her to him
and heard a moan she hardly recognized as her own escape from her lips as he moved to press his mouth
against her throat.

Steen had wanted to discover, to sample, to explore.
He hadn't expected to feel this sharp need, this eager
passion flare so quickly, so hotly. His hands dragged her
closer as he returned to capture her lips with a desperation he couldn't remember feeling in far too long. She
responded by diving deeply into his mouth, by giving as
good as she was getting.

He realized he was trembling, and felt a quick flash
of annoyance that she could bring him to that. He had
to back away, and he would. After one more stroke
down her sleek body, one more taste of the lips already
swollen from his kisses, one more moment lost inside
her. When he did pull back, he found he was more
shaken than he'd care to admit.

Frankie felt the hammering of her heart trying to slow
itself, felt the rushing blood try to ease as she caught her
breath. She jammed her unsteady hands into her pock-

ets but, unwilling to let him see just how he'd affected
her, she straightened her shoulders and raised her eyes
to his.

"You must practice a lot," she said, her voice almost normal. "You're rather good at that."

Steen wished his breathing was more even as he returned the look. Such a small woman to cause such an
explosion inside him. "I can't remember the exact date,
but it's been awhile since I've kissed a woman." But he
did remember that it had never felt quite like that.

"Oh. I see." Slowly, she turned and walked toward
the bedroom. If he thought her a coward, so be it. She
had to have a few minutes alone. Recovering from facing the eye of a storm took a little time.

"Mmm, that was delicious." Frankie put down her
napkin and leaned back in her chair. "What can I do to
convince you to give me your secret marinade recipe?"

Steen wiped his mouth and regarded her with mock
seriousness. "Well, if I had a computer, you could
check it out for me. But I don't. You could help me trim
the tree or be stuck with the dishes. Your choice."

"What tree?"

"I cut down a Douglas fir last week. It's out by the
back door." Pushing aside the kitchen chair, he stood.
"I've got to bring it inside and stick it in the stand so the
snow will melt off and the branches will lower. Then we
can trim it."

Frankie began to clear the table. "I choose the dishes.
But you go ahead."

Taking the dishes from her, he set them on the counter. "Leave this and come help me with the tree. It'll be
fun."

She stood her ground. "I'd rather not."

He stopped, examining her face. He saw reluctance, and something more. Something like anxiety. He touched her arm. "It's okay. Memories that bad?"

Turning to the sink, Frankie nodded. "Yes." She bent to load the dishwasher, hoping he'd drop the matter. Without another word, she heard him leave, and moments later, the back door closing. Releasing a deep breath, she leaned forward to gaze out the window.

Moonlight flooded the trees, causing shadows to weave over the snow-covered yard. The radio played a soft waltz in the background and she could hear the fire Steen had built earlier sizzling through the logs. His cabin was really very comfortable, cozy and warm—and she wanted desperately to leave it.

Not in recent memory had she had to come face-to-face with so many remembrances from her haunted background. She wasn't even anxious about getting to Eric's casino anymore. She was anxious to go home— back to the familiar, the everyday, the life she'd made for herself.

She was tired of seeing so many shadows from the past. Tired of Christmas trees and carols and hoopla.

And fearful. She was fearful of this sudden, this stunning reaction to Steen Olson.

Though they'd chatted almost normally throughout dinner, the awareness had crackled between them as surely as the fire had hissed and sparked in the grate. They'd shared one hell of a couple of kisses. It wasn't easy to set her thoughts aside and go on as if nothing had happened. Something had, and she wasn't sure what to name it. Now, when he gave her one of those long looks, his gray eyes seemingly trying to see deep inside her, she felt a slight fluttering, a quick shift of her heartbeat. On the one hand, she wanted him to kiss her again, to see if she'd imagined the power, the intensity. On the other, she feared he would.

Ridiculous! She was too smart to let a man get to her, too cautious, too mature. Wasn't she?

With short, angry strokes, she wiped the countertops. There was an undeniable attraction between them that pleased her even less than it did Steen. His answer was to rush out into the cold snow and wrestle with a tree. Hers was to damn near scrub the design off the tiled counter. But when they were both finished, the feelings would still be there. If only the snowplows would show up. Then she could be on her way home where she could begin to view these couple of days as a frustrating episode and nothing more.

And she could forget she'd ever laid eyes on one Steen Olson, ever been carried through the snow in his strong arms, ever been kissed senseless by him. Sure she would. With disgust, she tossed down the dishrag and marched to the bedroom.

The smart thing to do was to plead fatigue, to climb into his big featherbed and read until sleep would come. She'd thought they could be friends during this unexpected interlude. And then he'd kissed her like someone who'd moved light-years beyond mere friendship. As she undressed, she acknowledged the anger she felt was better aimed at herself. Because she'd kissed him back. Oh, yes. Quite royally, she'd kissed him back. And enjoyed every second of it.

Slipping on her robe, Frankie pondered the why of it. Matt had been her first man and after he was gone, there'd been no one. She'd reacted to the few men who'd wandered into her life since, with gentle affection and a distant friendship. She hadn't let herself think about what she was missing.

Unclipping her hair, she picked up her brush and began pulling it through the heavy strands. She missed the sparring with a quick masculine mind, the easy camaraderie such as she'd shared with Steen while he'd carved and she'd painted, the feeling of being more alive. She missed feeling like a desirable woman. And she fervently wished Steen hadn't reminded her that she missed all that. For it was exactly what she'd be walking away from when she left.

And leave she would, for as her mother used to say, she had other fish to fry. She had a life she'd painstakingly put together to replace the old, shattered one. This one was based on mature reality, not youthful dreams. No illusions. It was safer that way, infinitely safer. She made her way to the bathroom.

By the time she finished her shower and came out of the bath, Steen had the tree in its stand in the far corner of the room, stubborn clusters of snow already melting onto the plastic sheet underneath. He turned from stoking the fire.

His hair was damp and glistening from the snow, his cheeks ruddy from the cold, his eyes a slate gray as they watched her. Why couldn't she have been stranded with a grandfatherly type like Corbett, a man bright, witty and entertaining, but with thinning hair and fighting a paunch? Frankie thought irrationally. Why someone so damn appealing without half trying?

Steen bent and picked up two brandy snifters, holding one out toward her. "I poured us a drink."

She ran a hand through the hair she'd just blown dry. "I thought I'd turn in early. I'm a little tired. But I don't want to put to you out of your bed again, so I'll take the couch."

Nervous. She was nervous and he knew exactly why. He'd been a little jumpy himself since he'd given in to the need to kiss her. Chopping a whole stack of wood hadn't relieved the ache touching her had caused. Maybe they could move things back to friendly. Maybe. He had to try. He indicated the glass. "This brandy's a hundred years old, and I feel close to that after splitting a few logs. I'm harmless. I assure you."

Too late, Frankie thought, to convince her he was ever harmless. Nevertheless, rudeness was something she was never comfortable with. She walked to him and took the glass.

Their eyes met over the rims as they sipped. Frankie felt the heat from the fire graze her cheek, felt the liquid heat glide down her throat. She could smell the pine scent that clung to him. The drink was strong and she wished she were. The song coming from the stereo filled the room, something low and sultry. Her heart pounded in time, in reluctant anticipation, in undeniable need.

Quite suddenly, he wanted to hold her, Steen realized. To hell with differences, with a toast to friendship without entanglements. He took her glass and set it and his own down on the end table. Taking a step closer, he held out his arms. "One dance, and we'll turn in."

One dance. Could she chance it? Could she turn him down? Frankie moved into his arms. They closed loosely about her as he led her in time to the music. Her breathing became shallow. This felt like a mistake. It felt like madness. Yet it felt so good. How could that be?

Her hand in his was damp as he saw her shift her gaze to somewhere over his left shoulder, avoiding his eyes. A saxophone moaned in the background, the sound filled with longing. He guided her onto the wooden floor, away from the fire, into the shadows. His stomach muscles tightened as he placed her arms over his shoulders and shifted her body closer to his. Swaying with her, Steen wondered why he was putting himself through this exquisite torture when only a short time ago out in the snow, he'd vowed he wouldn't.

She could feel his heartbeat through her robe and his shirt, as erratic as her own, thudding against her breast. Unable to stop herself, she touched the hair curling at the nape of his neck, running her fingers through the softness.

All these years, she'd avoided this. It was so easy in San Francisco, dating a select few men she'd deemed tame and solid. A pleasant dinner, a concert, a play— then a quick hug and a brush of lips at her apartment door before she dashed safely inside. No hurt feelings, no soaring emotions, no racing hearts to contend with.

Only there was nothing tame or safe about the man who held her now, the man who in a day and a half had her emotions churning and her blood heating. The simple truth was, she liked Steen Olson. Too much. He was causing warm ripples of feelings inside her that were as surprising as they were unwelcome. She'd long ago deliberately turned from her sexual responses and buried them. Or thought she had. Trapped here alone in a cabin with an attractive man was no time to have them emerge, operable and screaming for attention. Even as she wondered how she'd come so far so fast, Frankie rested her head just under his chin, as if it belonged there.

He hadn't imagined it, Steen told himself. She smelled like wildflowers, soft and warm in his arms, and unbelievably responsive. She probably wasn't what he needed, but she was what he wanted. And he couldn't seem to stop wanting, to discipline himself not to touch her.

He'd thought her to be like Jessica, but realized that there was a major difference. Jessica had kept herself distant. Even during lovemaking, she'd always been in control of herself, single-minded. Frankie could be distracted with a touch, a look. He pictured her in his four-poster bed, imagined her wild and abandoned, carried away on the wings of passion as he already knew she could be. And his imagination was making him hard and hurting.

But there was more. She touched him deep inside where there were empty places waiting to be filled. He didn't know her, yet he knew her very well.

Frankie felt the change in him, the tightness of his body and the heat of his breath in her hair. She leaned away and stared into eyes hot and hungry. The song ended on a high note as she took a step backward.

She cleared her throat, knowing her voice would be ragged. "Thank you for the dance," she turned away, still shaky. "Where do you keep the bedding for the couch I can..."

"No. Take the bedroom."

He hadn't moved, his face still in shadow, so she couldn't read his expression. "It's not fair for..."

"Take the bedroom. I'll see you in the morning."

Frankie nodded. He needed to be alone and so did she. Quietly, she closed the door behind her.

Steen let his shoulders sag, releasing a bit of the tension that had him coiled like a finely wound spring. He had no one to blame but himself for his present condition. Cursing himself for a damn fool, he walked to the window and looked out at a large chunk of moon behind the snow-laden trees. From a distance, he heard the howl of a coyote, a desolate sound echoing in the still night air.

"I know how you feel, buddy," Steen muttered before turning back to his narrow couch.

Chapter Four

It was snowing again. Frankie couldn't believe her eyes as she stood looking out the window, gripping her coffee mug in hands that were white-knuckled and tense. It was the morning of the third day she'd been trapped here only fifty miles from her destination. Trapped and feeling frustrated, near desperation and definitely cranky. The fact that Steen had fixed himself a breakfast that would have fed two healthy lumberjacks, eaten it in high good humor and was now whistling to himself as he cleaned up was not helping her mood. People who were cheerful in the morning made her want to throw things.

"Penny for your thoughts," Steen said, drying his hands. She was not in the best of moods, he could see, refusing to eat, drinking cup after cup of black coffee as she stared outside.

"You'd get change."

"I think what we both need is a change of scenery," Steen announced.

Frankie was game. Anything to get rid of this closed-in feeling. But there seemed to be a few obstacles. She nodded toward the snowdrifts clearly visible through the high window. "How are we going to manage that? The roads are impassable and the path to your cabin is completely buried."

"We're not going on the roads. We're going to take a shortcut through the woods." He left the kitchen and walked toward the closet by the back door, noting that curiosity had her following. "I usually cut down a big fir and take it to Hannah, the lady who makes the blackberry brandy. She's baby-sitting with her granddaughter while her daughter's in the hospital having another baby. Emily's probably still there and we can't disappoint her and not have a Christmas tree to decorate."

Frankie looked skeptical. "Some of those snowdrifts are over our heads. We couldn't get very far. Besides, I don't have any warm clothes."

Rummaging through the closet, Steen's voice was muffled. "Ever try snowshoes, the kind that look like tennis rackets? They use them around here a lot. You can walk anywhere in them. And I'll fix you up with clothes. My sister left some things here if I can just find them."

"You didn't mention having a sister."

Arms loaded, he backed out. "She's twenty-two, ten years younger than me, a really bright girl. She's a junior in college in Reno." He dumped clothes on the couch and began looking through them.

Frankie went over and eased a hip on the sofa arm. "A junior. What's she studying?"

"Well, for a while there, I thought she was majoring in men, this one guy in particular. But she's finally sent him packing and settled down. She loves kids, wants to be a teacher." He handed her a down-filled jacket. "Here, try this on for size."

Shrugging into the jacket, Frankie decided to drop the matter of his sister. Unless she came riding up in a sleigh, chances were she'd never meet her. She looked down at herself. "I guess it fits."

"Sure does." He went back to the closet for the snowshoes.

Did she really want to trudge through the snow, to visit this Hannah and her granddaughter, mess around with a tree that was bound to get her thinking again? Perhaps the best thing would be to let him go alone, to stay here and read. Frankie took off the jacket. "Look, I think I'll pass on this walk. You go chop down your tree and..."

Steen faced her and played his ace. "Hannah has a phone." He hadn't told her earlier, sure that in her anxiety to get to Tahoe she'd have trudged out when the storm was in full force. But after their conversation about Eric Hanley, he'd decided he ought to give her the opportunity to make that call. Much as he disliked the thought of her leaving, he hadn't the right to prevent her from rushing to that jerk's side. Perhaps he wouldn't come for her, Steen mused.

Hands on her hips, Frankie studied him. "You sure know the right buttons to push with me, don't you?" In more ways than one, she added silently.

He came closer. "Do I?"

It was hard to answer with a dry throat. She started to turn away as he thrust something into her hands. "What's this?"

"Thermal underwear. Put it on. It's going to be a long, cold walk."

A long, cold walk was just what she needed. And so did Steen. Frankie went into the bedroom.

"Hold still, can you?" Steen wound the scarf around her neck and fastened it in front.

"Hold still? Eskimos sitting on ice floes and fishing all day wear less than I've got on. I won't walk, I'll waddle."

"Haven't you heard, the layered look is in?" He stood back to admire his work. "I think you look kind of cute."

Frankie shifted restlessly, bundled up like a toddler facing her first winter walk, complete with snowshoes the size of rowboats. "Cute? If I could move, I'd pop you."

Grinning, Steen pulled on a wool hat and grabbed his ax from the corner. "Ready?"

"Way past ready," she muttered, following him out the door, bracing herself for the cold. It wasn't too bad, she soon discovered. The sky was thick with heavy clouds but the snow was only falling lightly and the wind had died down. It was all so clean and seemed to stretch for miles, hanging from the trees like fine lace, snaking along the path between the thick trunks.

And the silence. It was utterly quiet except for their breathing, which soon became a bit labored.

"How you doing?" Steen asked after a while, turning to check on her. He thought she looked a bit like Lucy, the cartoon character in "Peanuts," all bundled up with only her face visible.

"Okay." She stopped behind him, trying not to huff and puff, straining to see through the trees. "There's not a house in sight. Just where is Hannah's place?"

"Through the woods, not far." He started forward.

There was that *not far* routine again. She trudged on, her eyes on the hazy horizon.

They'd been walking quite a while when they came to a small clearing bordered by tall firs. "Hey," Frankie called, "aren't you going to chop down one of these trees?"

Turning, he waited until she caught up. "No use dragging one from here. There're plenty right in Hannah's backyard. Want to rest a minute?"

"Yes." Without warning, her arms shot out and she fell backward onto the snow. Her laughter rang out in the clear mountain air. "Ever make angels in the snow?"

"Sure." Steen lined his body up next to hers and fell back, then moved his arms up and down to form the wings. "Only I'm not sure we'll be able to get up easily wearing snowshoes to check out our handiwork."

"Eddie Baines and I used to walk home from school together," Frankie told him, moving her arms. "In the winter, we'd compete, seeing who could make the best angel. He always won. Eddie had bright red hair and these long arms and he'd somehow scramble up without mussing the snow. I don't know how he did that." She gazed up at the murky sky. "I haven't thought of him in years."

"Did you ever have snowball fights with Eddie Baines?"

"You bet I did, and I won, too. Not every time, but often enough that he knew I could."

As he picked up a mound of snow in each gloved hand, Steen smiled at his mental picture of a young Frankie getting the best of the redheaded boy. "And did he ever wash your face with snow—" quickly, he rolled over, dropping snow onto her already rosy cheeks "— like this?"

But Frankie was faster than he'd estimated, even wearing stacks of clothing. She gave a quick push and sent him sprawling onto his back, then zeroed in on him, shoving generous globs of snow onto his cheeks.

"Try to zap me, will you?" Laughing, she spread more onto his chin as he shifted his head, trying to avoid her busy hands.

"Okay, okay, I give up." Steen encircled her with his arms, trapping her hands on his chest, enjoying the tension releasing laughter. In the tussle, she'd lost her hat and her golden hair framed her face, lifting softly in a light breeze. She lay atop him, catching her breath, her eyes deep green, her long lashes shiny with snow-flakes. God, she was beautiful.

The look in his eyes had her softening. Frankie moved her gaze to his mouth as her pulse picked up its rhythm.

"You want to kiss me, Frankie?" Steen asked, deliberately goading her.

Oh, yes, she wanted to kiss him, all right. She wanted that mindless loss of self, that slow slide into another world. Well, why not? Soon, she'd phone Eric and if he didn't come for her, at least she'd convince him to send someone to plow her out, for old times' sake. In mere hours, she'd be on her way out of here and, in the meantime, she'd be safe at Hannah's. Yes, why not?

"Do I want to kiss you?" Tipping her head to the side, she appeared to consider the thought. "Yes, I think I do." Excitement shivered through her, more devastating than the freezing temperature.

"Then ask me." He licked his lips while his eyes challenged her.

She smiled at the role reversal he'd led her into. "All right. May I kiss you, Steen?"

He liked the sudden husky timbre of her voice. "Yes."

The laughter left her as she tugged off her gloves. If there would be but one more time, she'd make it count. She raised her hands and framed his face, taking pleasure in the morning feel of his unshaven cheeks. Closing her eyes, she touched her lips to his.

As in everything she did, Frankie had intended to stay in control, to keep herself in check. But he opened to her, drawing her in, his arms urging her closer through the thick barrier of clothing while his tongue danced into her mouth. And she forgot all her intentions.

Who would have guessed that this big, rugged man would have a mouth so soft, so tender? Who'd have predicted he'd taste wild and hot, yet already somewhat familiar, as if she'd been waiting for his special flavors? And who'd have suspected that a woman who rarely gave men more than a quick kiss at the door would open her mouth and close her mind as she strained to press closer?

She tasted like the first sweet spoonful of thick, new honey in the spring and smelled like winter dreams and wildflowers. There seemed an innate shyness to her, yet he sensed her need to know more of him, as he wanted to know her. Steen fought the knowledge that knowing her completely would mean there'd be no turning back. He'd thought to have a friendship free of entanglements. They were two adults who knew what they were doing. He shoved to the back of his mind the hollow ring of that as he felt her reluctantly pull back.

Darker now, her eyes found his. She felt the need to say something. This kiss had been as the other, too powerful to ignore. "I think there's something to mountain air. I've never reacted quite this way before."

"I've also been known to slip things into the drinking water," Steen said, grateful that his voice was steadier than he felt.

"What a sneaky thing to do." Rolling away from him, Frankie scrambled clumsily to her feet, the snowshoes making her awkward. Spotting something in the snow, she bent to pick it up. "Look, an acorn. You'd think it would have been buried in all this snow."

Steen was up and at her side. "Lots of oak trees around here. It's probably a lucky acorn."

Frankie smiled at his flight of fancy. "Then you should have it." She placed the acorn in his hand, retrieved her hat and gloves, and scanned the direction they'd been traveling. "I guess we'd better be on our way."

Pocketing the acorn, Steen started out, welcoming the physical exertion.

Twenty minutes later, nearly out of breath, Frankie stopped. "I think I see something," she said hopefully. Since their so-called rest period, he'd been setting a marathon pace. Gamely, she'd kept up, but she was nearly worn out now. She hoped the house in the distance was Hannah's.

"Almost there," he called back as he marched on.

Distances could be deceiving in the mountains, Frankie discovered. By the time they reached Hannah's backyard, she was chilled to the bone and her legs

quivered from the unusual workout. She was also weak
with gratitude when the door swung open at Steen's
quick knock.

"Well, look who's here!" Hannah said, hustling
them both into her kitchen warmly fragrant with cinnamon and sugar. "What a day to be tromping around
in the snow," she chided, already unwrapping Frankie's scarf from around her neck. She shot a scolding
look toward Steen. "Just because you've got the con-
stitution of an elephant doesn't mean the rest of us do,
you big ape."

"Good to see you, too, Hannah," Steen said as he
wiggled out of his snowshoes. "Meet Francesca Taelor, only she prefers Frankie."

"Pleased to know you, Frankie," Hannah went on
as Frankie emerged from under layers of clothing. "My,
you are small, aren't you?" She glanced along her own
five-foot-eight-inch length. "I always wanted to be tiny.
Don't have the bones for it, I guess."

Hannah was younger than Frankie had expected, in
her mid-fifties, she'd guess. In her youth, she'd been
beautiful. She was still attractive with high cheek-
bones, intelligent blue eyes and rich chestnut hair pulled
back from her oval face into a braided knot at her nape.
She also had a knack for making a guest feel at home,
Frankie decided as Hannah settled them at her table
with fresh coffee and a plate of cookies still warm from
the oven.

"There, that should help chase away the chill of that
long walk," Hannah said as she set down cream and
sugar.

The kitchen was huge, reminding Frankie of the one
in the farmhouse she'd grown up in, with gingham cur-
tains at the windows and worn linoleum on the floor.

She sipped her coffee and watched Hannah mix cookie dough while she questioned Steen with all the audacity of the old neighbor she was. When she heard a shy voice from the archway, she looked up.

"Steen, did you bring me anything?"

"Now, Emily," Hannah warned. "Say hello to Steen's friend, Frankie Taelor. This is my granddaughter Emily."

The child smiled shyly at Frankie before returning her attention to Steen.

"But he *always* brings me something. Don't you, Steen?" the little girl insisted as she came into the kitchen.

"You bet I do." He stood and held his arms straight out at his sides. "Come find it."

What a lovely child, Frankie thought, with a wrenching heart. Her hair was long and blond, like Sara's might have been by now, though her eyes were dark brown and shy where Sara's had been deep blue and always laughing. Pressing a hand to her lips, she watched the little girl skip over to Steen and timidly pat down the pockets of his jeans in a game they were evidently used to playing.

Suddenly Emily's small face lit up as she spotted a bulge in the pocket of his plaid shirt. With a little triumphant sound, she touched the hidden gift. "There it is."

He bent lower. "Guess I have to give it to you since you found it."

Eyes dancing, Emily removed a small carved rabbit with one foot raised and a mischievous look on his face. "Oh, he's beautiful. I can name him Thumper, like Bambi's friend." She turned to Frankie. "We saw that movie last week."

Not trusting her voice just yet, Frankie nodded. She fought to bury the pain, the what-might-have-beens, and concentrate on the here and now. Steen took Emily onto his lap and was soon involved in a discussion as to why one of the bunny's ears stood up and the other bent forward while Hannah went on about the way he spoiled the child.

Spoiled, indeed, Frankie silently agreed. Even his smaller carvings easily sold for several hundred dollars apiece and he'd just given Emily one as if he'd picked it up in the corner drugstore. Then she noticed more in Hannah's hutch—plain wooden carvings and painted ones, crowded in among cut-glass vases and delicate china teacups. A small fortune, she realized since learning that Steen turned out the pieces sold as Olson Carvings.

Hannah dusted flour from her hands. "I see you noticed my collection." She winked at Frankie. "Steen's been bringing them to me for more than ten years now. There's many a collector who'd love to get his hands on those, 'specially some of his early pieces. Not that I'd ever sell a single one. Wrapped in love, they are. Right, Steen?"

Scooting Emily from his lap, Steen stood, looking a shade embarrassed. "I think it's time I got that tree. You want to help me, babe?" he asked Emily.

"Can I, Grandma?"

"If you bundle up, you can. Frankie and I'll finish up these cookies, then we'll see about making some supper."

Frankie eyed the cookie cutters lined up on the floured board. Reindeer, a bell, a star and a fat Santa, among others. "I'm not very good at baking."

"Nothing much to making cookies. I'll show you how."

Hannah was a hard woman to refuse. She fingered a metal cutter in the shape of a sleigh and watched Steen put his coat back on. He helped Emily into leggings and a heavy jacket, listening all the while to her chatter and giving her serious, thoughtful answers. But his eyes strayed to Frankie often. She had to get out of here. Too much was closing in on her.

"Hannah, would you mind if I used your phone?" she asked, rising and looking about for the instrument. She spotted it on the side wall and walked over.

"You sure could, if it was working." Hannah put a little muscle into rolling out her cookie dough. "Been out for two days now. Happens a lot around here during these storms."

Frankie sagged in disappointment. She couldn't resist picking up the receiver and listening. Nothing. She felt her frustration return full force.

Steen put his hand on her arm, his touch gentle. "They're probably working on it. Maybe it'll come on before we leave."

She nodded, too much in turmoil to speak. As she cleared her throat, she felt a small hand slip into hers, and looked down.

"Want to see the cookies I made?"

"Sure." She had no right to be rude to these people because of her problems. She let herself be led over to the counter where several dozen cookies in a variety of shapes were iced in an assortment of colors, resplendent with sprinkles and silver balls. "They're lovely." She smiled at the child.

"When I come back in, I'll help you decorate yours. If you want me to."

"I'd like that." There was something sad in Emily's eyes, something too solemn, too serious for someone so young. "How old are you, Emily?"

"Eight. I had a birthday last month and you know what I got?"

Eight. Dear God, eight. She kept the smile in place. "No, tell me."

"A kitten. I named him Mittens because he's all white with four black paws. Only he went outside and got lost." She turned to Steen who was pulling on his gloves. "Maybe I can look some more for him while you cut down our tree, okay, Steen? Mittens has been gone two days and he's probably cold and hungry."

Steen's eyes met Hannah's over the child's head. "I'll help you look for him, babe. Come on, let's go."

Frankie didn't believe in false hope. "Maybe he wandered to the road and someone picked him up. Was he wearing a collar?"

"Yes, a plaid one with a bell on it. But Mittens wouldn't go away with anyone. He's my cat." Emily pulled her cap down low over her ears. "He'll be back. I know he will." She walked toward the back door.

Steen gave his head a small shake, then followed her outside.

Frankie moved to the table. "I hate to see your granddaughter disappointed, but a kitten could never survive two days in that storm."

"I know that and you know that. But that child doesn't want to believe it." Hannah shook her head. "She's always been kind of in her own world, you know what I mean. Too serious. Her mother's like that, too."

A quiet child with huge eyes. How often people had said that about her, Frankie thought. She stared down at the rolled-out batter the older woman had placed in front of her. It looked like she had little choice. Picking up a cookie cutter, she shoved it into the pale, plump dough. "I understand your daughter's in the hospital. Did she have her baby yet?"

To her amazement, Frankie found herself chatting cozily with Hannah about her daughter, the weather, her cabin in the woods and the best recipe for cabbage soup while the cookie cutouts filled the pans. She absorbed the homey feeling, at first with hesitancy, then with a greediness she hadn't suspected in herself.

So this was one of the things she'd missed—two women sharing thoughts over their baking, the warm scents, the sounds of cookie sheets scraping over oven racks and bells ringing heralding another completed batch. Her mother had had little energy left to make time-consuming decorated cookies. She had baked a Christmas cake with fruit and nuts, a rare holiday treat. There were a few good memories, Frankie acknowledged.

They were nearly finished before she noticed the Christmas carols softly playing in the background. She'd forgotten how it felt to relax body, soul and mind, if indeed she'd ever known.

Home. Hannah's house felt like a home. Or like one should be. How hers could have been if... Frankie blinked back the rush of tears. *Please don't let me cry, not here.*

Hannah slipped the final batch from the oven and sat down with a relieved sigh while Frankie washed her hands and regained her composure. "The last batch, thank goodness. I usually don't make such a fuss at Christmas, living alone and all. But with Emily here this year, I decided to go all out." She rubbed her left shoulder. "I'm not as young as I used to be."

"You don't look old enough to be a grandmother," Frankie told her honestly as she rejoined her.

"I married young. I don't recommend it."

"Nor do I."

Hannah's shrewd blue eyes measured her before she nodded. "We'll get along, I can tell. I like you and I'm an excellent judge of character."

Frankie smiled at that. "Thank you."

Hannah returned to her subject. "I keep telling Steen. Marriage is for the lucky few. The rest of us strike out once and are smart enough to steer clear. But you can't shake that man's beliefs."

Frankie preferred to shift the focus of the conversation from Steen back to Hannah. "Are you divorced or did your husband die?"

She gave a mirthless chuckle. "I booted him out the door two years after I made the mistake of marrying him. I gave him a choice—me or the booze. He made his decision and I've never regretted mine. The only good thing that ever came out of our marriage was my daughter, Donna, Emily's mother."

"Yes, you're very fortunate to have them both." It was more than she had, Frankie couldn't help thinking. "How long have you lived here?"

"Over thirty years. I scraped together and bought this house shortly after Charley left. It's a good, safe place to raise a child. For twenty-five years, I drove to Tahoe and back every day, working for an insurance company. Retired six years ago, and not a day too soon."

"That's a long commute."

Hannah finished her coffee. "Yes, but worth the drive. City living's not for me. What kind of work do you do, Frankie?"

This she could talk about with ease. While Hannah removed the cooling cookies from their baking sheets, she explained her computer expertise and was surprised at Hannah's sharp questions and sincere interest.

Placing the lid onto the cookie jar, Hannah turned to Frankie. "Have you known Steen long?"

"No. I'm just someone the poor man's marooned in a snowstorm with." She told Hannah the story of the bus ride, the trudge to Steen's house, even her foolish attempt to leave in his Jeep.

Hannah laughed. "I guess you could find worse men to get stuck with for a few days. Steen's a gentleman, just not real smart when it comes to the opposite sex, like me."

Frankie's curiosity wouldn't let that lie. "You mean Jessica?"

"Oh, he told you, did he? Yes, Jessica. She hurt him quite badly, I think, more than he lets on. Afterward, he used to come over and sit staring into my fire. But he made himself get over her, and he still believes there's someone out there for him and he'll find her one day." Hannah shook her head in disbelief. "Stubborn man. I told him to steer clear of career women. He needs someone who'll give him more than half a loaf."

A warning from a caring neighbor? Perhaps. "Good advice, I'm sure. Some women prefer careers over marriage. Personally, I can hardly wait to get back to work, and then home. I have no interest in involvements." There, that should ease Hannah's mind.

"Nothing wrong with having ambition. Some people thrive on it. But sometimes it doesn't mix well with marriage." Hannah rose and opened the refrigerator. "You like pot roast?"

Frankie gladly shifted her thoughts. "Yes, I love pot roast."

Hannah began unwrapping the meat. "Yes, Steen's a mighty fine man," she began again conversationally. "Took that sister of his in when their folks died, and he was hardly more than a boy himself. Raised her real good, too."

"Steen raised his sister?" He hadn't given her many details when he'd mentioned his sister earlier.

"Sure did. Put her through college and she was quite a handful there for a while. He started up his carving business and now he ships all over the world. And he did it by himself, with no help from a living soul. You've got to admire a man like that." Hannah took out vegetables and put them in the sink.

"I do admire him." Frankie walked over and picked up the potato peeler. Hannah was making her feel a bit defensive. "As I mentioned, I've only known the man a few days." A few very nervous days that had somehow brought about several very thrilling kisses.

All right, so Steen Olson was good to his sister, a talented artist and a successful businessman. He probably had loved his mother, apple pie and the flag, too. And let's not forget that he was one hell of a kisser. Be that as it may, she still wasn't interested. And she fervently wished they would stop discussing him.

With effort, she dragged her attention back to Hannah who was now telling her how for years she'd hated to cook, but since her retirement she'd learned to love it.

"It gives me such satisfaction to try a new dish and have it turn out well." Glancing over, she stretched an arm about Frankie's shoulders and gave her a quick squeeze. "You're killing that potato, you know."

Frankie stared at the sliver in her hand and the sink full of peelings and shredded potato. So much for controlling her thoughts, she decided.

She'd just finished cleaning all the vegetables when Steen and Emily tromped in sporting red cheeks and a huge evergreen. Emily climbed out of her coat and announced that they had not found Mittens, but she was sure they would tomorrow. Her eyes were filled with such positive hope that Frankie had to look away. Had she ever had that kind of blind, childish faith? She doubted it.

Hannah put their dinner into the oven and then directed the placement of the tree, which seemed to take forever, Frankie thought. By the time they got it just right, she'd decided that the huge evergreen gracing the White House foyer couldn't possibly have had more discussion as to every correct angle and side.

Stifling a yawn, she'd hoped Steen would suggest they be on their way once the tree was happily residing in its stand, but the request died on her lips as he climbed up into the attic and brought down boxes of Christmas ornaments. Lord, she didn't want to do this, Frankie thought, feeling more trapped by the stifling holiday atmosphere than she'd ever been by the storm. Yet she couldn't see a way out, short of being rude.

She could have handled herself better if it hadn't been for Emily's presence. She was a sweet child, bright and pretty. It was her own fault, Frankie decided. If only she didn't see the possibility of Sara in every smile and gesture as the four of them hung ornaments on still damp limbs. When Hannah mentioned a salad, she almost raced to the kitchen to make it, leaving the tree trimmers to finish the job.

Steen reached toward the top, hanging an ornament shaped like a delicate teapot up high where no one could accidentally brush against it. He'd been watching Frankie on and off all day. Was it this business of old, hurtful Christmas memories disturbing her, or was there more? Several times, he'd seen her clutch her hands together tightly, hoping their trembling would go unnoticed. And he'd seen her eyes fill with tears she'd blinked away more than once. What was bothering her? And more to the point, when had her well-being become so important to him?

He'd just tucked the last empty box away when Hannah announced dinner. Emily raced him to the bathroom as she always did, chuckling when he let her beat him as usual. When he questioned how she was feeling, she mentioned missing her mother. And Mittens. He followed her to the table, feeling that right now, the cat seemed more on Emily's mind than her mother.

"Hannah, this is the best doggone pot roast in the whole state of California. Maybe the country." He winked at Emily. "Possibly the world. Would you consider marrying me?"

Emily giggled. "You can't marry my grandma. She's too old for you."

"I'll take magic pills and be her age real quick. Then I'll be your grandpa and you'll have to do everything I say."

Hannah joined in, not to be outdone. "Forget that. Give me those magic pills and I'll be twenty-five again. Then we'll see if you can keep up, young man."

"I'm sure I couldn't." Steen took another biscuit and shifted his gaze to Frankie. She was quiet, her eyes a little haunted. Maybe tonight, he could do a little probing. Perhaps it would help if she'd talk it out.

Steen thought it best that they start back right after dinner in case the wind had picked up again, causing more drifting. But Emily spoke up before he could voice his thoughts.

"Frankie, would you read my new book with me, please?" she asked as she carried her empty plate to the sink.

Frankie looked doubtful, torn between wanting to leave and not wanting to hurt the child. "Well, I . . ."

"Hold on, missy," Hannah said, taking in the scene with her shrewd eyes. "Don't go getting your tail feathers in a swivet. I'll read it with you after these folks leave. They've got better things to do."

"Do you?" Emily asked solemnly.

Better things to do than read a story with a child? The urge to gather Emily to her, to feel that small, warm body against her own, stunned Frankie. Swallowing with difficulty, she pushed back her chair. She could do this. She *had* to do this.

"I have nothing I'd rather do more than read with you, Emily," she said. "That is, if I'm not needed in the cleanup crew."

"We'll handle it," Steen said, rolling up his sleeves. He'd watched her nearly turn white, then get a grip on herself. He'd been about to help her out, but she'd made her choice clear. He turned to Hannah. "When are you going to have a dishwasher put into this place, Hannah?"

"I had one once. The silly thing kept jamming and overflowing. God gave us two good hands, unlimited water and then had someone invent soap. I think He meant for us to take it from there. Some inventions are more trouble than they're worth.''

From the corner of his eye, he saw Frankie sit down on the couch and Emily curl up next to her while Hannah went on muttering about an entire generation of spoiled people. Frankie's face was tight with repression as she began, her voice low.

'' 'Twas the night before Christmas, and all through the house . . .''

Steen had to give her credit. She made it more than halfway through before she suddenly stopped reading. Staring down at the pages, she bit down on her lower lip and closed her eyes. Wiping his hands, he watched her close the book and stand up.

''I'm sorry, Emily,'' Frankie said in a shaky voice. ''I'm very tired. Could we finish this another time?'' Without waiting for an answer, she swung desperate eyes to Steen. ''Could we leave now, please?''

She was holding herself in tight check, he knew. Too tight. Nodding, he went to the closet for their things.

Hannah's hand on her arm was meant to comfort as her voice was meant to soothe. ''Guess we wore you out, Frankie. Next time will be better, you'll see.''

The older woman couldn't possibly know of her problems, yet somehow, she understood in that timeless communication that women often shared that she was hurting. Frankie zippered her jacket, then embraced Hannah, holding her close for a brief moment. She smelled of cinnamon and powder and love. She pulled back only to see Emily alongside looking up at her.

''Will you come see us again? Maybe I'll have a new baby brother or sister by then. And Mittens will be back for sure.''

She heard Steen open the door as she held the child to her for a long, heart-stopping moment. Then she turned and strode out the door, not stopping to look back, moving hurriedly toward the footprints they'd made when they'd arrived.

He actually had trouble keeping up with her, Steen noticed. Driven by adrenaline, and whatever demons lived inside her, she slapped her snowshoes onto the crusty snow and marched ahead of him. They were halfway home before he called out to her.

"Hey, lady. Could you slow down? I'm out of breath."

She slowed gradually, then finally stopped. He came alongside her and saw that her head was downcast as she kicked at an icy wedge with the side of her snowshoe. The moonlight poured down on them, casting long shadows that raced between the trees.

"I'm sorry, Steen. I just couldn't handle another minute in there."

"Can you talk about it?"

Pulling off her gloves, she rammed them into the jacket pockets. "I don't know."

She needed to confront it, and he needed to know. "It's not just because your childhood Christmases weren't all that happy that you're upset, is it?"

"That's only a part of it."

Steen put his hands on her arms and moved her fractionally closer to where their bulky jackets were just touching. "Maybe talking about it will help."

She shook her head. "Nothing will help." She let out a shaky breath. She'd come too far. Somehow she'd suspected that she'd get to this point with him. She hardly recognized her own voice. "I was married when

I was very young, eighteen. Matt and I had a little girl, Sara. She was so beautiful, blond and blue-eyed.''

He felt a shiver race up his spine. "Was?"

"She and Matt both died when the trailer we were living in caught fire six years ago, the week before Christmas." She raised anguished eyes to his. "I loved her so much."

Breaking from his hold on her, Frankie ran blindly toward Steen's cabin, her vision clouding with tears, but somehow managing not to fall despite the clumsy snowshoes.

Stunned, Steen watched her go.

Chapter Five

Steen stood with one arm braced against the mantel, watching the flames catch hold and the wood begin to burn. One of the reasons he loved this cabin was this huge fireplace—the smells it produced, the comfort it offered. If only he knew the best kind of comfort to offer the woman he could hear pacing in his bedroom.

He'd let Frankie run on ahead of him, thinking she needed the time to compose herself. When he'd entered, he'd found her outerwear in a pile on a chair next to the snowshoes and the door to the bedroom firmly shut. He'd put away the coats, built a fire and decided to make hot chocolate. She had to come out sooner or later.

To lose both a husband and a child so tragically, and right before Christmas yet. Finally, he understood her aversion to this particular holiday and his heart ached for her. Her daughter would have been around Emily's age. Small wonder she'd been visibly upset at Hannah's granddaughter. He'd never have taken her there if he'd known. But of course, he hadn't and now she was hurting, perhaps reliving the nightmare. Steen stared into the fire, wondering what he could possibly say to her.

Their drinks were cooling. Just when he was trying to decide whether or not he should knock on the door, it opened. She'd changed into her brown jogging outfit. Her hair, looking freshly brushed, fell softly down around her shoulders. Though she was quite pale, she was once more in control as she came toward him. In that hesitant way she had, she stopped in front of him and looked up, her eyes red-rimmed but clear.

"I'm sorry."

"You have no need to apologize." He indicated the cup on the end table. "I made some hot chocolate. This woman I knew once told me that there's something about hot chocolate that makes anything easier to handle."

Frankie took a sip, letting the hot liquid warm all the cold places inside her. If only it could. She sat on the couch, wondering if she'd been wise to leave the bedroom. She'd regretted the outburst she'd been unable to stop and hated the tears that had followed. Normally, she had no trouble avoiding situations that would bring on the flood of memories. But since arriving here, there'd been the snow, and the paints and the whole Christmas scene. And Emily. The little girl with the sad eyes and her lost kitten had been the final straw.

Steen sat down, angling his body toward her. "They're about nineteen, maybe twenty inches wide. Think they're broad enough?"

Frankie pulled her gaze from the fire and looked at him. "What do you mean?"

"My shoulders. Pretty broad. If we were playing our guessing game right now, I'd guess that you rarely talk about the past. Maybe you should."

She let out a long breath. "Why? Talking about the past doesn't change anything."

"It can change your perspective."

"So the good doctor who tried to get inside my head after the accident told me many times. For nearly a year, he treated me for depression and general malaise, then said he'd done all he could and the rest was up to me. Most of the time, I'm a fairly well-adjusted, functioning human being. But once in a while, the memories crowd in and I lose control." She took a drink of chocolate.

"We all do, occasionally." Steen leaned closer, his arm along the back of the couch. "Did all this happen back in Ohio?"

Her hands curled around the mug. She would tell him, tell him and get it over with. "Yes. My parents were farmers. Even when I was young, only a few could make farming pay. Ours wasn't one of them."

"Farming's like ranching, I guess. Texas ranchers have the same problems. A few do really well. Others lose their shirts. How big was your folks' farm?"

She knew what he was doing, gently leading her into opening up to him. He was so kind that somehow she didn't mind. "Not very. Dad kept a few cows and grew corn and beans mostly. My mother raised some chickens and ducks and worked alongside him. I remember her back then as always looking tired, rarely laughing. She hated the life of a farmer's wife, hated being trapped by poverty and endless chores, by broken dreams and a loss of hope."

"And you helped on the farm too?"

"Yes, early mornings and after school. As I grew older, I begged my father to sell the farm and do something else, but he wouldn't. He had this thing about enduring whatever came your way. I felt like I, too, was a burden they had to endure. So I decided that I'd leave as soon as I was old enough. I had these big dreams, to work my way through college, to make something of myself. And then I met Matt Taelor."

Steen heard very little emotion in her voice, almost as if she were telling a story that had happened to someone else. He finished his drink and waited for her to go on.

"Matt's family owned one of the larger farms and they were doing very well. His father was a gruff man and his mother thought she was better than my family, better than anyone. She didn't like me from the first day Matt took me to their home, which was when we were both juniors in high school. But Matt didn't seem to care. And my mother thought Matt was wonderful."

"How did you feel?"

"I liked Matt well enough. But mom saw him as my way out of a life she was determined I wouldn't be stuck in. They couldn't afford to put me through college. I was used to hard work, but she didn't think I could do it on my own. Mom thought marrying Matt was a shortcut to salvation. And I felt it would relieve them of at least one of their burdens."

Steen felt infinitely sad. "So you got married."

She nodded. "Yes, we eloped right after graduation. Matt said his family would learn to love me as he did, but they never came around. We had no money of our own, of course, so we moved in with them. And oh, how I hated it. His mother looked down her nose at me, criticized everything I did. She had all these notions on how well-brought-up people lived. Men were the breadwinners and they were to be treated as such, catered to. Women never left their bedrooms unless fully clothed. They wore hats to church on Sundays and never let anyone see them with a hair out of place. They learned to cook and to sew and to keep house. To this day, I think I sleep in the nude and wear casual jogging suits around home because of all the restrictions Mrs. Taelor imposed on me those dreadful six months I spent in her house."

Frankie sent him a quick, embarrassed look over her intimate revelations, but saw he was listening intently, not smiling. She cleared her throat.

They had yet to come to the hard part, Steen knew. Beginning to understand more, he placed his hand lightly on her shoulder. "You left there after six months?"

"Yes. I was pregnant by then and I couldn't stand living in that house. We started looking at apartments. And then, my father died quietly in his sleep one night. Mom sold the farm and paid off all the bills, which were staggering. Soon after, she moved to Florida into a retirement community. The only thing left for me was this old secondhand trailer we'd used for occasional vacation trips when I was young. Matt and I fixed it up and moved it to a trailer park. It wasn't much, but at least we were alone. I...I often wonder what would have happened if I could have gotten along with Matt's mother, if we hadn't lived in that old trailer. Maybe then..."

He squeezed her shoulder. "We can drive ourselves crazy wondering about what-might-have-beens."

Frankie sighed. "I know."

"But you were happy living in the trailer?"

"Yes, the happiest I can remember. Sara was born and she was so perfect, so beautiful, such a good baby. Matt worked days as a shoe clerk and went to school three nights a week learning to be an accountant. His family had promised to pay for his schooling, but when we moved out, they turned their backs on us. Matt said he didn't care, but he had to work so hard. I felt like our marriage had placed such burdens on him and he was so young. I wanted to get a job to help out, but Matt wanted me home with Sara."

She was quiet so long, gazing raptly into the fire, that Steen wondered if she'd go on. "Then what happened?" he prodded.

Frankie took another deep breath. "Matt liked to make a big deal out of Christmas. Sara had just turned two and he'd brought home this large tree that barely fit in the living room of the trailer. It was evening, we'd put Sara to bed and we were going to trim the tree so we could watch her reaction in the morning. Only one set of lights didn't work at all, and we didn't have enough bulbs for the other set. Matt had a test in the morning so while he hit the books, I said I'd drive to the store and get more lights."

He watched her as she carefully set down the mug and twined her hands together as she stared straight ahead, her eyes focused on the past.

"It was bitterly cold, but not snowing. I drove into town and the first store didn't have any. I went on to the drugstore, bought the lights and started home. I heard the fire trucks from the highway and saw flames in the distance shooting higher than the treetops. I remember wondering whose house could have caught fire and feeling sorry for them. It wasn't until I'd turned down

our road that my heart stopped when I realized...when I saw whose..."

Her voice caught on a sob as Steen slid his arm
around her. She was crying openly now and unaware of
it. She held herself rigid as she continued.

"I jumped out of the car and ran closer, but a fireman grabbed me. The flames were everywhere and the
frosty air formed a kind of vapor that swirled around,
making everything hazy. I told him my family was in
there, my husband and baby, but he wouldn't let me go.
I struggled, but he held on. I stood there listening to the
terrible crackling noise of metal turning red-hot and
then sounds like wood crashing. There was billowing
black smoke everywhere. And the heat...I'll never
forget the heat...."

She looked wounded, cornered, like a rabbit in a trap.
Steen took a ragged breath. "It's okay. Let it out, it's
okay."

Frankie felt herself trembling and trying desperately
not to sob out loud. She hadn't realized that her face
was wet until she felt Steen gently wiping her cheeks.
She hated crying in front of him, but she couldn't stop.
So many tears for so many years. When would they dry
up? Turning, she lay her cheek on his chest and clung
to him, gripping his shirt in clenched fists, silently
weeping.

He held her, just held her, feeling helpless, feeling her
pain. He didn't know what to say so he murmured to
her gently, hoping his words offered some comfort.

Frankie wasn't sure how long she stayed in his arms,
absorbing the feel of him, the hard rock strength of
him. Finally, exhausted and spent, she eased back and
blew her nose.

"How had the trailer caught fire?" he asked.

"The gas heater had been working night and day because of the freezing temperatures. Something went wrong and there was an explosion. I was the one who insisted we leave Matt's mother's house, that we live in that old trailer. If I could have put up with her, maybe..."

The guilt of the survivor. He was first cousins with that feeling. Steen touched her chin with one finger and angled her face so she would look at him. "We all have to make decisions in our lives that could go either way. I hope you believe that you had nothing to do with what happened."

Frankie took a deep breath, straightening her shoulders. "I know I'm not responsible for the fire. I have no reason to feel any guilt—and I don't. But I...I miss Sara so much."

He pulled her into his chest. No guilt left, she'd said. And she believed she was handling it, but Steen had serious doubts. Finally, she pulled back and wiped her face dry. The sadness still lingered in the dark green depths of her eyes. Steen wished he could chase away all traces. "It'll get better. And one day, you'll fall in love again."

Adamantly, she shook her head. "No, never. I can't let myself care for anyone again. The next time would finish me. Besides, I consider myself a bad risk for any man."

"Not everyone we love dies so tragically, or so young. Living is a risk, Frankie. You can't..."

Quickly she stood, letting the anger take her. It was so much easier to deal with anger than hurt. "Who are you to tell me what I can do? Aren't you the one who said you wanted only friendships, that you'd rather live alone than get tangled with someone?"

He rose to face her. "You only heard part of what I said. I'd rather live alone than live with someone wrong for me. I know what I want—a woman whose first priority is a home and family. And me. I believe work and a career are important, but people we care about are more important." Steen shook his head. "I wonder if there are any women like that left."

"I was one once." Her voice was soft, low. She drew in a deep breath. "That was another whole lifetime ago. Now, I want only friendship from men. And occasionally, I need a man to make love to me."

Frankie raised an unsteady gaze to his. She'd tried this once before, with a man she'd dated for several months in San Francisco. She'd thought that perhaps making love with someone she liked would fill some of the emptiness inside her. She'd gotten as far as the bedroom, had even removed her dress. Yet she hadn't been able to go through with it. But this was different. Steen was different. Maybe... "So, do you want to go into the bedroom?"

He was totally taken aback. "What did you say?"

"I said, do you want to go into your bedroom and make love? I mean I know you're attracted to me and I certainly am to you. Why can't we be adult about this? I... I think I need you tonight."

She'd almost fooled him there. Then he'd seen her lower lip quiver and the uncertainty in her eyes. If ever he'd seen a woman who needed tenderness more than passion, she was standing before him now. "I don't think so. But thanks, all the same."

Frankie felt the heat rise. She'd wanted to be held, *needed* to be held. She'd thought it would be so easy to get him to make love to her, to blot out the world, to allow her to escape for a little while. Other women had told her how easy it was and she was certain she hadn't mistaken Steen's signals. Why then? She stared into his eyes, trying to read what was there.

Steen took her hand and pulled her down alongside him on the couch. He touched her hair, a caressing gesture, then gave her a gentle smile. "I'm not crazy about making love to puffy-faced women with runny noses." He snuggled her into his chest as his arm drew her close. "I wouldn't object to sitting quietly though and just watching the fire."

The sigh that came from her was filled with a mixture of relief and exhaustion. She curled her hand on his chest and he covered it with his own. Steen couldn't remember the last time a woman had evoked such compassion in him. He kissed the top of her head. "I'll take a raincheck, though."

She made a soft sound, then in moments her breathing deepened.

Asleep on his couch again, this time in his arms. It was getting to be a habit, one he was growing overly fond of. She hadn't had much happiness in her life so far. She needed someone, someone to care deeply for her, though she would not easily accept any man. As a matter of fact, there wasn't much that would be easy with Frankie. Still, there was something about her.

She moved him, touched him somewhere deep inside, causing a jumble of feelings in him, Steen decided. She was a woman struggling to live with her memories, fragile and vulnerable. For the first time in a long while, he began to think he may have run across a woman who could satisfy all parts of him—his heart, his mind, his body and the dark yearnings of his soul. She was like riding the roller coaster with all the anticipation, the thrills and the heart-stopping pleasure.

Smiling to himself, Steen closed his eyes. Even as a kid, it had always been his favorite ride.

The moonlight woke her. Frankie opened her eyes, squinting against the glare of the beams on the stark white snow. She stretched under the quilt, realizing that once more she had no recollection of being put to bed. Frowning at that thought, she got up and saw she was still wearing her clothes. Something to be grateful for, she decided as she glanced at the bedside clock. A little after two. An odd hour to be feeling restless.

She leaned into the high windowsill and peered out. Everything was silent, so still. There seemed to be no wind; not an evergreen branch stirring. Steen's storage shed was only yards from the back of the house and alongside it was a spacious dog run that must be for Red when his master was away. The sky was empty of clouds and the moon was nearly full. She saw a bright star and made a wish, then scolded herself. Hadn't she stopped believing in wishes and dreams and magic some time ago?

Turning away, Frankie sighed. The weather had definitely improved. Surely by tomorrow the snowplows would reach even this remote section. If not, she'd strap on those snowshoes and march the half mile out to the highway and flag down a truck or a bus or some moving thing. Enough was enough. She had to get out of Steen's house.

Because she was beginning to like being here too much—the peacefulness, the simple life, the quiet. And she was beginning to like Steen Olson way too much.

A shower would feel good right now, Frankie thought, but he was undoubtedly asleep on the couch and she didn't want to wake him. She stripped off her wrinkled clothes and climbed into her robe, then turned on the bedside lamp. In the dresser mirror, she examined her face. Fair-skinned people should never sob for hours, she decided, noting the shadows around her eyes, the slight swelling of her cheeks. No wonder Steen had turned down her offer to join her in his bed.

Foolish. What a foolish thing to do, to spill your heart out to a man about your unhappy past, cry all over his shirt, then invite him to make love to you. Her cheeks flamed at the thought. When it came to physical relationships in this modern day and age, she talked a good game. She had yet to translate that into action.

Besides, sex wasn't what she'd needed. She'd needed comfort, affection, simple human contact. The need to be held was a powerful craving, one that had gone unsatisfied for a long time. How remarkable that Steen had somehow understood that.

Frankie brushed her hair into some semblance of order, wondering if she dare venture out to the kitchen. She hadn't eaten much dinner and was suddenly aware of her rumbling stomach. If not food, at least a glass of milk would taste good. In her bare feet, she probably wouldn't disturb Steen. Moving quietly, she eased open the bedroom door.

Moonlight from the front windows dappled across his chest as he lay on his back on the couch, a colorful afghan twined around the lower half of him. The fire in the grate had dimmed to a few red embers, emitting a soft glow. As silently as possible, she made her way around the bulky furniture toward the kitchen.

In the light from the open refrigerator door, Frankie poured herself a glass of milk. She drank it down, letting the cooling liquid soothe her jumpy stomach. Perhaps it would also help her sleep. Strolling back into the room, she wandered over to the far window next to Steen's bookcase.

There was just enough light to make out some of the titles. Quite a collection, ranging from western history, to philosophy and even astronomy. It seemed the simple wood-carver had many and varied interests. He was not only attractive, but intelligent, as well. Not that it mattered to her, Frankie told herself.

The huge evergreen he'd cut down stood in the corner, a dark shadow, its branches tipped with shafts of light from the fire. He'd wanted to decorate it, but he'd held off because of her. A considerate man, a man of empathy. Tomorrow she would be on her way and he could put up his lights and hang his ornaments and forget her. As she must forget him.

Spotting a package under the tree, she bent to pick it up, then shot a glance toward the couch. He hadn't moved. When had he had time to wrap a gift? she wondered as she took it to the pool of moonlight. Not too large, wrapped in red foil with a soft white ribbon. The tag dangling from it read: Amelia.

Frankie was surprised by a sudden jolt of jealousy. Crazy. She put the package back under the tree. Probably one of his wood carvings. Who was Amelia? She didn't care. She *couldn't* care. Crossing her arms over her chest, she walked toward the fire.

But it wasn't the fire she stood staring at. He lay sprawled on his side, his back to the couch one arm under his head, the other dangling over the side. Dark hair matted his chest as it moved lightly with his breathing. He was strong and lean and hard, from the life he'd chosen to lead, the woodchopping, the hiking. His unruly hair fell onto his forehead and she fought the urge to brush it back, to feel the softness in her fingers. The mouth that had caused her pulse to race was full and tempting her still.

He wasn't her type, whatever that was. If she were setting up a scenario, she would pair him with a soft-spoken, traditional woman who loved to stay home, bake bread and raise babies, a woman Hannah would approve of. Someone fresh and clean, with no hurting memories nor a guilty past.

She was none of those things. She was fiercely independent, a city dweller needing her own space, wanting to do for herself and hating the thought of being beholden to anyone. And she was one of the walking wounded. Steen seemed like a man who needed an abundance of love and passion. Frankie wondered if she had any left to give.

Yet with all of that, it was *his* touch that made her blood heat, his face that plagued her dreams, his loving she wanted in the most basic way a woman wants a man. And she must not feel it. Closing her eyes, Frankie turned away.

His hand shot out and closed around her wrist.

Shocked, she swung back, her eyes wide. "I . . . I thought you were asleep."

"Did you?" Steen scooted up until he was leaning against the armrest, his eyes never leaving her face. He gave a quick tug to her arm and she was seated beside him, her hands flying to his chest to keep herself from falling atop him.

"What are you doing?"

"What were you thinking as you stood there looking down at me?"

She tried to stand, but his arms locked tightly around her. She could feel his heart steadily beating under her hand where it rested in the soft, curly hair of his chest. "Well, for one thing, I was thinking you were asleep."

"What else?"

She softened, remembering that this was the man who'd already turned down a visit to her bed earlier tonight. This was Steen, who wouldn't press. His eyes in the firelight were dark and aware, but she chose to ignore that. "I was thinking that I'm all wrong for you and that I'm glad that we've settled for friendship between us. Friendships last a lot longer than love affairs."

He raised a brow. "Had a lot of love affairs, have you?"

"No, but I'm sure that..."

"What I'm sure of is that I've never in my life wanted a woman more than I want you this very second."

Her heart was pounding so hard she was certain he could hear it. And still he just looked at her, his eyes hot and hungry, his mouth slightly open as he ran his tongue along his lips. Frankie struggled not to moan aloud as she felt her blood warming.

"Do you want to kiss me, Frankie?" he asked, but he wasn't smiling, wasn't teasing. Not this time.

"Please, no games. I don't want to play games."

"This is no game." His arms pulled her nearer, causing her robe to open just a little. Just enough. He saw the rise of her breasts and felt a quick response. She was a breath away, but he needed it to come from her. She was no longer sobbing through past pain. She was a woman sensually awakened and filled with need. A need as great as his. "What do you want, Frankie?"

His eyes demanded the truth. She couldn't lie to him the way she'd been lying to herself. "You," she answered, her voice a husky whisper. "I want you."

Chapter Six

She wanted him. Hadn't he known it all along, from that first stunning kiss they'd shared to that incredibly arousing dance? She wanted him and he wasn't strong enough to turn away from that wanting. He closed the distance between them and touched his mouth to hers.

From the fire in Steen's eyes, Frankie had expected a rough passion, a crushing, a devouring. But he was gentle, almost explorative, though he'd kissed her before. His mouth brushed back and forth over hers, sliding and caressing, stopping to include the corners, then returning to capture the fullness of her lips. Drawing her bottom lip into his mouth, he suckled softly, then more fiercely.

His hands on her back moved in lazy circles, not insistent, yet stimulating the skin under her robe, warming everywhere his long fingers touched. And still his lips merely played with hers. Losing patience, she drove her tongue into his mouth and felt the response she'd sought. His sharp intake of breath was followed by a deep moan as he met her thrusts with bold strokes of his own. For long moments, they tangled and danced, before Steen pulled back, his breathing unsteady.

Dipping his head, he rained quick kisses along her cheeks and chin, then moved to taste the tender skin at her throat. The soft sounds she made fueled the fire building inside him. Feeling the almost painful hardening of his body, he shifted on the couch and framed her face with his hands as he sought to slow down enough to savor. From the first, he'd seen her as a woman meant to be cherished, one meant for slow loving. Her eyes were the color of emeralds as she focused on him.

"Do you know how long I've wanted you?" he asked as his fingers moved into the thickness of her hair. "From that first minute when I carried you in the snow, when I had my face in your neck, and I couldn't get enough of the smell of you, when I wanted so badly to taste you. Did you know that?"

Frankie sighed, arching her neck to give him better access to the spot behind her ear where he nuzzled. He was giving her soft words and sweet sounds, romancing her. Because he was that kind of man. But she wasn't the kind of woman who needed them. She thought she ought to tell him that right up front, so he'd know their coming together was all about physical need and nothing about deep feelings.

"You don't have to give me flowers and love songs, the romantic build-up." She shivered as his tongue slid into her ear, her hands gripping his shoulders as his lips moved along her throat. "We're just a man and a woman offering each other pleasure for this moment. Nothing more, nothing less.''

Steen scarcely paused in his journey to learn every inch of her face. He knew what lay behind the words she was saying, recognized the protective guardrails she'd erected to keep him from reaching her inside. He'd play along, though he had no intention of playing by her rules.

Easing back from her, he reached to untie the belt of her robe as she sat facing him, her eyes watchful. Slowly, he slipped the material from her and saw the fire spread its warm glow over her silken skin. Her breasts were small and perfect and tightening with need as his fingers skimmed along the sides, then growing fuller as he cupped each one in turn. He heard her sigh as she closed her eyes, letting the pleasure take her.

"You are so beautiful," he told her before dipping his head to taste the soft flesh his hands had aroused. With a throaty sound, she let her fingers thread into his hair. For long moments, he gently plundered while she clutched him to her, then he raised his head.

"Do you think this intense wanting happens every time, with every man and woman?" he asked as his hands moved down along her ribs.

"Probably not," Frankie answered, her voice sounding foreign to her own ears. "As long as we don't let this get too complicated, we'll be all right. If we remember that you have a life and so do I. Then neither of us will be hurt. What we're dealing with here is only attraction."

Only attraction. He tried not to let her words hurt, because he was certain she was hiding the truth from herself. He pulled her up to him, a little more roughly than he'd intended, and heard her gasp as her breasts flattened against his chest. "Just attraction?" he challenged. He crushed his mouth down on hers.

Frankie felt her blood begin to race as he shifted, moving her on top of him, slipping her along the hard length of his body. She couldn't have said what happened to the afghan, but suddenly the only barrier between them was the thin briefs he wore, barely concealing the part of him that already throbbed against her. Oddly, she didn't feel naked or exposed; she felt on fire. On a soft moan, she opened her mouth and tasted sweet, hot desire.

Steen wasn't sure what was driving him, the need to make her see she was wrong or the need to love her as he'd been longing to since she'd first walked into his life. He did know he had to have her, her body and her mind, and perhaps then he could reach her soul. He felt a storm inside raging as his mouth consumed hers. She was small, almost delicate and she tasted so fresh and sweet. She smelled of aroused woman, a scent that sent his head spinning.

A little dazed, Frankie drew back from him. "You make me forget everything. How do you do that?"

"Maybe you need to forget, for a while. Maybe I do, too."

She fidgeted atop him, passion making her restless. "Make me forget, Steen." She touched her lips to his and felt her pulse begin to pound in parts of her that had been lying dormant for years. His mouth was hard against hers, almost bruising, and exactly what she needed.

The innocent air about her, the hesitancy that she usually displayed, was suddenly gone. And gone was his patience. Excitement thudded through Steen as her dark, rich taste exploded on his tongue. He felt her

tremble, felt her arch into him, and felt a wildness he
had only before imagined take over. His hands raced
along the satin smoothness of her slim body while he
squirmed free and tossed aside the last cotton barrier
between them. He rubbed against her and swallowed
her sigh of welcome. Arms tightening about her, he
deepened the kiss.

He was everywhere, his hands and his mouth, his
teeth and his tongue, touching her, kissing her, driving
her. Unable to believe she could be this helpless, Frankie
struggled against the waves, only to find herself losing
ground. When he rolled her onto her back on the wide
cushions of the couch, she dared to reach out and close
her fingers around him. She wanted, *needed*, to feel
him, to know him, to experience an intimacy she'd so
long denied herself. She'd had but one lover and she'd
been just a girl then. She was a woman now and knew
she'd never been this desperate, this frantic. With a
groan, she dragged his mouth back to hers.

She was suddenly wild beneath him, and Steen struggled to keep control. Their passion had built slowly over
the past few days, like sand in an hourglass patiently
drifting downward. Now it was raging, streaking like
the winds across a turbulent sea. His fingers moved into
the hot center of her while he watched her face. She
climbed slowly, and at that first trembling peak, her
eyes flew open in shocked pleasure. A rosy blush stole
over her features, and then, before she could catch her
breath, he shifted and thrust deeply.

Suddenly he was inside her and Frankie's hands
clutched at his back as she strained to keep up with him.
In moments, he had her soaring again. It felt like a
breathless race, like a storm out of control, building,
building. It felt like joy, like freedom. It felt like love.

Was it passion fueled by love or love fueled by passion? she wondered foggily. She didn't know. She only knew she no longer felt so alone. When she was sure it was impossible to fly higher, he showed her how.

Frankie took her time drifting back to the real world. Her system was slow on recovery, but perhaps it was also because she was reluctant to return. She'd been expecting physical release and had found instead a merging that had catapulted her into a beautiful sea of sensation. Her eyes closed, she clung to the glow of the aftershocks, unwilling to lose the feeling.

Steen had shifted his weight from her, but his arms had nestled her against him where she still lay, her skin damp from his loving. Had her memory dimmed or had this really been so out of the realm of her previous experience? She struggled to sort out her feelings while she hoped he'd say something, anything, that would make her feel right about giving in to her need for his touch.

He listened to her trying to slow her breathing, and the guilt washed over him. Just hours ago, he'd told himself he wouldn't rush her, that he'd handle her with the tender, loving care that all fragile things deserved. And then he'd yanked her down onto the couch and coaxed her into submission. Fighting a growing disgust with himself, he brushed the hair back from her face with a gentle hand.

"I'm sorry, Frankie. I shouldn't have..." He stopped, feeling her stiffen and pull back.

Wrong. She'd been wrong to give in to her feelings, to believe for a moment there that he had been as affected as she. Hadn't she schooled herself against letting her defenses down, against letting herself care? God, would she never learn? Tears of hurt, of humiliation building behind her eyelids, she scooted from the couch and grabbed her robe from the floor. "There's no need to apologize. It was . . . just one of those things." Quickly, she walked toward the bedroom, shrugging into her robe.

Running his hand through his hair, Steen sat up and reached for his jeans. If earlier he'd thought her not an easy person to deal with, he now thought her damn difficult. Why had she gotten upset at what he'd said? Perhaps he hadn't gone about his apology with finesse, but he'd been sincere.

When she'd told him about the death of her husband and child she'd touched something deep inside him. When he'd held her, letting her cry it out, letting her fall asleep in his arms, a tenderness he'd never known had been born. That his comforting touch had changed and rushed her into passion was not something he was proud of. His apology had been the beginning of his explanation, yet she didn't want to hear it.

Zipping his pants, he marched toward the bedroom. She damn well would hear it. He found her sitting on the bed brushing her hair.

"Look, I didn't mean to . . ."

"Yes, you already said that." She yanked the brush through almost violently.

"Usually, I have more control. I hope I didn't hurt you."

"I've been hurt before. I'll get over it."

Steen took a step closer. In the moonlight, he could see her eyes, ready to brim over. "Where? Where did I hurt you?"

"Inside. You hurt me inside." She stood, slammed the brush down on the bed and looked up at him. "I haven't been around much, I know. You'll have to forgive me if I don't know how to handle a man who apologizes for making love to me. But I'm a quick study. Give me a little time and I'll learn all the do's and don't's, the social niceties.''

Suddenly he realized they were talking about two very different things. "Damn it, Frankie, I didn't apologize for making love with you. I apologized for rushing you when I'd promised I'd keep my distance, for pulling you into my bed when you were feeling defenseless and exposed."

She searched her mind for reasons to disbelieve him, but as she looked into his serious gray eyes, she could find none. Yet she was afraid to believe. "Why should you care, one way or the other, if you hurt me? Soon, I'll be out of your life. It's as simple as that."

She was trying to retreat, to hide, but he wasn't going to let her. Not this time. "You don't seem to understand. I care about you and nothing's simple anymore."

Frankie closed her eyes, feeling suddenly on very shaky ground. This is what she'd feared, what she'd tried to run from, to guard against. Her heart, too, had ignored her strict warnings. Because she cared, too, more than she wanted to admit. Admitting would weaken her resolve, weaken her. She hated weakness. Opening her eyes, she looked into his.

"Don't care for me. I don't want it. I can't handle it."

Steen could see her closing off from him. He would lose her if he kept on along these lines. Backing off was never easy for him, but he'd learned it was often the best choice.

Lightly, he touched her hair. "I find it impossible not to care about you. Would you settle for a simple, caring friendship, with no strings attached?" He watched her absorb that as she decided to accept his terms. At last, she nodded.

He placed his hands on her shoulders, then slowly slid them around to her back, holding her in a loose embrace. "You're such a paradox. You came to my cabin, bristly and demanding, stomping your little foot when you couldn't make the snow stop and the Jeep do your bidding. You project this image of a cool, efficient businesswoman, strong enough to get along with tough casino managers. Yet you make angels in the snow, keep Hannah happy by baking cookies with her and you can spend hours contentedly painting spots on a carved fawn. Which is the real Frankie Taelor?"

She shook her head, feeling a shade confused herself. "I'm not sure. Maybe I've lost touch with the real Frankie Taelor. Maybe by now I'm just someone I invented to keep the world at arm's length."

He raised a questioning brow. "You know that about yourself?"

"Certainly. I'm not stupid. I'm also not likely to change, even though there are times when I wish I could." Times like now, Frankie thought. She sighed heavily. "I learned a long time ago that there's no point in wishing." Yet she had, only a short time ago, on a bright winter star.

"I disagree. There's *always* a point in wishing. How else do you make a dream come true?"

"Some dreams never come true."

"Then they're the wrong dreams. Don't tell me you don't harbor any dreams in the far corners of your heart?"

"A few. I told you about the house in Maui. But I no longer wrap my dreams around people. If I don't get my house in Maui, it'll be a disappointment, not a devastation. If I center my dream around a person, and something goes wrong, for me that would be self-destruction." She reached up and touched his face, already way too dear to her. "Can you understand my feelings on this, Steen, and stop trying to change my mind?"

He would have to, or lose her before he had her. "I'm trying, believe it or not. Tell me, did you believe me earlier when I told you that I'd wanted you from the moment I picked you up out there in the snow and carried you to my house?"

She shrugged, trying for nonchalance. "People say things in passion. . . ."

He moved his hands lower on her back, maneuvering her soft folds until she was pressed tightly against his arousal, once more straining to be free of his zipper. She sucked in a gulp of air as her eyes widened.

Never had anyone been so bold, so brazen with her. She'd always told herself if it happened, she would turn away from possible pleasure to avoid the probable involvement. Instead, here she was, reaching out, spreading her hands along the hard muscles of his chest, her head beginning to spin.

"Did you mean it earlier when you said you wanted me?" he persisted.

Her hands moved lower. "You mean you couldn't tell?"

"Maybe I just need to hear the words, even though you don't." The hell she didn't, much more than he. But she wasn't ready to believe them. "Do you think that men never feel less than self-confident?"

"Some men, perhaps. I've never met a man with your quiet assurance. And I understand why. You have work you love, and you're successful at it. You even know exactly what you want in a relationship, and one day I'm certain you'll find that special woman, too.''

Yes, he was beginning to discover what he wanted, Steen thought. But getting it wasn't going to be a piece of cake. ''It sounds like I have it all.'' He moved fractionally closer, rubbing against her, watching her breathing change.

In the morning, Frankie thought. She'd be on her way in the morning. But for tonight, he was here and he was hers. Throwing caution to the winds, she returned the sweet friction and saw his eyes darken. ''You do have it all. And you're a terribly exciting lover. Since you need to hear it, I'll tell you. Yes, I want you. I wanted you before and I'm not a bit sorry we made love. And I want you again.''

Steen kissed her eyes closed, his arms tightening about her. ''A man can't be an exciting lover unless his partner excites him.'' He lowered her to the bed and followed, his hand going to her belt. But before he untied it, he turned on the bedside lamp. ''I want to see you, not just in firelight.''

''Steen, I've never...''

''Tonight, we're throwing aside all the *nevers* of our lives. We're going to savor and enjoy and pleasure each other.'' He felt a shiver of apprehension, a fleeting glimpse of sadness. ''Because morning comes all too soon.''

Frankie didn't resist, couldn't resist. She lay back on the bed in the soft glow of the lamp and tried not to squirm under his heated gaze. Slowly, he unwrapped her, like a precious package, a gift. She hadn't thought it possible but she, who had always felt shy even under a cloak of darkness, soon felt beautiful under his silver gaze, his reverent fingertips as they trailed along her skin.

"I want you to trust me, to know I won't hurt you. I want to make love to every part of you. I want you to forget every other man you've known." He took the tip of her breast in his mouth and felt the answering response.

"There have been no others, not since Matt."

He waited for the elation, but felt only the sadness of her empty years. He lifted his head to study her face and knew she was waiting for his reaction. She'd revealed so much to him tonight. He wanted her to have no regrets in the morning. "Then let me show you how it can be between us."

He moved his mouth down her, his tongue teasing, his hands caressing. He wanted her steeped in deep, dark pleasures. He wanted her to feel revered, to feel desirable, to feel as if it were her first time. With more patience than he thought he possessed, he seduced her slowly until her skin quivered and her breath came in shallow puffs.

Willingly, Frankie let him lead her to the next plateau. She stretched a hand to free him of his jeans so she, too, could touch and explore, but he moved just out of reach and pulled them off himself. Dreamlike, she lay back and let the mists close in on her.

His hands were large, rough and callused, and felt oddly electrifying against her skin. His face was shadowed with a day and a half's growth of beard, and felt wonderfully masculine rubbing along her cheeks. His lips, wet from her own, moved to whisper in her ear, words that made no sense, words that thrilled her nonetheless. He stroked with tenderness, devoured with ferocity, then gentled her with sweet kisses. Gasping for air, she whirled along wherever he would take her.

For the first time, perhaps ever, Steen felt completely unselfish in his need to please, in his desire to love a woman. He'd taken her with a wild abandon the first time. Now he filled her slowly, his movements held in desperate check, stretching the moment, seemingly endless. Frankie floated with it, trusting him.

One together. She'd heard it said before, but hadn't believed it possible. Pressing her lips to the pulse at his throat, she wrapped her legs around him and let herself dream the impossible dream. For now, for just this moment, anything was possible. His heart beat against her breast, in rhythm with their movements. She had made this strong man tremble with desire, weak with passion. She and no other had made him quiver with excitement and race toward completion. Giddy with the knowledge, Frankie held on.

Braced on his elbows, Steen brushed the damp hair from her cheeks and touched her lovely face. Her eyes fluttered open. "That's right, Frankie, look at me." He slowed a little, knowing she was almost there. "I want to see you when the dam breaks. I want you to know who's loving you."

As if she could think, as if she could do anything but feel. Yet his dark eyes beseeched her and she could not refuse. "Steen, oh, Steen," she whispered, then felt the waves close in as he plunged deeper. Just before her eyes lost focus, she heard him breathe her name. Burying her face in his throat, she let go of the world as he poured his love into her.

She awakened to the roar of an engine and the scrape of the snowplow. Bright winter sunlight poured through the window as Frankie opened her eyes and blinked into the glare. The truck was clearing Steen's road and by the sound of it, she could tell it wasn't far. She had to talk to the driver.

Moving to rise, she encountered an obstacle. Steen's arm was across her midsection, oddly familiar, oddly disturbing. She glanced over and saw his eyes were still closed. Despite her need to rush, she lingered to gaze at his face. It had been more than six years since she'd awakened naked and her limbs tangled with a man. And such a beautiful man.

Sighing, she carefully removed his arm and turned back the covers. Quickly, she dressed and left the bedroom, grabbing the down jacket as she scooted out the front door. Steen had shoveled the snow from the porch yesterday and a dozen feet in front of the cabin. Hurrying forward, she was relieved to find that the cab of the truck was facing her. Arms waving wildly, she ran down the walk and at last caught the driver's attention.

It took her only a few minutes to scribble down Eric's name, phone number and a sketchy description of where she was. The driver agreed to call him for her on his next break. Frankie thanked him and made her way back to the cabin, her thoughts in a turmoil.

Would Eric send someone for her, or just ignore her request? A hard one to call. She'd give him a few hours and if he didn't show, she'd think of a new plan. Hannah's phone was probably working by now. Or she could see about freeing Steen's Jeep from the ditch she'd gotten stuck in. Shivering, she stepped into the cabin. She needed to pack, to take a shower, to...

He was leaning against the arch of the kitchen doorway, wearing his jeans and an unbuttoned plaid shirt, his expression unreadable. Averting her gaze, she slipped out of the jacket and rubbed her chilled hands together.

Steen had known the instant she'd awakened, had in fact been awake himself for some time before that, watching her sleep. But he hadn't let on, trying to guess what she'd do as he'd listened to the plow come closer. She'd done exactly what he'd figured she'd do. Despite all that had been between them last night, she was leaving. Why did it hurt so much when he'd known all along she would go at the first opportunity?

"Coffee's on," he said, pleased his voice was rock steady. "It'll be done by the time you finish your shower."

She took a step toward him, then looked up. "I don't know what to say. I've never lied to you. I have obligations, to Eric and my other clients."

"You don't have to say more. I understand. I'll make some breakfast." He turned to the kitchen.

"I'm not hungry. Coffee will be fine."

Food was the furthest thing from his mind, too. Steen stood at the kitchen window, watching the snowplow finish its lumbering chore. Then the driver would be off, calling her casino manager who would undoubtedly double-time it over to pick her up. Damn! He walked to the coffeepot and willed it to hurry.

It was possibly the longest morning in recent memory, Steen decided. She's come out of the bathroom, showered and dressed and packed, and had sat sipping coffee. Like two polite strangers, they'd talked about this and that. He'd wanted to say something significant, meaningful, but he couldn't come up with the right words. Maybe they'd said it all last night. So they waited.

By noon, Frankie was restless, pacing about the room, checking her watch. When at last she heard a car approaching, he saw her hurry to the window. The limousine was dark and sleek, very much like the man she rushed out to greet on the porch, then led into his cabin.

"So this is where you've been lazing away the days while I've been losing a fortune." His small, darting eyes took in the room and summarily dismissed the entire cabin. "Can't say I approve of your vacation choices."

Her lips a thin line, Frankie turned from the new arrival to Steen, hoping to hurry the introductions, to get going. "Eric, this is Steen Olson, of Olson Carvings. He all but saved my life. Steen, this is Eric Hanley of the Diamond Nugget in Lake Tahoe."

He was short with pale skin, dark hair and an arrogant look about him that had Steen clenching his teeth. He admitted ruefully to himself that he wouldn't have liked Eric Hanley if he'd just found the cure for cancer. Keeping his gaze level, he reached to take the man's outstretched hand, noting it was soft and pampered.

"Olson Carvings," Eric said, brushing hands. "I've heard of you." Again, his gaze swept the room, falling just short of insolent. "You don't *live* here, do you?"

Steen didn't know if it was the man himself, or his tone that irritated him more. He kept his features even as he jammed his fists into his pockets, wondering what it would feel like to rearrange Eric Hanley's smirking face. "Actually, I do. I used to live in a lean-to about six trees south of the front door. Maybe you saw it on the way in?"

Eric narrowed his eyes, reassessing the man. With a dismissing grunt, he turned to Frankie. "You ready? You got a lot of time to make up for."

"I'll be right with you." Glancing at Steen, seeing the control he was hanging on to, she made for the bedroom. She heard Eric go outside without another word.

If she could just get through this day, Frankie thought as she picked up her bag. Then she could... She nearly collided with Steen who was blocking the bedroom door.

"He's a peach of a fellow. I can understand why you're rushing to help him out of a tight spot."

She took a deep, fortifying breath. "I told you I don't even like the man. I'm helping him out because it's my *job*. It's what I do, what I am."

His eyes were dark, questioning, hurt. "Is it?"

"Yes. Look, Steen, I thank you for all you've done for me." The words stuck in her throat. Such a pitiful thing, mere thanks after *all* they'd shared. "You have to agree, I've never..."

"Lied to me. I know." He hoped his eyes weren't as bleak as he felt. He took her bag and walked her to the door, then helped her into her raincoat. Touching her shoulders, he turned her to face him. "One question."

"Yes?"

"Are you lying to yourself?" He saw her face pale as his question hit its mark. He wasn't particularly proud of himself, but he wanted her to think about it.

"You don't fight fair."

"You should know something about me, Frankie. I don't fight at all." He brushed her forehead with a kiss. "Be happy."

She stayed a moment longer, her hungry eyes memorizing him, then turned abruptly and walked out.

It was late when she finished. Stifling a yawn, Frankie rose from the chair in the computer terminal room and stretched to relieve the kinks in her neck and shoulders.

The repairs had taken longer than she'd hoped. By nine in the evening, part of the casino was functioning and now, at ten to midnight, all was once more operable. Since the gambling area was open night and day under normal circumstances, already the bright lights were blinking and the steady thud of coins in slots could be heard mingling with the low, excited hum of voices.

She'd have thought Eric would be elated. Instead, he'd been leaning against the desk watching her the last half hour, his face sullen. Rearranging her features into a smile she didn't feel, Frankie looked up at him. "There you are, at long last."

"Yeah, at long last is right. You sure took your sweet time about it, baby." His voice was hard, unforgiving.

Frankie gathered up her manuals, once more the cool professional. She'd be damned if she'd let this arrogant jerk intimidate her. "As I explained in your limo, the delay was unavoidable. You can mail my check to the usual address. I think I'll go to my room now," she said, feeling bone tired.

Eric pushed away from the desk. "About that check. We need to discuss the amount. Since you didn't get here at the agreed upon time, we'll have to make some adjustments."

Wearying. This was all so wearying. "Oh, I don't think so, Eric. I arrived as soon as was humanly possible. I can't walk on water and I can't drive through snowdrifts higher than the rooftops. That storm is a recorded fact that I believe would be considered an Act of God in a courtroom. Do you want to play that game or give me the amount called for in our contract?"

His small eyes narrowed for a long moment, then he put on his affable smile, throwing a beefy arm around Frankie. "You're a mite touchy, lady. We can work things out."

Fighting a shudder at his nearness, she moved away and through the door. "I rather thought we could. I'm really tired. Good night, Eric."

But he wasn't giving up that easily. Falling in step beside her, he escorted her to the elevator. "I still think you should reconsider that offer I made you last year. You could do worse than working full-time for me."

The last thing she wanted to do right now was rehash his ridiculous offer. He'd wanted her to move into the hotel, be on retainer, float back and forth between his three casinos and be available constantly. He'd also implied rather pointedly that his glorious presence came with the job. Frankie tried not to look repulsed at the mere thought as she shoved in the elevator button.

"I prefer living in San Francisco. And I love the freedom of free-lancing, as I told you before."

His soft, pale hand reached up and turned her chin, forcing her to look up at him. "We'd be good together, Frankie. And you'd never want for a thing."

It wasn't the first such offer she'd received since leaving the relative safety of working for a corporate outfit. She'd had no trouble turning any of them down, either. "I appreciate the thought, Eric, but it's just not the life I want."

Suddenly, his arm shot around her, pulling her close to his thick body as his dark eyes turned suggestive. "What do you want, Frankie? Don't you get lonely, out on the road so much? Don't you miss having a man around, someone to warm you on those cold nights? I'd be real good to you."

Frankie smelled expensive whiskey and imported cigars on his hot breath. She felt the fury leap into her eyes as she pulled herself free of him. "What I want is for you not to touch me, ever again. Our arrangement is business, strictly business. If you forget that again, I won't be returning." The elevator doors wheezed open. Grateful that the car was empty, she hurried inside and pushed the button for her floor.

Color moved into Eric's face as he glared at her. "I'm not used to being turned down."

"I'm not used to being bullied," she said as calmly as she could manage. At last, the doors closed and the elevator moved.

Sighing, Frankie willed the car to hurry. She needed the privacy of her room and the oblivion of sleep. She'd long suspected Eric Hanley of wanting more than her computer expertise, and knew he was capable of pushing hard to get what he wanted. Too bad because she'd hate to lose this account. But her peace of mind was more important than money.

Inside her room, she flung her manuals aside and went to the bag she'd left on the rack. When she'd arrived, Eric had rushed her so that she hadn't had a chance to unpack. Reaching inside, she pulled out her cosmetic case and her robe. Turning toward the bathroom, she heard something fall onto the carpet.

A small item, wrapped in plain tissue paper. She bent to pick it up. Throat tightening, she tore the wrappings and removed a beautifully carved Christmas tree. She sat down on the bed, her eyes filling.

The gift he'd been working on and it had been for her. *When you give something you've made yourself, you give the recipient a part of yourself,* Steen had told her. She rubbed her thumb along the string of lights that wound around the delicate branches. Why a Christmas tree? she wondered, then the answer came to her. Steen wasn't one to push, yet he'd left her with a gentle but powerful reminder.

He'd given her far more than a small wood carving, and taken a risk in reminding her. He'd given her a taste of love, a night she would remember for all time. He'd given her several days of peace and contentment in his home. But she'd left him anyhow, knowing she'd hurt him sooner or later. Because she was no good for him. And she was no good for Eric Hanley, either. Most of all, she was not even good for herself.

Be happy, he'd said as she'd walked away. Curling her hand around the smooth wooden piece, Frankie lay down on the bed and let the tears fall.

Chapter Seven

It didn't seem like Christmas Eve morning. Steen sat on the thick rug in front of the blazing fire untangling the third string of lights and wondered why.

All the trappings were present. Earlier, Emily and Hannah had driven over in Hannah's new Land Rover, bringing him a holiday fruitcake smelling of raisins and brandy and issuing an invitation to dinner. He'd fashioned a wreath from discarded evergreen fronds and hung it on his door. Even now, the familiar carols were serenading from the stereo. Soon, the tree would be decorated. Yet something was missing.

Not some*thing*, Steen told himself as he scrambled to his feet. More specifically some*one*. Frankie.

In just a few short days, he'd gotten used to her presence, her scent, her slow smile. More than gotten used to. He'd begun to fall in love with her. And he was sure she wanted no part of that feeling or of him. Plugging in the lights, he saw that they were all working. He began to string them on the tree.

Steen thought he knew himself as well as any man. After the pain of his youth, the traveling he'd done to try to get over his grief, seeking the absolution that can only be found inside a man, he'd finally moved to the Sierra Nevada Mountains. Here he'd taken the time to heal himself, to become whole again. And he'd seen that Amelia got the support and loving care she needed to grow up into the fine young woman she now was. None of that had come easily to him.

And though he hadn't consciously sought someone, that special someone who would make his life complete, he'd nonetheless known that one day he'd be open and receptive to her. In his loneliness, he'd reached out to Jessica, but fortunately he'd discovered before either of them had gotten badly hurt that they could never have made one another happy. So he'd waited.

He'd been content with his life, but there'd been a void, one he'd seldom acknowledged, an emptiness inside that his work and friends couldn't fill. When Frankie had come along, literally falling into a snowbank and into his arms, he hadn't had a bright flash that this was the one. There'd been no comets in the sky, no bells ringing, no hallelujah chorus.

No, it had been far better than that. It had come slowly, in soft moments, in simple pleasures they'd shared, in gentle laughter. It had grown when he'd shared her pain over her loss, when he'd held her as she'd wept for things that could never be. And it had flared, then settled into a sure, steady flame when he'd made love to her and she'd touched much more than his body. She'd touched his heart when he'd been wondering if anyone could.

Anchoring the last bulb, Steen stood back and examined his handiwork. Not bad. He reached for the gold roping that would catch and reflect the lights. What would Frankie say if she were here right now? Could he ever get her beyond the pain of Christmases past? Could they build new memories, loving ones, to replace the hurtful ones?

For he had touched her heart, too, though she was too stubborn, too single-minded to admit it. And still she'd left. He tossed the tail of the rope onto a low branch and picked up a box of ornaments. He stared at them unseeingly as his mind relived yesterday morning when she'd driven off with that pompous ass with the pasty skin and the pudgy hands. Hands that he fervently hoped weren't touching her this very minute.

She wouldn't permit it, he told himself. He'd been the first man to touch her in six years, since her husband had died, and he seriously doubted if she'd give in to her needs easily again. But when she had, she'd responded like the fragile crocus that grew outside his door, opening to the sun and reaching for the warmth.

She'd be back. He had to believe that. Wasn't he the one who'd told Emily that she had to believe when she'd cried over her lost kitten? Had he deluded the child, as well as himself? No. He would not give up. He was a man who didn't fight, he'd told Frankie, but that wasn't exactly true. He didn't fight the way people expected him to. But he fought nonetheless.

The Christmas tree carving he'd slipped into her overnight bag was one way of fighting. He'd taken a chance, giving her something that would hopefully bring back a flood of memories every time she looked at it. Memories of the two of them together over the past days. She could shove it away in a drawer, but could she shove it out of her mind?

Stretching to hang a delicate hand-painted ornament that had belonged to his mother, Steen jumped as he heard a car approaching. When he peered out the window, he felt a slow smile form. Another wish come true. Hadn't he told himself she'd be home for Christmas?

Swinging the door wide, he smiled a greeting at the woman who ran toward him.

Not a single seat available on any airline going from Lake Tahoe to San Francisco, not even on the small commuter line. Frankie hung up the phone and walked over to stare out her hotel window. She should have expected the crowded conditions since it was Christmas Eve day. Now she was stuck here, this place she'd been dying to get to, for another day, perhaps two. The thought had her shuddering.

Her work was done and the hours stretched before her, endlessly boring. She wasn't fond of gambling and knew no one in town except Eric Hanley and a few other casino managers. And after the way Eric had come on to her last night, she most decidedly didn't want to spend any more time in his uneasy company.

She watched the wind swirl about the legs of the few passersby on the street below. Very little snow was accumulated here in town, although it looked quite cold. Maybe she could pass the time doing a little shopping before the stores closed for the holiday. Since she hadn't gone to Maui and was in the thick of Christmas here in the States, perhaps she should get a couple of gifts. She should remember Reenie, the one neighbor in her apartment building that she socialized with occasionally. And, of course, Corbett.

Corbett. She hadn't talked to him in a while. Smiling, she went back to the phone. Corbett always knew how to get her out of her doldrums. When he answered on the third ring, she greeted him warmly.

"Hey, Francesca," he said in his low, somewhat theatrical voice, "good to hear from you. Is the sun shining in Maui?"

Frankie sat on the bed. "I wouldn't know. I'm in Tahoe." Quickly, she told him of Eric's late-night call, the storm and the small cabin in the woods, touching lightly on her rescuer.

"What'd you say his name is?"

She hadn't said, but she could almost see Corbett seated at his Hepplewhite desk, narrowing his eyes speculatively as he drew on one of his gold-tipped cigarettes. "Steen Olson. Are you familiar with Olson Carvings?"

"Who isn't? There's a whole assortment of rather spectacular Olson Carvings decorating the Christmas windows in several of our better shops in town. And I wouldn't be surprised if some of his smaller pieces aren't in Gump's. You mean to tell me you were rescued by *that* Olson?"

"Yes."

"What's he like?"

"Oh, kind of reclusive. Quiet, like most artist types." And kind of slow to warm to people, kind of compassionate, kind of wonderful.

"And handsome?"

"Mmm, I suppose so. In a rugged, outdoorsy way." Frankie crossed her legs, wondering how much her voice was revealing. It was time for a subject change. "How's your weather?" Lord, how lame that sounded.

"Rainy. Tell me, what did you two do for four days and three nights trapped in this little shack in the woods, being strangers and all?"

"It's not exactly a shack. He's got some antique furniture you'd really appreciate."

"But you said it was small."

"Well, yes. A large living room as you walk in, a decent kitchen and . . ."

"One bath, one bedroom?"

"Yes, and this big wraparound porch that . . ." *One bedroom.* He'd trapped her. There were still times when Corbett made her feel about seventeen even though she'd been over twenty when she'd met him. Frankie cleared her throat. "He has this huge couch facing the fireplace. That's where guests sleep." Most guests. *Oh, God!*

"And we did leave, on snowshoes, and walked several miles to his neighbor's house. A motherly type who fed us homemade Christmas cookies." Frankie ran a hand through her hair. It had been a mistake to call. The things that she'd enjoyed so much sounded mundane in the retelling.

"Sounds so *homey.* Why is it I can't picture you hiking in the snow? You hate cold weather. You don't even own a heavy coat."

"I borrowed some clothes." She stood, shoving a hand into the pocket of her slacks. "So, are you having your usual Christmas Eve bash for unattached males and beautiful but lonely women?"

"Certainly. Are you sure you can't fly home in time?"

"Not a seat to be had. I may have to rent a dogsled to get out of this town. I feel like a prisoner of that jolly man in the red suit who's downstairs playing the slots even as we speak. You haven't seen anything until you've run across Santa collecting quarters in a cardboard bucket."

"And how is Eric the Terrible, still as slimy as ever?"

Corbett had come with her once when she'd had a job to do for Eric and the two men hated each other on sight. "Afraid so. We had a few words last night, not very pleasant ones. I think he's finally realized I'm not going to move into his penthouse suite."

"Are you going to see him again?"

"Probably not. He seemed fairly angry...."

"Not Eric. Your rugged wood-carver."

Taken aback, she dragged the phone cord to the window, buying a little time. "I don't know." And that was the truth.

But she'd waited too long to answer. "Are you all right, Francesca? You sound a little...distracted?" His voice had lost its teasing edge and was suddenly filled with the concern that always brought tears to her eyes. "Did this quiet man get to you?"

She swallowed past a sudden lump. "No, no. I'm tired, that's all. I just wanted to wish you a good Christmas."

"I wish you were here. I'd hug you till your ribs popped."

Blinking rapidly to clear her vision, Frankie smiled. "I'll take you up on that when I get home."

"What are you going to do tonight?" Corbett knew how she felt about Christmas and the concern in his voice deepened.

"I don't know. Walk around and watch people lose money, stay out of Eric's way."

Corbett released a puff of smoke. "How far away is this cabin in the woods?"

"Fifty miles or so. Why?"

"Not so very far, is it? Promise me something, honey?"

"What's that?"

"That you'll be careful."

"Yes, I will. Bye, Corbett."

Slowly, she walked back and replaced the receiver. *Are you going to see him again? Fifty miles. Not so very far, is it? Be careful.*

Corbett had given her a lot of valuable business advice through the years. But he'd never presumed to give her advice on her personal life. Yet that had sounded suspiciously like a warning.

She had to get out of this room and get some fresh, cold air on her face, Frankie decided. Quickly she grabbed her coat and handbag and headed for the door.

Two hours later, Frankie returned to the Diamond Nugget with a shopping bag full of gifts and some clothes for herself. She was mighty tired of recirculating the few things she'd brought along. Spreading out her purchases on the bed, she chose a soft cowl-necked navy sweater and matching wool slacks, smiling at the red-cheeked woman in the mirror. There was something to be said for bracing winter weather enhancing the complexion.

Slipping on the leather boots she'd bought, she acknowledged that she'd always hated winter. But that had been before Steen had taught her to enjoy walking in the snow and sitting in front of a roaring fire while the wind whistled outside. And he'd taught her with gentle touches, stunning kisses and trembling hands how it felt to be loved, to be loved so thoroughly that she'd scarcely had the energy left to breathe. With determination, Frankie reached for her hairbrush. She simply had to stop thinking along those lines. Grabbing her purse, she thought it might be a good idea to stroll about the casino.

It turned out to be a rotten idea. The bright lights looked falsely gay and the thrumming music, the raucous laughter and the screams of delight from the winners soon had her head pounding. But she kept on walking, hoping to divert herself from her melancholy thoughts and to avoid her solitary room.

She saw a young couple evidently lose the last dollar they'd set aside for gambling leave dejectedly. She heard a chubby tourist berate her husband who refused to leave the machine he kept steadily pumping dimes into. She watched an older woman sitting alone at a blackjack table, cigarette dangling from her lips and one arthritic hand curled about a small pile of chips, give her a measuring glance through the smoke. Vacationers, tourists, holiday revelers. They didn't look very happy; not any of them.

All alone on Christmas Eve with strangers for company and the dream of breaking the bank driving them on. Did she look as pathetic, as lost, to others as she found some of these people to be? she wondered. In the coffee shop where she sat sipping her coffee, she noticed a young couple in their thirties and two little boys perhaps eight and ten. They laughed together as they ate burgers and fries and sipped on malts, oblivious to the world around them, content in their own special world, the family unit. Feeling inexplicably sad, Frankie finished her coffee and headed for the elevators.

She'd had enough of this, enough of feeling excluded, on the outside looking in, as she so often had

felt as a child. Why she was letting all this bother her
now when for years she'd hardened herself against the
pain of being alone, *choosing* to be alone, she wasn't
certain. She only knew she felt like screaming and very
well might if she didn't get away soon.

Arriving at a decision, Frankie entered her room and
went to the phone. She'd rent a car, go for a drive. She
thumbed through the yellow pages. It was such a beautiful section of the country. Spectacular mountains,
scenic overlooks. She let out a sigh as she found the
page with car rentals. Who was she kidding? She knew
exactly where she wanted to go.

Did this quiet man get to you? Corbett had asked her.
Here, in the silent privacy of her room, she could answer honestly. Yes, he had. He mostly definitely had
gotten to her. And she hadn't the faintest idea of what
to do about it.

The first place she phoned had a small compact
available and she quickly made the arrangements.
Feeling better already, she hurried to pack. She'd just
go for a little while, take him the gift she'd bought, a
sort of thank-you for her tree and his warm hospitality.
Maybe she'd pick up some groceries, in the event he
hadn't freed his Jeep yet and been unable to get to the
store. Neighborly like. Nothing special. Smiling, she
zipped her bag closed and went back to the yellow
pages.

She'd go visit Steen, but there was someone else she
wanted to see, as well. But first, she'd have to see if she
could find a pet store open on Christmas Eve. One that
sold kittens.

"My mouth's on fire, but that was *so* good," Amelia said as she leaned back in the kitchen chair. "You

still make the best chili this side of the Rio Grande. Maybe on both sides."

Steen pushed back from the kitchen table and smiled at his sister. "Every Texan worthy of the name knows how to make chili."

"You should see the stuff they pass off at the dorm as chili. It's nothing more than beans floating around in some gray liquid. And not a chili pepper in the whole pot." She wrinkled up her small nose. "Awful."

"Well, I'm glad you made it home, even if it was because you missed my chili and not me." Though Amelia hadn't lived here in years, they both thought of the cabin as home. He'd missed teasing her, missed having her around, he thought as he studied her.

She was still a little too slender, but she'd regained most of the weight she'd lost over the past year. Her eyes, the same deep gray as his own, had also lost that rebellious edge he'd hated. She was more like she'd been as a teenager, seemingly happy to be alive. This is what he'd wanted for her and he was enormously pleased that, after several detours, she was finally getting there.

"Oh, I miss you, all right," Amelia went on. "I sure could have used your help on this last term paper. Economics is really *not* my subject. I thought I'd have to spend my entire Christmas break working and studying, but I got lucky. This guy named Ken Dickson helped me put it together. He's a real whiz."

Steen struggled to keep his features even. "Am I going to meet this economics whiz?"

Amelia burst out laughing. "You should see your face. Not to worry, big brother. Ken's nothing like Troy. And he's only a friend." Sobering, she placed her hand on his arm. "I really did learn my lesson with Troy. He cost me a year in my studies, but I'm back on track now." She dropped her gaze, toying with her napkin. "One of the reasons I wanted to come home was to show you that I'm all right again. That and to thank you for being so patient with me. I...I don't know what got into me for a while there."

He felt the tension ease from him. "You fell in love and you went a little crazy. It happens to the best of us. The problem was you picked the wrong person."

"*Does* it happen to all of us? Have you ever been in love, Steen?"

"Don't you remember Jessica? I cared a lot about her, but like Troy, she was the wrong person."

Amelia played with a lock of her long, auburn hair. "How do you know when it's the *right* person? And is there really a *right* person, or are some people just luckier than others, or more willing to compromise?"

She was forcing him to think a little too deeply about some things he hadn't quite figured out himself. Steen rose to clear the table. "I think compromises are necessary in every relationship. As long as you don't compromise and settle for someone just because. Just because he makes a good living or likes the same things you do. Because then you lose out on the passion, the fire that makes it all worthwhile." He shot her a grin over his shoulder. "And without the passion, you might as well get yourself a cat instead."

Amelia joined him at the counter. "I had a little taste of passion with Troy, and it nearly wrecked me. Maybe I just can't handle strong feelings."

Steen turned to her, his eyes intense. "Yes, you can, and don't settle for anything less. There's a man out there somewhere who's going to teach you all about passion, but a man who also cares for you. For the real you, deep inside, someone who cares about answering all your needs, not just sexual. A man who'll love you more than he loves himself, not a user like Troy. That's worth waiting for, a love like . . . like Mom and Dad had.''

A look of sadness crossed her face. "You still think about them a lot?" At his nod, she went on. "So do I."

Steen bent to stack the dishes into the washer. "Sure. How can we not? At least they died together. One wouldn't have wanted to live without the other, I always felt."

"I felt that, too. You aren't blaming yourself, are you?"

Slowly, he closed the door of the dishwasher. Was he? Or was he kidding himself that he was handling things, like Frankie thought she was? No, he really didn't think so. He'd had twelve years to adjust. "Not really. I know I didn't do anything wrong, though at the time I was afraid I might have. But living with a tragedy that you can't blame someone for can be awfully hard on you, too. You have to learn to forgive yourself for all the imagined wrongs."

She reached up and gave him a warm hug. "You're such a good man, Steen, and you were a good son. I just wish you'd meet that special someone who'd love you the way she should." She angled back to smile mischievously into his eyes. "And supply all that passion."

He thought of Frankie as she'd threatened him with a mound of snow, her cheeks red from the wintry day. He thought of her as she'd sat at this very table, concentrating on painting the fawn. And he thought of her beneath him on his big bed, her green eyes hazy with desire. "It'll happen one day."

"How can you be so sure?"

"You've got to believe. Some things you can't explain. You just *know* they'll happen." He swatted her with the dish towel. "Now, how about you and me going out and building a snowman? I think we need to work off that fattening lunch."

"Good idea." Amelia followed him into the living room where her jacket lay on a chair. "I miss Red. When are you going to go get that ornery old dog?"

"When I get my Jeep out of the ditch at the fork in the road. I probably can't get anyone with a truck to help until after Christmas."

Amelia pulled on the second boot. "How did you get it stuck there anyhow?"

His back to her, Steen swung open the door. "I didn't. It's a long story. Come on, let's go."

Banking her curiosity, Amelia followed her brother outside.

It was snowing again. Not heavily but nonetheless coming down steadily. Driving along Highway 50, Frankie realized she didn't mind the snow this time. She'd resigned herself to the fact that she couldn't fly home for several days so the weather became unimportant. Perhaps she was getting soft, she thought as she glanced down at the small calico kitten that lay curled next to her on the car seat.

Touching his velvety fur, she smiled. She hadn't given him a name because that would be up to Emily. The kitten was only six weeks old, barely weaned from his mother. She'd had a little trouble settling him down when they'd first started out. But after he'd explored, sniffed and poked into every corner of the car, he'd come back, snuggled up to her and quickly fallen asleep.

He wasn't Mittens, but she hoped Emily would take to him anyway.

But how would Steen take to her returning in such a cavalier fashion after the way she'd walked away from him? Or was he, in that quietly accepting way he had, expecting her? And just what signal was she sending him by her unexpected return visit?

Frankie let a semi that was really rolling pass her, the afterwave rocking her small car. She knew that Steen would never buy the story that she'd rented a car merely to deliver his thank-you gift. Nor even that she'd come to bring Emily a kitten. Those calm gray eyes would look right through her. So what then?

How about the truth? her conscience prodded. Perhaps if she were sure of the truth, she might tell him. The truth was she did want to thank him, for sheltering her, for putting up with her, for the beautiful carving. All of which she could easily have told him in a note written from San Francisco.

Time to face some hard facts. She wanted to talk with him again, to share a drink by the fire, simply to look at him. She wanted more—to touch him, to kiss him, to lay with him and feel his lean, hard body close up against hers. Oh, Lord, she couldn't tell him any of that. Yet it was true, every word.

Desire, passion, love—they were words she'd removed from her vocabulary years ago. Because giving in to them led to pain and loss. When you cared about someone, you gave them power over you. She'd vowed she'd never let anyone have that kind of power over her again. Yet with Steen, she yearned. Oh, how she yearned.

She noticed that she was almost to the turnoff to his road. The thing was, she was stuck here for at least two more days. He'd agreed to a caring friendship and that's how she'd put it to him. If he could keep to that, she would and they could share a few good hours together, some happy times. Then she'd go back to her life, and he'd remain in his. What harm could there be in friendship? After all, neither of them was overburdened with friends. Yes, she was sure he'd agree. Wearing a pleased smile, Frankie turned onto Steen's property.

She passed the Jeep, still wedged in the ditch and felt a momentary pang of guilt. She should offer to have it hauled out of there. She parked some distance from the house, wanting to surprise him. Nestling the kitten inside her jacket, she set out on foot, her new boots crunching in the hard-packed snow. She'd just come around the final bend when she noticed a car parked alongside the cabin. Almost at the same moment, she heard the laughter of two people, one low and rumbling, the other high-pitched and definitely female. Frankie stopped in her tracks.

They'd been building a snowman, but the opportunity to stuff new snow down her neck was obviously irresistible to Steen. The woman tried to get away, but he was too fast. Down she went and be quickly followed, his hand holding a wad of snow raised high and threatening. The woman squealed as she tried to wiggle away, but he caught her and they both laughed as the snow found its mark.

Her hair was a rich reddish-brown, her face young and alive and her reflexes very good. She gave a hard shove and reversed their positions. With lightning speed, she straddled his chest and stuffed snow in his ears, on his cheeks and into his dark hair.

"Thought you had me, did you?" she asked, daring him to retaliate. Her gloved hand dropped another clump down the front of him, inside his jacket. Steen's protest died on a bubble of laughter as he twisted out from under her clever hands, toppling her into a pile of snow.

Frankie hugged the warm kitten to her chest. Why should she care if Steen was wrestling with some woman in the snow? She had no ties on him. They were just friends, new friends at that. Besides, she didn't want him.

Or did she?

This wasn't the moment to ponder that. As quietly as possible, she started to turn back. But her movements must have caught his eye, for suddenly she heard Steen's voice.

"Frankie! Hey, Frankie, where are you going?"

She turned to stare at him as the woman scampered to her feet and tossed her long hair off her face. If only she'd have gotten away before he'd spotted her. But she hadn't. Giving him a weak smile, she took several steps forward. "Hello, Steen."

He dusted the snow from his pants and went to her. "Come here. There's someone I want you to meet."

It certainly hadn't taken him long to replace her, Frankie thought. And with such a young woman at that. Obviously, the night she'd spent in his bed had meant much less to him than to her. Willing herself to stay calm, she put on a smile.

Steen touched her arm. "I'm glad you came back," he whispered before turning her toward the young woman. "Amelia, I'd like you to meet a friend of mine, Francesca Taelor. Frankie, this is Amelia. My sister."

In the process of reaching to shake the woman's hand, Frankie stopped and swung her gaze to Steen's face. "Your sister?"

He felt his lips twitch as he watched the play of emotions on her face. So she'd been jealous there for a moment. That's why she'd been about to run away again. Good. Jealousy was a start. He nodded. "Yes, my sister. Remember, I told you about her?"

She felt like smiling and gave in to it. "Yes." She shook Amelia's hand heartily. "It's good to meet you."

Amelia's head was tilted to the side, her eyes flickering from one to the other. She returned the warm handshake. "You, too, though I feel at a disadvantage here. You evidently know about me, but I don't know anything about you. Have you known Steen long?"

"Oh, we're old friends," Steen answered for her.

The kitten chose that moment to squirm through the opening in Frankie's jacket and greet them with a plaintive meow. Smiling, Amelia reached to pet the tiny head.

"Well, look at you. How adorable. What's his name?"

"I haven't named him." Frankie looked over at Steen. "I brought him for Emily, to replace Mittens. That's why I came. A Christmas present for Emily."

He didn't ask why she hadn't driven right over to Hannah's and given the kitten directly to the child, why she'd come to his cabin first. He merely smiled. "That's good of you. We're invited to Hannah's for dinner tonight. It's sort of a Christmas Eve tradition."

"Oh, Steen," Amelia said with a frown. "I hope you won't be upset if I beg off. One of my friends who lives in Tahoe has invited some of the girls who weren't able to get home for Christmas over for a couple of days, kind of an extended hen party. We're just going to kick back, eat too much and talk all night."

"That's fine. But then I think we ought to go inside so you can open your present before you go. And so I can get into a dry shirt." He slid an arm around Frankie, dying to know if she had her things in the car but determined not to ask. "Maybe we'd better find some milk for that little guy."

"I picked up some items at the grocery store," Frankie said. Catching Amelia's inquisitive look, she made a dismissing gesture. "You know, for the cat. And I brought a few things for dinner. Steen's been so generous that I had to reciprocate."

"Yes, he's like that." She sent her brother a pointed look. "Why don't you get the groceries from the car, Steen? And why don't you and I go in and warm up by the fire, Frankie? I'm pretty wet myself."

Falling in step beside Amelia, Frankie followed her inside.

Steen busied himself transferring two sacks of groceries from Frankie's car to the house, smiling to himself when he saw her overnight bag on the back seat. But he left it there. He didn't want to push, especially not in front of Amelia who, he knew, was fairly bursting with questions already.

He set out a saucer of milk for the kitten as the two women settled themselves in front of the fire. Though he wasn't certain it was the right thing to do, he left them alone and went to the kitchen to put away the things Frankie had brought. Sometimes it was best not to interfere, but rather to let two people get acquainted on their own. If they didn't hit it off, he'd soon know.

Curious, he poked his nose into the first bag and found a box of lasagna noodles and several cheeses.

He'd told her once that he loved Italian food. Did she plan to stay long enough to make some for him? Whistling, he checked out the other sack, trying to ignore the low voices in the other room.

"Otherwise I'd be a senior this year," Amelia was saying, "but I lost a year because of this creep I let myself care for. He quit college so I decided education wasn't for me. I squandered the money Steen had given me for school to live with him in this dinky little apartment." She shook her head. "Crazy. I wish I was more like Steen. He's always in control. Have you ever been in love like that, where it makes you act crazy?"

Frankie had never met anyone more outspoken, especially on such short acquaintance. She wasn't sure if it was Amelia's youth or just her personality. "No, I'm more the cautious type." Yet she was here, wasn't she? And for her, that was pretty crazy. "I understand Steen raised you after your parents died. You must be very close."

Amelia stretched her slim legs toward the fire, drying her jeans. "Yes. Even through all this stuff with Troy, Steen's been so understanding. We've been through a lot together. I was only ten when the accident happened. It shattered my whole world, I can tell you."

"Death can do that to you." Her heart went out to Amelia, left orphaned so young. But at least she'd had a caring brother.

"Yes, it was devastating. And then, when Steen took off and left, I thought I'd die. The people in the foster home were good to me, but . . ."

Frankie frowned. "What do you mean, Steen took off?" Leaving a ten-year-old sister—it didn't sound like the Steen she'd come to know.

Amelia sent a quick look over her shoulder and could hear Steen whistling in the kitchen. "I thought you were old friends."

She ignored that. "But didn't Steen raise you?"

"Well, yes. I was twelve when he came back for me and we moved to this place in L.A. We lived there awhile, but he didn't like the kids I met in school. Some of them had quite a bit of money and they were kind of wild. That's when he bought this cabin and we moved here. At first, I thought it was the end of the world. But it grows on you." Amelia nodded toward the bedroom. "That was my room and Steen slept right here on this big, old couch. I spent my teen years here. We had dogs and cats and I'd feed the deer and Steen would take me hiking and fishing. And he'd drive me to school twenty miles one way every day."

First he left her, then he was so devoted? She hated to quiz anyone, but she needed to know. "Amelia, where was Steen those two years while you were in a foster home?"

Suddenly, Amelia looked worried. "I thought you knew."

Though she badly wanted to know, she had no right to badger this young woman into revealing a confidence. "No, and I understand if you'd rather not say."

Amelia was thoughtful a long moment. "Can I ask you a question?"

"Certainly."

"Steen's never been one to talk much about his personal life with me. I'm ten years younger, so maybe he still thinks of me as a kid. But I'd really like to know. How do you feel about my brother?"

The lady played hardball. Odd how a day ago, perhaps a couple of hours ago, she'd have given her an evasive answer. But that was before the churning had begun in her stomach, before she'd begun to suspect there was more to Steen Olson's past than he'd let on. For the first time, Frankie's need to know about someone overshadowed her need to stay uninvolved. "I care about him. Will that do?"

Amelia's serious gray eyes, so like Steen's, studied her and then, finally, she nodded.

"So where was he?"

"Running."

"Running? I don't understand."

"Running away because he felt responsible for the accident that killed our parents."

Stunned, Frankie tried to gather her thoughts. "Why would he feel that way?"

The young girl sent another look toward the kitchen. "I think you'd better let him tell you the rest."

Still whistling, Steen came into the room and stopped in front of them. "So, ladies, should I throw another log on the fire?"

Frankie studied his strong features, the kindness in his eyes. Responsible for two deaths? No, not this man. Impossible.

Chapter Eight

"Oh, Steen, they're beautiful," Amelia said, her dark eyes wide with delight. Carefully, she lifted the pearls from their black velvet box. "They were Mom's, weren't they?"

"Yes. Turn around and I'll help you put them on."

Holding her long hair out of the way, Amelia turned her back to him as he fussed with the fastener. "You had them in your safety deposit box all these years, right? I remember you telling me about them ages ago, that you were saving them for me." Her hand touched the necklace almost reverently before she turned to hug her brother. "Thank you so much."

Frankie sat on the far end of the couch, the kitten curled up asleep beside her, and watched Steen and his sister. There were only the two of them left in their family, yet they were so close. She'd never had a sister or brother and felt a pang of envy for all she'd missed.

Her childhood memories focused on a mother who, though kind and loving, had been weary and distracted, and on a father who'd been mostly silent and brooding. Two people who never should have married because they so obviously hadn't made one another happy. What a waste.

"I love all my gifts," Amelia said, stacking the boxes she'd opened with such glee, that had held a silk blouse, a robe and matching slippers and several record albums. She sent Steen a radiant smile. "You spoil me and I love it." With youthful energy, she jumped up to bring him a brightly wrapped box. "Now, it's your turn." She placed the package on his lap, then sent Frankie an apologetic look. "I'm sorry, I didn't know you'd be here or I would have..."

Frankie brushed away the apology. "I love watching you open your gifts, really."

Steen had the box open and his face broke into a smile as he held up a multicolored sweater. "So you finally finished it." He got to his feet and pulled the sweater on over his shirt, smoothing it over his long torso. "Fits fine." He reached to hug her. "Thanks."

"I was a little worried," Amelia confessed to Frankie. "His shoulders are so broad. I've been working on that, off and on, for two years."

"I can't knit, crochet or any of that," Frankie told her. "Patience isn't my strong suit. I seem to prefer instant results."

Steen bent to gather up the wrappings to toss onto the fire. "You're patient enough to paint."

"That's different. Painting relaxes me. Sewing frustrates me."

"I know what you mean. I can't tell you how many rows I had to yank out and start over. I wanted to give

Steen something I made myself, but it's likely the last one he'll get.''

"One of a kind, a collector's item." Steen rubbed his hands together. "How about some eggnog, ladies?" At their nod, he went to the kitchen, pleased that Amelia and Frankie seemed to like one another.

He'd sensed a little tension in the air when he'd joined them earlier, but perhaps he'd only imagined it, for they were talking like old friends since. Yet several times, during the gift-opening ceremony, he'd caught Frankie studying him, her eyes measuring. Was it just this Christmas hoopla that had her somewhat quiet and thoughtful? Or was she regretting her return visit? Later, after Amelia left to join her friends, he meant to find out.

"Here we are," he said, handing glasses all around.

"What shall we drink to?" Amelia asked.

Steen held his glass out. "How about to friendship?" His eyes locked with Frankie's. Her full lips parted into a small smile and he fought the urge to kiss her right here in front of Amelia.

"To friendship," they all said together, and clinked glasses before sipping.

Amelia glanced at her watch. "It's getting late and as much as I hate to miss sharing dinner with you two at Hannah's, I'd better run." Picking up her jacket, she shrugged into it. "Steen, are you ever going to get a phone in here? I didn't even know if I'd catch you home when I started out."

He helped her gather up her things. "I hate phones. Ninety percent of the callers want to sell you insurance or wash your carpets. Who needs it?"

Amelia went on tiptoe to kiss his cheek. "It's those other ten percent that make having one worthwhile. See you in a couple of days, big brother." She turned to Frankie who rose to say goodbye. "I'm glad you're here to spend Christmas with Steen. He tends to get a little moody around the holidays."

Don't we all? Frankie thought, yet she'd never have guessed that Steen would. "It was good meeting you, Amelia."

"You, too. I hope to see you again." Amelia gave her a fast hug, then headed for the door.

Frankie sat back down as Steen carried his sister's bundles out to her car. Total opposites, she decided. Amelia was open and natural, talking about herself, her past, her mistakes, as easily as if they were old friends. But Steen, though warm and caring, was cautious with his conversations. As a matter of fact, it would seem he'd deliberately left out a few pertinent facts.

She was well aware that her past had influenced her work choice and her solitary life-style. Did Steen also live and work hidden away in the woods with no phone and no close neighbors because of something in his past? She hadn't even considered that. But she was certain of one thing. The gentle, compassionate man she knew as Steen Olson could never do anything deliberately to hurt anyone, much less the parents he spoke of so lovingly.

The door closed as Steen walked in amidst a whirl of white flakes. "It's snowing harder," he said as he walked over to the fire, blowing on his hands to warm them. "We might be marooned here again."

Frankie got up and moved to him. Learning that he, too, had had a troubled past had subtly altered the way she viewed Steen. She wasn't certain just what it was, not yet. She was certain that she'd done the right thing in coming to him. Slowly she reached to trace along his lean jaw. "I certainly hope so." She saw the reaction in his dark eyes as he slipped his arms around her.

"I want to kiss you. For hours now, I've wanted to kiss you."

"I want that, too." Her mouth locked to his as he dragged her close to his hard body, and suddenly Frankie's world felt right again. His tongue claimed entry and she let him in, reacquainting herself with his taste. Oh, how she had missed this. A day and a half and it had been long, so long. Since he had taught her how loving could feel, she reached for more like a desert walker reaches toward a rain shower. Her hands moved up into his hair as she molded herself to him, returning the kiss with all the wildness he could so easily provoke in her.

Home. She was home, back in his arms, and Steen felt his heart soar as he deepened the kiss. She'd been hesitant at first, and he could tell she'd come reluctantly, giving him a transparent story about a kitten for Emily to justify the trip. But she wasn't kissing him hesitantly or reluctantly. She was kissing him with open hunger and he gloried in it.

His lips had moved to her throat, pushing aside the soft wool of her sweater, when he heard tiny mewing sounds. Turning together, they smiled at the kitten standing on the couch, looking at them curiously with his head cocked.

"I guess we'd better take him to Emily," Steen said. "Besides, Hannah gets annoyed if we're late for dinner." He thought of their last visit there, how she'd all but run from Hannah's house. He hated to disappoint his neighbor, but he wouldn't want Frankie upset again. "Would you rather not go?"

She'd rather have stayed, rather have continued, but she leaned back from him and shook her head, unwilling to disappoint Emily or Hannah.

"We won't stay long." His lips returned to hers, lingering, losing themselves in her softness. "Mmm, hold that thought and we'll pick this up later."

Her eyes were cloudy with the beginnings of desire. "I can't seem to lose that thought, much as I've tried."

"Is that so bad?"

"It could be."

He held her to him, speaking close to her ear. "Let's not overthink things. You're back and that's what matters. Let's just go with our feelings and no questions, no probing thoughts for now, all right?"

Frankie had a lot of questions, but they would wait. Maybe Steen was right. Maybe they could snatch this moment out of time and float with the feeling. They could at least try. "Okay," she said, then gave him a quick kiss. "You carry the kitten and I'll drive."

Emily ate dinner with the kitten curled up and asleep on her lap. Too excited to eat much, she held a biscuit in one hand and kept the other on his soft fur. She turned bright eyes to Frankie. "Did I tell you thanks yet for getting me Rascal? He's so cuddly."

"Yes, child," Hannah interrupted, "you've told her three or four times. Now eat some dinner."

"When Mittens comes home, he's going to love Rascal as much as I do." She gazed down at the small bundle. "They'll have such fun playing together."

Feeling a little helpless, Frankie met Steen's eyes across the table. There seemed no way to make the child forget Mittens. Only time would take care of this one, she decided. Taking a bite of chicken, she also decided that she was handling this visit much better than the last. Emily wasn't quite as sad-eyed as before, although she noticed Hannah's shrewd gaze studying her every chance she got. But it was Steen's look she found even more disconcerting. He couldn't seem to keep his eyes from her. On the one hand, it embarrassed her. On the other, it pleased her enormously.

What woman didn't want to be openly admired and frankly desired? A week ago, she'd have turned from it. But Steen had changed her and she wasn't sure how to handle the new Frankie who couldn't seem to wait to leave so they could fall into his big featherbed. Her cheeks flushing, she bent to her dinner, trying to think of a subject that would distract her thoughts.

"I can't believe your daughter still hasn't had her baby," she said to Hannah. "Is there a problem?"

"False labor, the doctor called it. He released her, then the next night, she started with contractions again. They've got her in the hospital, and they've stopped again." Hannah shook her head. "Looks like that baby's got a mind of his own already."

"Is it a boy? Did she have the ultrasound test?"

"No, she said she wanted to be surprised. But *I* know it's a boy. I can feel it." She patted Emily's hand. "I was right about this little one, wasn't I, honeykins?"

"Grandma, I'm not hungry. Can I please go see what Steen brought me?"

"Don't you think you ought to let the man finish his dinner before you start pestering him?" Hannah rose to get the dessert from the refrigerator. "How does this look, pumpkin pie with whipped cream?"

"It looks great," Steen said, shoving back from the table. "But I think we should wait until later to have some. If I don't take Emily to her present, it's going to be buried in snow out there."

Hugging the kitten, Emily slipped from her chair. "What is it and why'd you leave it outside?"

He winked at the two women still seated at the table. "You'll see. Come on, let's bundle up. I don't want you to catch cold on Christmas."

Hannah smiled tolerantly. "I believe he's more excited than she is," she confided to Frankie.

"Frankie, will you hold Rascal for me until I get back?"

"Sure." She took the soft bundle from Emily and set him on her lap. The cat didn't even stir.

Getting up to pour coffee, Hannah sent her young guest an inquisitive glance. "We were over at Steen's this morning. Didn't see you around."

"No, I got a ride yesterday and went to Tahoe. I had a commitment I had to fulfill."

"But now you're back."

"Well, yes, temporarily. There were no plane seats available due to the holiday so I thought I'd come by. It was nice of you to have me to dinner again."

"I've always got room for one or two more at my table." She put her hand atop Frankie's and gave it a squeeze. "It was thoughtful of you to get that kitten for Emily."

"I only hope that . . ."

Hearing the back door bang, she turned to see Emily already dashing out in search of her gift. Steen walked over to the table.

"Hannah, that was a wonderful dinner." As she nodded in acknowledgment, he moved his gaze to Frankie, touching her shoulder in a gentle caress. "I won't be long." He turned and went outside.

With just a touch, just a light touch, he could make her whole system hum. Amazing. Frankie took a sip of coffee. "As I was saying, I only hope this kitten will help Emily get over the loss of Mittens."

"Maybe. We all handle loss in our own way, even children."

Frankie couldn't help wonder how much Hannah knew about Steen's past. "How long have you known Steen?"

"About ten years, I'd say. He moved Amelia into that cabin of his when she was just about twelve. Said the big city was no place to raise a child. I agree."

"I met Amelia today. She's lovely. I'm still amazed that Steen changed his whole life to raise a sister."

"She's family, honey. I know Steen's never been sorry."

Frankie stared into her cup. "Most men would have considered a young sister a burden, a handicap to their success." She knew about burdens. She'd been one to her parents and even to Matt. It wasn't a good feeling.

Hannah shrugged. "I suppose so, but Steen isn't like most men. He knows that things that are worth having come at a price, for all of us. When I threw Charley out years ago, I knew it would cost me a lot more than mere money to go it alone, to raise my daughter. But it was better than having her grow up in an atmosphere of fighting parents. All decisions come with a price tag. We just have to decide if paying that price is worth it to us. It was to Steen—and to me."

"You're probably right."

Propping her elbows on the table, Hannah leaned forward. "Let me tell you a little story. I've got two sisters. The oldest one, Helen, had polio when she was a girl. She's got one leg that's pretty useless and she kind of drags it. Most folks would call Helen a cripple. But she's married to a fine man who loves her and she's got three grown children and a good life. People like being around Helen.''

Hannah paused to taste her coffee before going on. ''My other sister, Clara, is a fine-looking woman, pretty as a picture and not a mole on her perfect skin. But her husband walked out on her years ago and she's never gotten over it. She's locked her feelings away and has very few friends, because she's bitter and nasty to everyone. People don't look at her and see a cripple, but I do. There's all kinds of handicaps in the world, but the worst ones are the ones we give ourselves. Don't you see?''

She saw all right, Frankie thought. She saw that this simple woman who lived back in the woods was much more than she appeared to be. She was a woman of substance despite her down-home ways. Or maybe because of them.

She gave Hannah a sad smile. ''Yes, I see. But sometimes, changing isn't as easy as it sounds. Perhaps Clara *wants* to be less bitter, less angry at the world for what happened to her. But she can't.'' Or perhaps she didn't want to try again, fearful of being hurt. Frankie could relate to that perfectly.

''Ah, but she should try, and try again. There's this man she's been seeing for two, maybe three years. Burt's a nice guy, works at the same bank where Clara does. She's so wrapped up in that job of hers that she can't see that that man's crazy about her, though I surely can't figure out why.'' Hannah shook her head sagely. ''It's a mistake losing time, putting off being with someone you care about. You think you'll wait awhile, talk tomorrow, settle things then. Maybe even tell him how much you care. Sometimes tomorrow's too late.''

Hannah was so warm and motherly that it didn't seem strange to Frankie discussing personal feelings with her, though they'd known each other only a brief time. "I hadn't thought of it quite like that."

Hannah turned to Frankie. "I tell Clara, reach out, be glad for every minute you have. Life is about laughter and loving, about enjoying and sharing what you've got with others. Otherwise, what's the point of us being here at all?''

Frankie found herself envying the older woman's strength, her outlook. "You're quite a lady, you know that, Hannah?''

Embarrassed, Hannah stood to get the coffeepot. "Listen to me going on so. Get me wound up and I don't know when to quit."

The back door burst open, letting in a blast of cold air. "Grandma, come see," Emily called. "A sled. Steen made me a sled.''

"Just what we needed," Hannah grumbled as she made her way to the door. But there was a smile on her face as she poked her head out the door to enthuse over Emily's gift.

Frankie sat staring into the coffee she didn't want. *There're all kinds of handicaps in the world, but the worst ones are the ones we give ourselves.* Without knowing her background, had this astute woman seen right through her? Did Hannah view her as handicapped, an emotional cripple who'd done it to herself? Perhaps, but she didn't know the whole story, didn't know that she *had* to protect herself from suffering the kind of pain that went with caring deeply. Like Clara, she was afraid and readily admitted that fact to herself.

It was one thing to care as two friends might for one another. And quite another to care so deeply that you don't know where his joys and sorrows begin and yours end. That kind of caring—all right, let's label it loving, Frankie admitted to herself—could cripple you.

No, she was right to keep it to friendship and a mutually satisfying physical relationship. No one would get hurt that way. She felt confident that she could make Steen see that that's all they would ever have between them—friendship. As she heard him and Emily pile in through the back door, she stood, wondering how long they were expected to stay. She was anxious to be alone with Steen.

"Steen," Hannah said as she helped Emily out of her snow-crusted boots, "if you'll throw another log on, we can open the gifts before we dig into that pie. What do you say?"

"Sounds good." Steen studied Frankie's face as she watched the little girl squirm out of her outerwear. She looked pensive, but otherwise all right, with no traces of the frightened-doe look. He went to get the logs.

In no time, they were settled around the Christmas tree and Hannah, her cheeks red from the nearby fire, opened the gift Frankie had brought her.

"Why, this is too pretty to wear. My aprons get a real workout. Look at this lace. Lovely." She leaned over to warmly embrace Frankie. "Thank you, honey. It's real sweet of you."

Frankie watched Hannah's strong, capable hands trace the colorful embroidery design. This gift-giving business, one she'd not been a part of for so long she could scarcely remember the last time, had its moments, she thought, realizing the woman was genuinely pleased. It wasn't that she was ungenerous but rather that she'd purposely spent the last several Christmases in Hawaii among strangers, safely uninvolved in the emotions of the season. Yet now, as she watched Emily rip the paper from a present in a rush of childish impatience, she found herself glad to be a part of this small celebration.

The adults watched Emily work her way through her pile of gifts—some clothes from her grandmother, a doll and some puzzles and books that her parents had sent to be opened tonight, and a huge stuffed koala bear for her room at home. Then it was Steen's turn.

"I was hoping you'd come through with another batch," he told Hannah as he uncovered two jars of her homemade jam and a bottle of her blackberry brandy. "This should take me through the winter. Thanks, Hannah."

"Open mine next, Steen," Emily prodded. "Grandma helped, but I did a lot of it myself."

"You know I like those gifts best, don't you, babe?" His fingers undid the clumsily wrapped package under Emily's watchful eye. Carefully, he removed a framed photo. "Well, I wonder who this is."

"It's me, Steen. It's called a silhouette. You sit in front of a light and you draw a picture of your shadow on the wall. Then you cut around it with scissors and paste it on white paper. I did the cutting. Do you like it?"

"I love it."

"Think it looks like me?"

"It's close, but you're much prettier in person." He winked at her and gave her a long hug.

As if remembering her manners, Emily turned to Frankie. "I didn't have time to make you one, but I could do it later. If...if you'd like one."

Frankie gave her a big smile. "I'd love that. Thank you."

"I see a package under the tree for Frankie," Steen said bringing it over and handing it to her. "Mighty big, too."

Frankie wrinkled her brow at Hannah, looking genuinely surprised. "You shouldn't have."

"At my age, I do what I please, honey. Open it."

Tearing the tissue paper, Frankie unwrapped a large bedspread. Holding it high, she saw it was hand-crocheted, an ecru lace in an intricate pattern. "This must have taken you hours and hours."

"I do needlework evenings while I watch TV. I hate to sit idle, just watching shows, you know. If it doesn't fit the style of your home..."

"This is lovely enough to go in any bedroom. But I can't accept this, Hannah. It's too much. You scarcely know me."

"Steen brought you and that's enough for me. It'll please me no end to think you'll use it on your bed."

"As soon as I get home." Frankie leaned toward Hannah only to find herself enfolded in a big hug. The woman's warmth and generosity all but overwhelmed her. She'd done a lot of traveling, met a lot of people, but none who'd made her feel as welcome, as accepted as these had this week. She met Steen's dark eyes over Hannah's shoulder and felt a quick rush of emotion. It seemed there was little she could do to avoid sentiment lately. How was she ever going to get back on track? she wondered as she pulled back from Hannah.

"Hey, did you hear that?" Emily asked, jumping up. "Someone's ringing bells outside." She ran toward the door.

"Now, who do you suppose that is, coming after dark like this on a Christmas Eve?" Steen went to help her with the heavy door while Frankie turned to watch.

"Santa. It's got to be Santa," Emily guessed.

"It wouldn't surprise me at all," Hannah said as she stacked the boxes out of the way. "It's been that kind of week."

Hadn't it just? Frankie thought. A week to remember.

"Ho, ho, ho," a deep voice from the doorway chimed.

Emily giggled and Steen smiled a welcome as Hannah explained to Frankie.

"That's Ben Carson, our neighbor about half a mile toward the creek. He's been putting on that same old Santa suit every Christmas as long as I can remember, going around to all the houses where there're kids. Ben's kind of skinny, but his heart's real big."

Skinny was right, Frankie thought as she watched Santa stomp in in his knee-high black boots. Even the pillow he had belted in front of him didn't do much to pad his long, lanky frame. But his red hat bobbed atop his gray hair, his cheeks shone ruddy and his mouth smiled through his fake white beard. When he asked Emily if she'd been a good girl all year, her eyes were wide with the faith of a child who saw only what she wanted to believe.

"Mostly all year, haven't I, Grandma?"

"Yes, Santa," Hannah said as she motioned Ben closer to the fire where he could warm himself. "Emily's a good little girl."

"That's what I like to hear." Santa rummaged around in his deep bag and placed several brightly wrapped packages on the brick hearth. "Looks like these belong here." He sat down on the ledge and sent Hannah a quick glance. "Sure could use a hot toddy, Hannah. Real cold out there tonight."

"I'll make it, Hannah," Steen said from the kitchen doorway. "Want to help me, Frankie?"

"Sure." She rose to join him.

"You know where all the fixin's are, Steen?" Hannah asked.

"You bet." He reached for Frankie's hand and led her around the bend to the far cupboards. But instead of taking down glasses, he pulled her into the circle of his arms and buried his face in her hair. "Mmm, you smell like gingerbread and sweet, sweet woman." He nuzzled, moving his lips to her throat.

Frankie inhaled deeply, enjoying his rich masculine scent. "You smell pretty nice yourself, Mr. Olson." And he felt so good, his lean body hard up against her. Her response was instant and avid.

He felt the change and smiled. Christmas was fine; it was wonderful. But it couldn't compare to the wonder of holding this one small woman close to his heart. He dipped his head and took her mouth.

In moments, Frankie was lost in sensation as his tongue took possession of her mouth, staking a claim, making it his. How had she lived so long without knowing this incredible high? And how would she ever live without it after she left him?

She warmed him more quickly than the fire, Steen thought, more potently than any hot toddy, in places he'd thought would forever remain chilled. She set him aglow, set him to dreaming, to hoping again. The need to possess her was so strong, so real, that his knees were suddenly weak and trembling. That had never happened to him before. Steen eased back from her before he embarrassed them both.

"I guess it wouldn't do to have Santa catch us smooching up a storm in here instead of making his drink."

"Mmm, I guess not. Don't forget where we left off, okay?"

He grinned. "Fat chance." He reached for the mugs.

Frankie licked her lips, the taste of him lingering on her tongue. She hoped she didn't look as thoroughly kissed as she felt. "You people really get into this Christmas thing around here. A skinny Santa yet."

Steen put the kettle on to boil, then poured Irish whiskey into four cups. "Old Ben gets a kick out of dressing up for the kids. He and his wife, Ada, have nearly a dozen grandchildren, yet he still gets pleasure from traipsing around to all the outlying cabins. You should see the rabbit suit he wears at Easter."

Frankie leaned against the counter and crossed one foot over the other as she watched his preparations. "That I'd like to see."

His back to her, he dug in the refrigerator for the eggnog. "You can, next spring." He didn't give her time to disavow a return visit in the future. "Do you really like Hannah's spread?"

"Yes. It's beautiful. Did you think I was just being polite?"

Straightening, he returned to the counter. "You're pretty hard to read most of the time."

"Oh? When is it that I'm not?"

He raised his eyes to hers. "When I hold you, when I kiss you. I know exactly what you're thinking then." He saw the color move into her face and smiled. "And you're thinking it right now."

Blushing. Good Lord she was blushing, when she'd seldom done so even as a teenager. "Pretty sure of yourself, aren't you?"

"Sure that I can excite you, yes. Beyond that, I'm sure of nothing." He reached for the kettle and poured boiling water into the mugs.

"Then you're one up on me. I'm not sure of anything, period." She had been, before meeting him, before touching him had begun to cloud her mind and make her question her goals.

Steen set down the kettle and moved close to her. "You doubt that you excite me?" Taking her hand, he moved it down between them, curling her fingers around the hard evidence. She gave a small, shocked gasp. "Never doubt again," he said.

Frankie's eyes were wide and dark green with shock as he throbbed against her hand. But she didn't let go as her blood began to heat. "You do the most outrageous things, then lead me into doing them, and for some reason, I don't stop you. I wonder why that is."

His hand snaked beneath her sweater and cupped the fullness of her breast as he watched the pulse at her throat begin to do double time. "This isn't outrageous, Frankie. This is a man and a woman revealing how much they want each other. Can you think of anything nicer than that?"

She could scarcely think at all, which was why she pulled back, casting a guilty glance toward the kitchen doorway. Necking in other people's kitchens. Whatever had happened to her good sense? Frankie wondered, straightening her sweater. "No, I can't, but I can think of better places to continue this."

"You may have a point there." Too easily, she could make him forget where he was, Steen thought, taking a deep, calming breath. He got out the whipped cream and began to top off the drinks. "Did you ever get caught as a teenager necking in the back seat of a car?"

"No!"

"Honestly? I thought every young kid went through that stage."

Frankie touched her cheeks, trying to cool them. "Not me. I met Matt when I was only sixteen, and he was definitely not the back-seat-of-the-car type. He was almost as shy about sex as I was. His mother's ultra-proper upbringing, I imagine. There was a long list of things we didn't talk about, according to Mrs. Taelor, and an even longer list of things we didn't do." She was telling too much again. Making a dismissive gesture, she handed him a tray. "That was all a long time ago."

Perhaps, but the effects lingered on. A proper son who became a shy lover. Steen felt that his first instincts had been right—that she'd responded with such surprised delight and unbridled enthusiasm to his love-making not because it had been a long while for her. Because she'd *never* known such freedom in her marriage bed. Somehow, the thought pleased him enormously that he'd been the first man to have really touched her. Perhaps he could one day convince her to let him be the last. He felt a ripple of surprise that he felt so strongly, yet knew he did.

Steen picked up the tray of cups. "As soon as we drink these, we can make our excuses and leave. Do you mind a scalded mouth?"

With a teasing glint in her eyes, she smiled up at him. "Some sacrifices are worth the cost."

In the living room, Steen passed around the hot toddies and Emily's plain eggnog. By the looks of the mounds of discarded wrappings and ribbons, he guessed that Santa's presents had been most welcome.

Taking off his hat, Ben took a hot swallow and smacked his lips. "Sure beats the cookies and milk I get at most houses," he said with a wink at Emily.

The little girl's face was once more solemn. "Did you see my kitten outside, Santa? He's white with four black paws and his name is Mittens. He's lost and trying to find his way back to me, I know he is."

"Her cat's been gone for quite a few days now, Santa," Hannah informed him.

Ben quickly put two and two together. "Nope, I didn't. White's pretty hard to spot in the snow. Maybe some other little girl or boy found him and took him home." He motioned toward the calico kitten asleep on the cushion by the hearth. "Looks like you got a real fine replacement."

"Rascal's not a replacement. He's a friend for me and for Mittens when he comes home. You can't replace animals or people, Steen says. Right, Steen?"

Steen slid his arm about the child's slender frame. "That's right. But sometimes, we have to let go of the pet or person in our lives and realize that we'll have to live without them."

"But you said that if only I believed, Mittens would come back."

"Not quite, babe. I said that if you believe strongly enough, things will work out for the best. That's not always exactly the way we want them to work out."

Rascal picked that moment to awaken, stretch and meow for attention. Gathering him to her, Emily looked up at Steen. "Does that mean you don't think Mittens is coming back?"

"I don't know, Emily. I do know that in the meantime, you have Rascal to take care of, and he's counting on you."

She nodded, trying to look brave. "I'd better get him some more milk." Hugging her pet, she went to the kitchen.

Ben finished his drink and stood. "She's not giving up, is she?" He stuck his hat on his head. "Who knows? The cat may return. Stranger things have happened."

Frankie had about had it with all of them offering the child a fairy tale to believe in. "A kitten couldn't possibly survive for several days in that weather. Sooner or later, Emily's got to face that."

"Don't know about that," Ben said, hoisting his belted pillow up higher. "Years ago, Ada and I lived on a farm and we had this collie dog named Pepper. Bright as a button she was and loyal to a fault. But we were moving to the city two hundred miles away and we thought she'd be better off staying on the farm with its wide-open spaces. So we left her with the new owners. Well, Pepper had other ideas. She set out and went looking for us. One day, I get this call from a policeman. He'd found her wandering around, still wearing our name tag. The man who bought our farm told him where to find us. She was less than two miles from our new house." Ben picked up his near-empty sack. "Can't figure animals any more than we can figure people. I wouldn't fault the child for believing."

Frankie had listened politely, but she wasn't buying. "Tell me, Santa, did you make that story up?"

Ben shook his head. "No, ma'am. Gospel truth." He nodded to Hannah and Steen. "Good to see you again, but I've got to run. Two more stops to make tonight before I go home."

"Sure appreciate your coming by, Santa," Hannah said walking with him to the back door.

"We've got to be going, too, Hannah," Steen said, leading Frankie to the coat closet. Helping her into her jacket, he saw her frown. "What's wrong?"

"Do you honestly believe that dog story?"

Steen turned her to him, pulling her close by the lapels of her coat. "I honestly believe that if I can't be alone with you soon, I won't be responsible for my behavior."

She smiled up at him, warming at his heated look.

"Forget lost kittens and wandering dogs for tonight and concentrate on me and what I'm going to do to you when I get you into my four-poster bed. Can you handle that?"

Yes, she could certainly handle that. "Lead on, McDuff." And she hurried him to the door.

Chapter Nine

Frankie turned her face into the shower spray, then ducked her head and let the water rinse the shampoo from her hair. She hadn't really *needed* a shower, but she'd needed a little time alone to think and to prepare herself. For Steen.

She wrung out her hair, then turned off the water. Reaching for a towel, she let out a deep sigh. She'd never practiced the art of seduction, had scarcely been aware there was such a thing. She'd been so young, married to a man nearly as inexperienced as she, living in the unfriendly atmosphere of her in-laws' home with very little privacy. In short order, she'd been pregnant and often nauseated, then uncomfortable and bulky, feeling anything but sexy. Later, in their small trailer, it seemed the baby had stolen her energy and her enthusiasm.

And so here she was, deliberately preparing herself for a lover. How far we've come in such a sort time, she told herself.

Drying her hair, she pictured him sitting on the couch waiting for her. The fire would undoubtedly be going and he'd have poured some brandy for each of them. And, before she'd come into the bath, she'd seen that he had a large box wrapped and under the tree with her name on it. That worried her.

Since Matt's death, she'd never accepted gifts from any of the men she'd known. Gifts made her feel uncomfortable, beholden to the giver, somehow obligated. That's why she'd bought herself diamond earrings, letting the world know that if she wanted nice things, she could afford them and would get them for herself. Those earrings had become a symbol of her independence. Corbett knew that about her and he'd given her only things that would be used up, such as a good bottle of wine, imported crackers and her favorite cheese and occasionally he'd given her flowers.

And now there was Steen and he'd already given her an expensive carving, and her first impulse had been to give it back. But she couldn't hurt him that way. Instinctively, she knew he was a sensitive man—another reason why she found it ludicrous that he could be responsible for anyone's death.

How was she going to get him to tell her more about the accident that killed his parents? Not an easy topic to slip into the conversation. Yet she couldn't just let the issue slide. She needed to know, if only to dismiss the whole thing. And perhaps he needed to know that, as a friend, she believed in him. After all, wasn't that what friends were for?

Frankie lathered fragrant lotion on her skin, telling herself it wasn't for the special scent but because winter dried her skin so. She glanced at her overnight bag, at the small gifts she'd purchased for Steen in Tahoe just before she'd picked up the kitten. Impersonal presents, of no great value. She only hoped his to her were of a like nature.

She reached for the new robe she'd bought on her shopping spree that morning. A soft satin, it fell to the floor and had long, full sleeves and a deep neckline. It had been on sale, she justified to herself, and, to her credit, she hadn't purchased the matching nightgown. That would have been too obvious, to suddenly show up in an enticing nightie after she'd already confessed she never wore them. Had she subconsciously even then been thinking of driving back here to Steen?

What was Steen thinking this very minute? she wondered as she belted the robe. That she was quite brazen, terribly forward and decidedly eager to share a man's bed. She shook her hair back and smiled into the mirror. And it was about damn time.

As she continued to stare, she saw that her eyes held a hint of uncertainty. Not nearly as brave as she would like Steen to think she was. Taking a deep breath, she picked up her bag. Time to find out just how brave.

Steen looked up as she walked to the couch where he sat at the far end looking relaxed, very much as she'd pictured him. The room was dark except for the firelight that played on his strong features, turning his skin a rich bronze. His hair was wind-tossed, giving him a rakish air. He had changed into a well-washed gray sweatshirt with Bugs Bunny chewing on a carrot on his chest and a pair of comfortable gray cords. On his feet were huge fur-lined slippers that made her smile.

Not exactly an outfit designed to drive a woman mad with desire. However, because it was Steen, she thought he looked outrageously sexy. She took the drink he held out and sat down near enough to touch him, though she didn't.

Her eyes were as dark green as the satin robe she wore, her skin almost translucent in the glow of the fire. Steen inhaled her special scent and felt his stomach muscles tighten. Touching his glass to hers, he saluted her. "Here's to our first Christmas together."

He was doing it again, implying there'd be more, dragging them into the future together. But she wouldn't contradict him tonight. She took a sip, locking her gaze with his over the rim. For a long moment, she lost herself in the dark depths of his eyes, thinking she could sit just so, looking at him for hours while the heat of the brandy seeped through her.

Steen broke the look and reached for a package, placing it in her lap. Silently, he waited for her to open it.

"How did you know I'd come back?" Frankie asked as she set down her glass.

"I took a chance."

"I want to thank you for the beautiful carving of the Christmas tree."

"I didn't want you to leave here without some small reminder of your detour to my cabin."

As if she needed one, Frankie thought. Fumbling with the ribbon, she slid back the paper and lifted the lid. A dozen jars of paint and an assortment of brushes were nestled in green tissue paper. Though she'd schooled herself to be polite but indifferent to presents, this one moved her nonetheless. Picking up one of the brushes, she ran her thumb through the soft sable.

"I don't know that I'll ever use these, but..."

"If you get the urge to paint again, you'll have them. And the offer to work with me still stands."

"Thank you." Perhaps she would take it up again. It was a good way to lose herself and to do something she enjoyed. She set the box aside and reached into her bag that she'd placed on the floor. She gave him an apologetic smile, as she handed over the gifts. "I didn't have time to wrap these."

He opened the small box first, and grinned like a kid. "Where did you find raspberries at this time of year?"

She'd bribed the cook at the hotel, but she wasn't about to tell him that. "I have my sources."

"Christmas morning, we'll have raspberries and cream. I love decadence." He attacked the other box, ripping the lid in his eagerness.

Just like a little boy, Frankie thought. Christmas and ball games turned men back into children.

"Hey, Georgia O'Keeffe." He opened the book, admiring the reprints. "She's one of my favorite artists. I have her painting in..."

"In your bedroom. Yes, I noticed. The poppies."

"I love what she does with colors." He leaned to touch his lips to her cheek. A friendly gesture. This night, he wanted to linger and savor and draw out the pleasure. He reached to the table and handed her a small box. "One more for you."

Nervously, she fingered the tiny package. Trouble usually came in small boxes. "The carving and the paints were surely enough." Cautiously, she peeked inside. Sitting on a white wedge of cotton was a circular band fashioned from very dark wood. Lifting it out, she examined it closely. "What is this made of?"

"The acorn you found that day in the woods. I carved it into a ring for you." He saw the reluctance on her face and hurried to explain. "A friendship ring. Your initials are on the inside, see?"

Forcing herself not to make this an issue, Frankie touched the initials, then slipped the ring on the third finger of her right hand. Holding it out for him to see, she angled her hand this way and that. "A good guess on the size."

"It's not exactly diamonds, but . . ."

"I don't want a gift of diamonds." Even this was too much. But how could she refuse a gift he'd made and initialled for her? "I didn't know you could carve an acorn."

"Lady, I can carve anything." He set the packages aside, took a large swallow of his brandy and stretched out his legs, leaning his head on the couch back. "I can't remember a better Christmas. How about you?"

Frankie drew up her legs and angled her body toward him. "I have to admit it's been better than many I've had." She placed her hand on his arm. "Maybe because you're easy to be with."

"Am I?"

"Easier than most."

"For whatever reason, I'm glad you're here." He touched her hair, letting the silken strands drift through his fingers. "Very glad."

Frankie examined her feelings and found she could be honest with him. "I'm glad I'm here, too." She was also curious and felt the time had come for a few answers. She'd bared her soul to him earlier. Would he open up to her? She searched his face and decided to chance it.

"Steen, would you tell me about your parents' accident, why you felt responsible for their death?" She watched his eyes leap to hers, then saw the disappointment as he realized who'd told her.

Feeling a little as though a fist had slammed into his gut, Steen took a steadying breath. "Didn't she tell you all of it?"

"No, and please don't be angry with Amelia. You told her we were old friends and she thought I already knew."

He should have remembered Amelia's chatty nature. He blamed himself for not telling Frankie about what had happened sooner. Perhaps then, it wouldn't have sounded as serious as it now did.

"My father was born in Europe and believed in the old-fashioned work ethic. Although he could well have afforded to put me through college, he felt I should work at least part-time, so I'd appreciate the education he'd never had. Like most teenage boys, I was crazy about cars and hung around gas stations and auto repair shops. I learned a lot and pretty soon, I was repairing my friends' cars, then their parents' cars. By the time I got into college, I had more work than time to do it in."

He paused for a sip of his drink, then reached to take her hand. She laced her fingers through his and he continued. "I was home on summer vacation and had just finished installing a whole new brake system on my father's car for this trip they were going to take. They never went anywhere, always saving their money, but for years they'd planned this visit to Minnesota to my mother's brother. I finished working on the car, washed it for them, and Amelia and I watched them drive away on a sunny Saturday afternoon. The call came scarcely two hours later. They'd been killed instantly, hit broadside at a busy intersection because their brakes had given out.''

"Oh, God! But you said they'd been brand-new.''

He nodded, letting out a trembling breath. "They were. The sheriff came out to tell us in person. I'd just turned twenty and the news hit me hard. We'd always been a close family. Amelia was ten and inconsolable. It was awful.''

Frankie squeezed his hand in sympathy, giving him time.

"Dad's best friend was his attorney, Pearce Jensen. He helped me get the bodies brought home and arrange the funeral. Pearce took Amelia to the services, but I wouldn't go. I couldn't look at my parents dead. I blamed myself, fearful that I'd installed the brakes incorrectly.''

It was difficult for her to picture Steen as young and vulnerable. She'd only seen him sure and strong. "I'm certain no one but you thought that.''

Steen sighed heavily. "There was an investigation and the experts said that the brakes were faulty, not my installation. They put the blame on the manufacturers. Pearce immediately filled a lawsuit on our behalf. But I was young and stubborn and hurting. I figured I should have let a pro install the brakes and maybe he'd have noticed that they were faulty. I wanted someone to blame for the death of those two good people and I was the likely candidate.''

She touched his face, trying to ease his pain. "I know a little something about self-blame. It's a terrible thing to live with.''

"Yes, it is.'' A sigh trembled from him as he turned to face her. "I drove myself nuts with it. Every time I saw one of our neighbors, I felt they were blaming me. So I did something I'm not proud of. I ran away."

Because she'd known this was coming, she held on tighter to his hand. "That's when you traveled all over?"

"Yes. I looked at Amelia and she was a thin, sad-eyed version of the bright young girl I remembered. I wanted to help her, but, at twenty, I didn't know how. So I took off. Pearce found a foster home for Amelia." He turned to her, his eyes filled with lingering guilt. "A real nice guy, right?"

"You shouldn't condemn yourself. You were young and you had a lot to deal with—the loss of your parents, misdirected guilt, the sudden responsibility of a child. Your whole world had turned upside down."

"Yeah, that's about how I felt, all right. But good old Pearce didn't give up. Not on me and not on the lawsuit. While I spent months traipsing around the world like some gypsy trying to forget, he kept in touch and kept working on the case. It took two years, but we won a settlement for two hundred fifty thousand. A lot of money but then, we'd suffered a lot of pain."

"So that's when you came back and settled down?"

"Yes. Pearce found me and told me it was time I came home, stopped indulging in self-pity and faced things, that Amelia needed me. His words jolted me back to reality and made me see that I couldn't have prevented what happened and that I'd have to live with the loss of my parents. Accidents happen and sometimes, there's no one to blame.

"I couldn't just drift and let strangers raise my sister. So I went back and, you know, it was like I'd been away at college and now had come for her. She didn't censure me, didn't hold my long absence against me."

"Perhaps that's why, when she needed your understanding with that boy recently, you kept believing in
her."

"Probably. Anyhow, there were too many memories
in Texas, so I got an apartment in L.A. and contacted
this man who'd seemed impressed with my carvings.
Just about the time my work started catching on, I discovered that although most of Amelia's school friends
were from wealthy families, they were a wild bunch, not
the sort I wanted her to associate with. So I bought this
cabin where we could both be safe." He squeezed her
hand. "You see, we're not so different. I need to feel
safe, too."

"I guess we all do. Have you ever gone back to Texas
since, to make your peace with your old neighbors and
realize they didn't blame you?"

"Yeah, I did, once. With few exceptions, most were
welcoming. Running away, to some people, means
you're guilty of something. Weakness of character at
the very least."

Frankie felt a quick stab of anger. "How could anyone not believe you were innocent? On top of all you'd
been through? But didn't they know you? Couldn't they
tell what kind of person you were?"

For a long moment, he just stared at her, absorbing
the intense way she'd leaped to his defense. Up to now,
Amelia had been the only one who'd always believed in
him unconditionally, even through those difficult years
when he hadn't been there for her. Did Frankie even
suspect what a gift she'd given him? "People believe
what they want to believe, despite anything you say or
do."

She nodded, understanding more. "That's what you meant when I left, when you said that you don't fight at all."

"I fight, for what's mine and for what I want. But not by trying to change someone's mind about something they believe. I know that doesn't work. I've come to grips with the guilt I felt as a young man. I know I wasn't responsible. As to the way others feel, well, people have to come around on their own."

"The ones who didn't believe in you aren't worth a hoot," she stated emphatically.

Steen smiled at the way she'd narrowed it down to what really mattered. He wondered if he deserved this kind of blind faith. He felt that he was a decent person, but far from perfect. Could Frankie with her hurtful past accept a flawed man, one who was falling in love with her? "You're right, they aren't." He angled more toward her, his hand sliding around her slender waist. "Do you see why I understand how you felt after the fire?"

"Yes, and I thank you for telling me what happened."

He trailed the backs of his fingers along her cheek. "I should have told you sooner, but I didn't know how you'd feel and I thought you might . . ."

At his pause, she looked up. "Blame you, not understand why you ran? Is that what you thought?"

"Well, laying your tarnished past on an acquaintance is always a gamble."

She touched his face as he'd caressed hers. "Is that what I am to you, Steen, an acquaintance?"

He wanted to shout it out, to tell her that he thought of her as so much more. But he was wary. The doe's eyes came to mind. Frankie might not run from the truth about his past. But she might bolt if he pressed their relationship beyond the friendship they'd agreed upon. He touched his lips to her forehead. "No, you're more. A friend. A loving friend."

For the first time, Frankie thought that his definition sounded too inadequate to describe what had developed between them. Yet she'd been the one to insist on that definition.

She felt the gentle flutter of his lips at her temple as she heard the distant clang of a warning bell from deep inside her. Deeper. She was getting in deeper and deeper with Steen. She knew she should stop just as well as she knew she would not. She wanted this man, wanted him to make her forget the harsh realities of both their pasts. Perhaps together they could erase a few hurts and soothe one another, at least for a little while. She wound her arms around him, feeling comfortably drowsy, feeling warm, feeling safe.

He nuzzled her cheek. "I wonder, can you guess what I'm thinking right now?" His voice was already thick and unsteady as her sweet fragrance surrounded him.

She chuckled low in her throat, a rich female sound. "I think so. Pretty much what I'm thinking, I'd wager." She lifted her head to look at him. "I've never made love with a man who wore a Bugs Bunny shirt and furry slippers before."

"Good. I like it when I can give you firsts."

"You've given me more firsts than you know." At the look on his face, she felt herself melt inside, slowly, surely. She closed her eyes, moving into his arms. "Sometimes the way I feel about you frightens me." It was a big admission for her.

"You never have to be frightened with me, Frankie. You can let yourself go. You'll be safe with me."

Let herself go. The thought beckoned, tempting, frightening. To do as she pleased with this exciting man. To explore, to experiment. The allure was too great to turn away from.

Pulling back, she traced the contour of his lips with trembling fingers. Her other hand on his chest felt the quick lurch of his heart. She touched her tongue to his lips, tasting, tantalizing, then slid inside for the flick of an instant. More boldly now, she returned and their tongues met in a fiery duet. Steen's arms tightened around her as they leisurely stroked in perfect imitation of a slow mating.

The kiss flowed through her like fine wine, drugging, addictive. She reached for more, pressing closer, yet not close enough. Her hands on his back roamed restlessly, loving the feel of his hard body. He scarcely moved, letting her lead. Her lips left his and traveled along his jaw and higher to kiss his closed eyes, then back to his mouth to swallow his low moan.

The whole day had been like foreplay, Steen thought as he held on, trying not to rush her. Talking with her, eating dinner with her, being with her had sharpened his need. Memories of the night she'd spent in his arms rocketed through him as he shifted her now and dipped his head to taste her throat. Her hair fell backward, a golden red in the firelight, and he shoved his hands into its thickness as his mouth moved lower.

The material of her robe felt nearly as sensuous as the silken skin it covered. He closed his lips over the soft peak of her breast through the satin and felt her flesh reach out to him. He moved to savor the other while her fingers dug into his hair, his scalp, pressing him tightly to her.

How could he have known that this cool blonde with her diamonds would match his fire with a blaze of her own? How could he have guessed that her touch would erase all thoughts of any who had come before her? How could he have suspected that she would hold the key to the other half of his soul?

On a long breath, Steen pulled back and stood. "No couch tonight." In a swift movement, he bent to pick her up and carried her into his room. At the bed, he paused with her still in his arms. "I love holding you like this."

"Mmm, another first for me, the day you carried me in from the highway. No man had ever carried me before. Suddenly, you were no longer a stranger, but a man I couldn't help responding to, despite the snow and cold."

He set her on her feet. "Let's see if we can come up with a few more firsts." He slid the robe from her shoulders and heard the soft sound it made as it dropped to the carpet. He took a step back, his eyes memorizing every beautiful part of her. He saw her shiver and wondered if it was from a sudden chill or from his heated gaze. Pulling back the covers, he urged her to the bed as he stepped out of his slippers.

"Wait," Frankie whispered. "I want to undress you."

A willing victim, Steen raised his arms. Slowly, she pulled the sweatshirt from him and tossed it aside. Her hands moved to his chest, rubbing and stroking. He felt the heat spread as her fingers moved to the waistband of his cords. She unsnapped the opening, then shifted her attention higher, placing soft kisses on his chest, his shoulders, the muscles of his upper arms.

"I'm not very experienced at seduction."

"You're doing fine." He swallowed hard as she touched the zipper, trying to lower it. Any moment, she would give up and let him free himself, he thought. But she did not.

Steen sucked in a deep breath of air as Frankie slid one hand inside, protecting him as she eased the zipper slowly down with the other. She shoved the pants down and he quickly stepped out of them, impatiently awaiting her next move. Turning her hand, she inched her fingers beneath the band of his briefs and closed around him.

"Oh, Steen," she sighed, going on tiptoe as she put her face into the hollow of his throat. It felt so good to hold him, warm and throbbing with life. She'd longed for this, this slow loving.

He could stand very little more of this torturous ecstasy. He lifted her arms and placed them on his shoulders, then pulled her closer, lifting her, cradling her against his hardness. Locked together, they swayed, letting the delicious teasing pleasure pour through them.

Frankie's breasts flattened against his bare chest as he led her into a stunning kiss, hot and hungry and impatient. They fell back onto the bed, never losing their grip on one another. Feeling driven now, she deepened the kiss, needing more intimate contact as she pressed her yearning body into his. When her hands fumbled at his briefs, he reached to struggle them off. At last, they were skin to skin, the contact electrifying.

Passion ruled him now as Steen put his mouth to one rosy nipple, then the other, abandoning all pretense of patience as he felt an equal fury take her. He grazed his unshaven face along the delicate skin of her belly and heard her soft sigh. Glancing up, he saw her head moving restlessly on the pillow while her green eyes watched him. He knew she was scarcely aware that her body was arching and thrusting toward him as she sought the release only he could give her now. Letting the unbearable tension build, he slid lower.

Steen sent her whirling then, reveling in her stunned response as she jolted in his arms. Clutching her hand, he watched her climb, watched her give herself up to pure sensation. Finally, he moved up to smile into her dazed eyes as she struggled back from the churning vortex. The surprise, the soft pleasure on her face stirred in him feelings so strong as to bring tears to his eyes. Awash in emotion, he could put only one name to it. Love.

When she could take a normal breath again, Frankie brushed the hair back from her face, not meeting his eyes. She'd guessed there was more to lovemaking than her limited experience had shown her. She just hadn't imagined how much. She felt a flush of embarrassment, yet also felt wonderfully alive. When he tipped her chin so she would look at him, she tried to explain.

"I've never . . . that is . . ."

"I know. Another first." His hands framed her face. "I love you, Frankie."

Her reaction was instantaneous. "No! Please don't say that."

"Shh. I will say it. I must say it."

"I don't want this. I can't . . ."

He knew of only one way to stop her. His mouth closed on hers. The kiss was long and very gentle and when she finally looked at him, her eyes were once more soft. "I ask nothing of you in return, nothing you can't give freely. But I'm so filled with the feeling that I had to tell you."

Emotions churning, Frankie shook her head. "But that's not fair to you."

"Love seldom is." He buried his face in the space between her breasts, his hands moving to arouse her again. He knew she was trying to channel her reactions, but was losing the battle. He also knew how to make her enjoy the loss.

In moments he had her helpless again, her hands urging him to join with her. Using his last ounce of control, he shifted and entered her. He was hot, he was cold, he was screaming for release, but he went slowly, letting her catch up. When he was certain she was with him, he moved faster, surer.

Suddenly Frankie was flying again, flying on the wings of desire. She watched his beautiful face as he controlled his movements. Her hands were slippery on his back as he thrust, withdrew, then thrust deeper still. If this was a caring friendship, she welcomed it. If this was passion, she'd only just learned it. If this was love, she'd never known it before.

Feeling surprisingly safe in the arms of her lover, Frankie let go of the world as she joined Steen in his.

Chapter Ten

The space alongside him in the bed was empty. Steen sat up with a start, looking about the room. Her robe was gone, but her bag lay open on the chair beneath the window. The door was ajar and from the other room, he heard the soft sounds of a woman humming. With a relieved sigh, he shoved back the covers and got out of bed. It would seem Frankie Taelor had not jumped ship. Not just yet anyway.

Grabbing his terry-cloth robe, he shrugged into it while he let himself remember the long, loving night he'd spent holding her in his arms. Though he'd slept some, much of the time he'd just watched her sleep and let his thoughts wander. What would it be like if Frankie would come around? he'd asked himself.

She was everything he'd wanted in a woman, and then some. She was kind and caring, thoughtful, gentle. Yet she had fire, the passion he'd spoken of to Amelia, in and out of bed, and a bit of a temper that usually amused him more than annoyed him. Life with Frankie would never be boring.

He belted the robe and ran a hand through his hair. But she'd experienced soul-shattering pain, watching a husband and child die before her very eyes. She thought she'd buried it and was handling it well, but was she? Could he make her forget, make her happy? How would she feel about making this house their main base? How would he feel about all the traveling her job called for? What about children? He wanted several, yet would the memory of her Sara prevent her from trying again? So many questions. Heading out the door, Steen wondered if today he might learn some of the answers.

He found her in the kitchen watering the plants on the windowsill. Leaning against the door-frame, he stood for a moment appreciating how lovely she looked in the sunlight streaming in through the window. Her golden hair hung loose and free, framing her face as she bent to sprinkle an African violet, murmuring to it gently. So she liked plants, though she'd told him she didn't keep any herself. A paradox. There were a lot of things about Frankie that puzzled him.

Turning, she spotted him and her face broke into a slow smile. She stood there holding the watering can as color moved into her face, and he could easily imagine what she was thinking, what she was remembering. He walked closer, his arms going around her slender waist, and bent to kiss her mouth. So soft, so utterly responsive. His whole system sighed a welcome to her nearness.

"Good morning, sleepyhead. Coffee's ready."

"Why didn't you wake me?"

"You looked too peaceful. Did I wear you out?" Her green eyes sparkled as she teased him.

"It would seem so." He slid his hands low on her back, angling her body so that she pressed tightly against him. "But I'm rested now, and awake."

She felt a slight movement through the fabric of their robes. "So I see." She planted a small kiss on his unshaven chin, then nuzzled the spot with her lips. "Have you ever worn a beard?"

"No. Do you like beards?"

"I think they're sexy."

"I think *you're* sexy."

"I think we'd better replenish your energy." She moved out of his arms to pour his coffee. Handing him the cup, she freshened her own. So very new, this morning bantering, with the undercurrent sensual awareness always present. It felt good, it felt right. Too right.

She took a hot sip, memories of the previous night flooding her mind. Again, she'd acted like someone she scarcely recognized. How long before that intensity, that fierce need for more and still more, would taper off? Since she'd never known it to such a degree before, she hadn't a clue as to how soon life would become humdrum and ordinary again. She did know that nothing lasted forever.

"Are you ready for Christmas morning breakfast?" Steen asked as he poked his head into the refrigerator. "We could even have it in bed." He glanced over his shoulder at her. "Would that be a first for you?"

Frankie turned and put on a smile, for him and for herself. She would take this day, this one last day, and make it into a warm memory, one that she could take out of storage when she was back home, and relive it again and again. Tomorrow would come all too soon and with it, the harsh jolt of reality.

Joining him, she draped her arm over his shoulder. "Yes, it would."

"Then it's high time you had the pleasure." He pulled out the raspberries. "Let's do it."

Though he was a big man, he could move pretty fast when he had a purpose, Frankie thought. In no time, he had a tray laden with raspberries and cream, scrambled eggs and tiny sausages, heated muffins and sliced tomatoes. Walking carefully, he carried it into the bedroom. While she propped the pillows against the headboard and scooted into position, he set the food on the nightstand, then joined her.

"Straighten your knees, lady, so we can balance this tray. Easy now, there we go." With his fingers, Steen gathered up a cream-coated raspberry and popped it quickly into her mouth. He smiled as she closed her eyes appreciatively. "Heavenly, right?"

"As close as mere mortals are apt to come. More, please."

He gave her another. "You can feed yourself, you know."

Frankie sent him a mock frown. "So that's how it is, the cold morning after." She scooped up a forkful of eggs.

"Just let me chow down a little energy and we'll see if we can warm up your cold morning after."

"Promises, promises," she muttered between mouthfuls.

Steen moved swiftly, gliding his hand inside the opening of her robe, his fingers closing around the soft mound of her breast. As she gasped in surprise, he leaned close. "Do you doubt that I'll deliver?"

Feeling her flesh swell in his hand, she shook her head. "Not for a minute."

He kissed her nose, then returned to his breakfast, pleased to see it took her several moments to catch her breath.

"Tell me, is this how you used to spend Christmas mornings when you were a boy?"

"Eating raspberries and cream in bed with a half-naked woman? Nah, my mom frowned on that sort of thing."

She giggled because that's the kind of morning it was. "No, silly. I mean a leisurely breakfast because you'd opened the gifts the night before, or did you open gifts in the morning before breakfast?"

Steen buttered a muffin. "My father believed in tradition. We celebrated Christmas just as he had in his parents' home in Sweden. On Christmas Eve, we had a big dinner, rather late, then we all went to church service, after which Amelia and I went to bed. That's when he and my mother would wrap the presents and put them under the tree."

She pictured him as a young boy trying to fall asleep so the night would pass quickly. She, too, had tried to hurry the night, but for other reasons. So it would be over and the feeling of missing out would ease. How differently they'd grown up, mostly because one house had been filled with a hopelessness and the other with love. But she didn't want to think about either today.

"And in the morning, the two of you would rush to see what Santa had brought you?"

Steen finished a sausage and nodded. "That's right, only sometimes it was barely light outside when we'd be in there trying to wake my folks. They were such good people. My mother had lost two babies before she finally had Amelia and they were so happy when she was born. We had to keep up the pretense of Santa well into my teens for her, but I played along. Or maybe I was afraid that if I said out loud that there was no Santa, that there'd be no packages for me." He laughed at the childhood memory. "Sounds like I was a strange kid, right?"

"Not so strange. Even now, you feel that if you believe strongly enough, things will work out. Isn't that what you told Emily?"

"Yes, I do believe that."

Frankie wished she did. She set down her fork and angled to face him. "Tell me about some of your best Christmases." She wasn't sure why she wanted to hear about those good times. Maybe to verify that someone somewhere had had them.

The wistfulness in her voice nearly clogged his throat. Swallowing, he leaned back on the pillow and began to tell her about the year he'd been eight and he'd awakened to a low yelping sound and discovered a puppy he'd promptly named Cheetah because he'd been going through his old Tarzan movies stage. And the year Amelia had been about five and he a worldly fifteen and wanting to sleep in, but he'd allowed her to drag him downstairs anyhow. And they'd found that their father had just put the finishing touches on a dollhouse he'd made for his daughter. Steen realized that he'd stayed up all night in order to surprise her.

"There were actually tears in his eyes as he watched the pleasure on Amelia's face while she examined the tiny pieces of furniture he'd made. She still has the house and everything in it. You should see the carvings. The man had talent and the patience to do fine work, but he didn't believe he could make enough money doing what he loved." Steen finished his coffee and set the tray aside.

"At least he passed his talent and patience on to his son."

"I guess so, but think what a business we could have had together if Dad had lived." He shook his head in regret. "No, not really. He would have insisted I finish college and go into some business I'd have hated because he didn't think Americans respected people who worked with their hands."

"Obviously, they do." She curled her fingers around his arm, moving close to him. "He'd be so proud of you today."

He turned toward her, his arm encircling her. "I like to think so." Nuzzling his face into her hair, he breathed deeply. "You smell so good."

"That's a lingering raspberry scent you smell."

Steen set the breakfast on the floor, then eased back so he could look into her eyes. "I don't think so. Do you see all that sunshine pouring in on us?"

She squinted toward the window. "Yes. Do you think it's melting the snow?"

"Maybe. What I want to say has nothing to do with snow." He felt a quick tensing of the muscles along her back as his hand continued to caress there. He didn't care. Some things had to be said, tension or not. "We talked about this before. Men, and sometimes women, often declare their love in the dark, in a moment of passion. Small wonder they're not believed. Here, in the daylight, in the sunshine, I want you to know that what I said last night is just as true this morning. I love you, Frankie."

She drew back, the fear taking over. He was going to spoil the day. "I've asked you not to say this."

"I know. You're afraid."

Her eyes flew to his. "Damn right I am, and you should be, too."

Steen touched her cheek, his voice strong and reassuring. "No, no fears. Love is all there is, sweetheart. It's all we've got. It doesn't get any better than this. You'll see. One day, you'll agree. Meanwhile, just take. I don't mind giving. I've got years of giving stored up."

His dark eyes were filled with feeling, and very sincere. Frankie wanted so badly to let him take her, to fly away with him, to trust him to keep her safe from pain. But he couldn't, she knew. No one could. Only if you stayed alone and uninvolved could you stay free of pain.

But he believed, he honestly believed. He would make such a beautiful life partner for someone. She wished she'd have met him years ago, before she'd lost hope. She took his hand, twining her fingers through his. "I can't believe you're real," she whispered.

"I'm real, all right." He pulled her closer, aware of the inner struggle going on inside her. A breath apart, he touched his lips to hers briefly, gently. "Feel how real."

She felt the familiar trembling begin. "This is crazy. *You're* crazy. People don't fall in love in a few days."

His lips were on her throat and he felt her shiver, then clutch at the material of his robe. "Sure they do. Sometimes in hours, in minutes."

"No," she protested, realizing she was losing the battle if not the whole war. "It's the sentimentality of the season, that's all."

Unfastening both their robes, he aligned her body more perfectly with his. "Right. Santa Claus and all that bunk." He skimmed his hands along the contours of her back.

She felt the heat softening her, felt the hard length of him seeking entry, and couldn't suppress a moan. "Yes, it's bunk."

"Reindeer and angels and snow." Flipping her onto her back, he hovered over her, braced on his elbows. He trailed his hand between their damp bodies and felt her arch as his fingers slipped inside, making sure she was ready for him. "And carols and cookies and..."

Giving up, giving in, giving more than she'd ever given before, Frankie opened to him. "Oh, be still and just love me," she said and pulled his mouth down to hers.

Steen thrust deeply and filled her completely.

"I never thought I'd learn to like winter."

Gripping her hand in his, Steen guided Frankie along a narrow snow-covered path through the woods. "Another first?"

"I guess so. In Ohio, the winters are so long and on the farm, there were things you always had to do outdoors, no matter the weather. I'd go into the barn and some mornings it would be so cold that the hay in the horses' stalls would be mixed with ice. The poor animals hated it as much as I did."

Ducking under a low-hanging branch, he helped her around the bend. "And your father, did he hate it, too?"

"Probably, I don't know. He never said. He'd inherited the farm from his father, who'd died working the land just as he did."

"How is it that your mother ever married him if she hated the farming life? She must have known that's what he'd do."

Frankie shielded her eyes from the glare of the sun on the white snow, pausing to lean against a bare tree trunk to catch her breath. Walking while wearing so many clothes was tiring. "Oh, she had a really good reason. She was pregnant with me. I was fifteen when I figured it out after finding their marriage certificate in a trunk in our attic."

"And it shocked you?"

"No. It explained everything, why there was no love between them, why she hated the life she led. It wasn't just the hard work and the farm. She took care of my father and was good to him, but she never loved him."

Steen braced his arm against the tree at her back. "Maybe she didn't love your father, but I'm sure she loved you, and still does."

Frankie let out a ragged sigh. "I believe so, but it was never like you had. You grew up in a household where love between your parents and you and Amelia was something warm and wonderful. I've heard of that Ozzie-and-Harriet type family, but I've never really seen one up close. Only on television, in movies and books. My parents coexisted under the same roof, my mother growing ever more frustrated and my father enduring. Matt's parents' marriage was arranged, if you can believe that sort of thing is still going on. Two well-to-do families merging their children and properties. They didn't quarrel or even raise their voices in the six months we lived there. Well-bred people never do, I was informed. They just use one another, tolerate one another, and literally lead separate lives, each going their own way." She raised her eyes to his. "No shining example there, either. Are you sure you're remembering your childhood accurately and not making it all up?"

She tried to hide the sadness with a skeptical smile but he saw it anyway. Saw it and wished he could forever eliminate it from her. "My memory's right on target. How about when you and Matt moved out and lived in the trailer? Wasn't your marriage good then?"

Abruptly, she pushed off from the tree and began walking again. "I don't want to talk about my marriage."

Puzzled, Steen followed. She hadn't faced whatever still troubled her. He took her hand, changing the subject. "It's not much farther now, so we have to walk more quietly. If the deer hear us, they'll take off."

The deer. She'd concentrate on the deer they'd come out to see, so she wouldn't have to think about all the distressing things that Steen so often dredged up somehow. Emptying her mind, Frankie walked beside him breathing in the cold, pine-scented air. Huge evergreens on both sides of them stretched toward a blue cloudless sky, clusters of snow weighing down their lower branches.

A blackbird changed locations high above their head with a flutter of wings and a cawing sound that echoed in the stillness of the woods. The only other sound was the light steps their boots made in the fresh snow. It was a lovely sunshiny day and Frankie fervently wished she could keep her mind on the beauty all around her instead of on unsettling thoughts of the past. Or on her disturbing awareness of the man who held her hand.

It was time to leave, perhaps past time. Steen Olson was getting to her, the incredible strength of his tenderness, the caring ways, overwhelming her. He was making it difficult if not damn near impossible for her to remember her firm resolutions, her life's plan. If running away was the coward's way out, then she would be a coward. She was fighting for her life here. There was no way she could survive loving as fiercely as Steen needed, demanded, to be loved.

Suddenly, Steen stopped and went very still. He turned to Frankie, his finger on his lips signaling her to be quiet. They were one row of trees from the edge of the clearing. Slowly, he stepped close to the trunk of a tall maple, moving to one side of it while he guided her to the other.

His voice was the merest of whispers. "Look, over there."

Frankie broke into a smile of pure delight when she spotted them, a stately doe and a spotted fawn, very much like the one she'd painted. They stood perhaps a hundred yards into the clearing, near the salt lick Steen had placed there. Neither moved as the doe cocked her head, listening. So beautiful, Frankie thought. She'd never particularly been awed by animals, having grown up on a farm. But this was wildlife, free creatures who survived without man's help. Squeezing Steen's hand, she kept her eyes on the pair.

Moving slowly, Steen withdrew from the pocket of his jacket a plastic-wrapped piece of shaggy bark he'd cut from a tree in his backyard. It was covered with lichen, the algae substance that was a real treat for deer and very scarce in the winter. When he was certain the deer were comfortable with their scents, he took several steps forward, drawing Frankie with him. With hand signals, he motioned her to remain as still as he was. Eyes on the doe, he held out the bark and waited.

Her hunger for the treat overcame her wariness. Nudging her young one into the safety of the trees, the doe turned back to them and slowly began to walk over.

Ten feet away, she stopped to study them with her dark eyes while she sniffed the air.

Heart thudding, Frankie could do nothing more than stare in fascination. Finally satisfied, the doe came closer, then stopped right in front of Steen. Lowering her head, she flashed her tongue out for a quick taste, her eyes on the man that held the bark. Trusting him more fully, she took several more licks, longer each time. Amazing, Frankie thought.

The doe raised her head and stood as if waiting. Moving slowly, Steen bent to place the bark atop a mound of snow. She didn't move for long minutes, then dipped her head and grabbed the edge firmly in her small mouth. Seemingly in no hurry, she looked back at Steen, then shifted to Frankie, as if including her in the thanksgiving. Turning, she walked regally back toward her fawn who waited where she'd left him. Nearly there, she looked back over her shoulder one last time. Then she began to run through the thicket, the fawn following on his spindly legs. In moments, they were lost among the trees. Frankie let out a breath she hadn't been aware she'd been holding.

"If I hadn't seen that with my own eyes, I never would have believed it," she whispered, almost afraid to break the eerie silence of the forest.

"She's beautiful, isn't she?" Steen turned her into the circle of his arms, glad he'd been able to show her the deer up close.

"How long have you been able to tame wild creatures?"

"That doe's been coming around about two years now. She knows me, she trusts me." He tilted her chin, capturing her eyes. "How long before you'll trust me?"

Not one to miss an opportunity, was he? "I made love with you, didn't I? The first man in six years. That took more than a small amount of trust."

He tapped a finger on the left side of her chest. "When will you trust me with your heart?"

"Steen, we've been through this before. Please don't push."

"I'm not pushing. I'm asking." He had to ask and ask now. Because he knew that soon, maybe tomorrow, she'd be gone. He could see it in her eyes. Perhaps regretfully, but she'd be gone.

Frankie took a step back, then another. "Okay, I'll give you an answer. Probably never." Growing angry, she threw him a challenging look. "I never lied to you and I resent your trying to back me into a corner."

He felt defeated, yet compelled to go on. "Why'd you come back, Frankie? And don't give me that bull about a kitten for Emily."

"I told you . . ."

"You don't love me, you dislike Christmas, so what was it then? Was it sex? Was it because I showed you a side of yourself you hadn't seen, a sensual side?"

"I've lived without sex before. I can do it again."

"Are you sure?"

"I don't have to listen to this." She started down the path back toward the cabin.

"You're a warm, loving woman, Frankie. Why won't you face that?" Striding after her, he caught her by the arm and swung her around to face him. "What are you afraid of? Why won't you let yourself love me?"

"Let me go!"

"Is it because you're still mourning Matt? Is it because you've never let yourself get over his death?"

"No."

"Despite what you told me, are you blaming yourself for that fire?"

"No, I . . ."

His hands on her upper arms were harsh now, his voice demanding answers as he forced her to look at him. "Are you still in love with your dead husband? Is that it?"

"No!" A sob caught in her throat as she tried to pull away, away before the dam burst.

"Tell me, damn it!"

"I never loved Matt. Never." The tears came now, flowing freely like the truth she'd hidden from him. And maybe from herself. "I married him for all the wrong reasons, just like my mother did with my father. I used Matt. And he died when it should have been me. I liked him because he was so good to me, but I didn't love him, only Sara. God, how I loved my baby. I've never loved a man, no man, not until . . ." With a choking sound, she finally pulled free of him and ran, ran from the stunned look in his eyes.

But she'd scarcely gone ten yards when she fell, going down in a snowy heap. Steen was at her side, pulling her to her feet, pulling her to the shelter of his arms. She cried then, deep wailing sounds coming from the depths of her soul, clinging to him as he held her. He could only hold on, his hand smoothing her hair, his voice murmuring words of comfort he hoped might penetrate her pain.

That was one he hadn't considered. She hadn't loved Matt. That only increased her sense of guilt. He wasn't sure how long he stood there in the silent woods while she wept. He wasn't sure what to say when she finally reached into her pocket for a tissue and blew her nose.

"I seem to do this a lot with you," Frankie said, wiping her eyes.

He kept his arms loosely about her. "I've confessed a few things to you, too. You may not have seen the tears, but they were there."

How did he always know the right thing to say to make her feel better? She owed him the truth, though she hated saying the words. She'd denied them so long, so very long. Raising her eyes to his, she saw only compassion. Maybe it was time.

"I don't know why really, but Matt fell in love with me, almost from the first day we met."

Steen smiled. "I know why. It happened to me, too."

Frankie frowned, unable to handle his declaration right now. "Please don't make this any harder for me to tell you."

"You don't have to..."

"I want to. We dated for two years, but we were only high school kids. He started asking me to marry him long before graduation. I liked him, but I knew I didn't love him. I also knew his family thought I wasn't good enough for him. My mother kept hammmering away at me, that I shouldn't wind up like her, that I deserved a chance. Matt was a good boy, she said, and he'd make a fine husband. His family loved him and would accept me in time. I let her convince me. I knew it was wrong, but Matt offered me a way out and I took it."

She looked at him then, her green eyes pleading for understanding. "But I swore I'd never let Matt know I didn't love him. I was a good wife. He wanted a baby and, though I felt we were both too young, I threw away the birth control pills. And I kept that trailer spotless, cooked all his favorite dishes, gave him comfort, encouragement. Everything but...but love."

"Don't, Frankie. You don't have to go on." There was a look of such anguish on her face that he could hardly bear it.

"Steen, I don't think I know how to love. I thought I loved my mother, but I let her talk me into something I shouldn't have. I tried to love my father, but he turned away from both of us. And Matt...Matt would be alive today if he'd never met me. I loved Sara, but it didn't keep her safe. Don't you see? Some people just don't have a knack for loving. They..."

"That's crazy. None of that was your fault. Everyone needs love, everyone *can* love."

"I'm a very bad choice for you to love, Steen." She turned and pointed. "Look behind me. You can't see it clearly, but it's there. Tons of baggage I'm hauling around. Baggage that has nothing to do with you. Run while you can. Run."

"I would, maybe, if I could. It's too late."

"No, you're wrong. I'll only hurt you. You need to forget me. This... Look on this as a pleasant interlude, a..." She saw the quick pain in his dark eyes and choked back a whisper. "You see what I mean, I'm hurting you already." Pulling free of him, she shook her head. "Let me go home, Steen. It'll never work out between us. I haven't anything to offer you except more pain, and you've had a fair share of that already."

Slipping his arm around her, Steen headed them back to the cabin. "Let me be the judge of that. I'm not giving up on you. I think you're just beginning to face up to a lot of things. I have faith that you'll work them out, that you'll see that you belong with me."

Frankie blew her nose, then thrust both hands into her pockets. "How long have you had these masochistic tendencies?"

He swung her about, leaning down until they were nose to nose. "Loving you is the best thing that's ever happened to me, understand?"

Tired. She was bone tired and weary of thinking. "No, I truly don't understand."

"You will, one day. Now, let's go back. Are you hungry? I could fix some dinner."

"I couldn't eat a thing."

"What would you like then?"

There was only one thing she could think of that would take her mind off everything. "I'd like you to make love to me." One last time. Slowly, for the memory would have to last a very long while.

He kissed each of her eyes, then lingered over her mouth. "*With* you, not *to* you. To you suggests that you won't be participating."

She gave him the ghost of a smile. "Oh, I'll be participating, all right."

Tightening his arm around her, he stepped up their former pace. "Then let's go home."

Home. When, if ever, would Frankie Taelor regard his house as her home? Steen asked himself. He could take her home now and love her all night long. But what would the morning bring?

In the morning, Steen woke to the muffled sounds of someone moving about the room, quickly dressing, quietly packing. It took all his willpower to lie still, to feign sleep, to let her go. If Frankie could leave him so easily again, then he would not stop her.

No man wanted a woman who remained against her free will. Eyes tightly closed, the blanket clutched in his fists, Steen lay waiting for the sound of the door closing.

Chapter Eleven

Frankie set down the phone and waited for the elation. Long minutes passed and nothing happened. Sitting down at her desk, she sighed heavily.

Dina Jones, the Realtor from Maui, had been fairly bursting with excitement over her good news. The owner of the house Frankie had been wanting for two years was making a job change, necessitating a move to the mainland immediately. While the price hadn't lowered, the sellers were seriously motivated and ready to entertain a reasonable offer. Though she had several parties interested in this property, Dina had called Frankie first. Should she act immediately, Dina wanted to know, and submit an offer before someone else snapped up this wonderful house?

Frankie's prolonged silence on the line had hinted of more than surprise at the news to Dina. Had she lost interest? the realtor wanted to know. Had she? Frankie asked herself.

She truly didn't know. Ordinarily, she'd have been thrilled, elated, excited. But nothing had been ordinary since...since she'd gotten stranded ten days ago in a snowstorm. Realizing it was unfair to keep Dina dangling, she'd told her she'd have to think things over. Amid warnings that she just might lose the house if she delayed too long, Frankie had assured Dina she'd phone her back shortly. And tell her what? she wondered.

Getting up to pace, Frankie took a turn around her spacious living room, then went to the wall of windows and stood gazing out at the bay. The early-afternoon sun played on the shimmering water, but even nine floors up she could see whitecaps, attesting to a chilling breeze. It was, after all, the twenty-ninth of December. And three days after she'd snuck out of Steen's cabin in the early-morning hours, feeling like a coward.

Rubbing her arms, she sat down on the corner windowseat and acknowledged that she still felt cowardly. After their walk in the woods and her soul-wrenching confession, he'd taken her into his bed. There'd been a poignancy to their lovemaking that had brought tears to her eyes again, as if Steen, too, had felt it might indeed be their last time. He had that sixth sense about him that seemed to look into her mind in a way that both frightened and warmed her.

Drawing her legs up, Frankie hugged her knees and let herself remember how just before the early light of dawn, she'd awakened as never before with Steen's mouth on hers and his hands arousing her sleeping flesh. He'd been all flash and fire and fierce heat as he'd had her soaring before she'd been fully awake, another astounding first. But then, he'd introduced her to a lot of firsts, she thought as she twisted the small ring on her finger, the one he'd carved from an acorn.

But she'd run, run from him and her feelings, driving to the airport as if ghosts had been riding in the back seat. And perhaps they had been. Ironic that Steen had feared she might not understand his need to run from a situation. She understood it all too well. She'd flown home, arriving in the late afternoon, and spent the remainder of the day keeping busy sorting through accumulated mail and returning phone calls.

She'd spent half an hour talking with her mother who'd chatted on about all the activities she was involved in with her friends in Florida. Frankie was glad she was busy and happy.

The next day, she'd gone on a local appointment, and then flown to Albuquerque on a quick consultation the following day, returning home last evening. She'd kept busy so she wouldn't have to think about whether or not she'd done the right thing in leaving Steen so abruptly. And now, here she sat, pondering a big decision, what to do about the house on Maui.

Far below, Frankie watched the gulls circle round and round the shoreline, then skitter back out toward deeper water. She felt like one of those unsettled birds, undecided whether to land or fly farther out to sea. She'd never been an indecisive person, not until recently.

Outwardly, it would seem she had much going for her. Despite Eric Hanley and his implied threats, her business was doing well, her savings account growing. Glancing around her apartment, she knew she was pleased at this home she'd made for herself. Her Hawaiian dream house had suddenly become available and, with some penny-pinching, affordable. She had friends, challenges, seemingly everything. Why, then, did she feel nothing but this restless ennui that had plagued her since her return?

Stretching out her legs, Frankie leaned back against the frame and closed her eyes. She knew the answer. Because although she'd run from Steen, put miles between them, he was with her still. In her mind, in her memories, in her heart. Dear God, what to do?

Already she missed him, craved him, needed him. How had she let this happen? Pressing a closed fist into her stomach, she felt the hard lump of dissatisfaction churning. She was doing him a favor by leaving him; if only he could see it. He deserved so much more than a damaged woman, one it seemed that even Hannah had been able to spot as an emotional cripple. Even after sobbing out her guilt to Steen over marrying Matt when she didn't love him, only to lose him in a dreadful accident, he hadn't judged her. He'd held her tenderly, made her forget her past with his loving ways. But in the cold light of morning, she'd remembered again, as she always would. She couldn't saddle Steen with that kind of disability.

She knew she was being a coward, but the instinct for self-protection was strong. What if she let herself love Steen, and something happened to take him from her? Could she handle another loss, or would this one finish her? Wasn't it better to break it off now, when the love was just blossoming?

But there was more at issue here. Could she take her hard-won freedom and hand it to him, give in to him, become half of a whole? Would their joining forces strengthen them, or weaken each?

Even a wild deer trusted Steen, felt safe with him. Truth be known, she did, too. But she wouldn't, couldn't tell him. She didn't deserve him. He would forget her and meet someone whole and healthy in mind and spirit and she would make him happy. Meantime, she'd call Dina Jones and explain that she'd changed her mind. Though the Realtor would never understand, the house in Maui had recently lost all appeal for Frankie.

Rising, she walked to the phone and was about to pick it up when it rang. Hesitating a moment, she let it ring once more before answering.

"Well, Francesca, it's about time I found you in," Corbett greeted her.

Frowning, Frankie sat down. There'd been two messages on her answering machine from Corbett, and she hadn't yet found time to return his calls, perhaps subconsciously avoiding him. Corbett had a way of seeing through her that was unnerving.

"Good to hear from you, Corbett. I'm sorry I haven't gotten back to you. There was so much to do when I returned, and yesterday I had to fly to New Mexico for the day."

"No problem. I knew you'd surface sooner or later. How are you?"

"Fine. How about you? Did your Christmas party go well?"

"Certainly. Don't my dinners *always* go well? Of course, we pined away for you...."

Frankie found herself smiling. "You're a wonderful liar and I've missed you." With a rush of unexpected emotion, she realized it was true. Other than her mother, Corbett was as close to family as she had and, though he hovered a bit too much, she was fond of him. She seldom let him know though, and now heard the pause at the other end as he took note of her comment.

"I, too, Francesca." Corbett let out a whoosh of smoke. "But we're about to remedy that. Tonight, a very special dinner, at my place. Seven o'clock. Informal and don't be late."

She'd long ago gotten used to Corbett issuing invitations as if they were commands. She just wasn't sure she was up to one of his five-course extravaganzas. "It's sweet of you, Corbett, but I'm a little tired and . . ."

"Dear lady, I'm not asking you to *cook* the dinner, merely to *eat* it. You do still eat, don't you?"

Frankie laughed. "Yes, now and again."

"I know you've been clumping around in the backwoods for days on end, but I'd hoped you hadn't become as uncivilized as the bears you undoubtedly ran across."

"No bears, but I did see a deer tame enough to eat from your hand."

There was the slightest pause while he digested that. "Fascinating. It sounds as though your rugged woodcarver took you back to nature, and you enjoyed the trip. Did he?"

He was baiting her and they both knew it. "There's a lot to be said for the peace and quiet of country living."

"Really? You must tell me all about it tonight."

No, that she wouldn't do. "Is there anything I can bring?"

"Just your lovely self."

"Corbett, did you invite others?" An outgoing man, he thought twelve was an intimate number at the table and Frankie didn't think she could handle that this evening.

"Is there someone you'd like me to invite?"

"I'd rather it would be just the two of us."

"Then the two of us it shall be. See you at seven, Francesca."

"Yes. Thank you." Hanging up, she acknowledged an odd uneasiness, then shook it off with determination. Corbett was her best friend. She'd probably feel much better after a relaxed evening listening to his endlessly entertaining stories.

Reaching for her phone book, she scanned it for Dina Jones's number. She'd get this call over with, then head for the shower. And she'd stop overthinking everything and put on a happy face, Frankie decided. She was beginning to bore herself.

Steen gripped the ax handle firmly, swung it up, then brought it down, splitting the log with a satisfying crunch. The two pieces fell from the tree stump to the ground. He reached to the pile and placed another chunk of wood on the stump. Pausing a moment, he stopped to lean on the ax handle, gazing at the large assortment of wood pieces littering the ground at his feet. He'd split half a cord of wood and still hadn't released all his pent-up energy.

Sighing, he gazed up at a clear blue wintry sky and let his thoughts focus in on the cause of his restlessness. He hadn't heard a word from Frankie since she'd left three days ago. Would she ever come around again, or did she intend to quietly slip out of his life, to pretend that all they'd shared had been a pleasant interlude?

After her sudden departure, he'd gone through several stages of reaction. Anger, certainly. Disappointment. Resentment. And finally, he'd settled on one. He simply missed her.

He'd never particularly minded being alone, often had even preferred it. But since having Frankie here, the days without her stretched out long and lonely for the first time. Not a good feeling.

She'd seemed happy here much of the time, contented even. But even if she would return, how long before the quiet life would bore her? Would she quickly tire of small-town living, this woman who had a lovely apartment in San Francisco and had traveled extensively? She'd lived in a little Ohio town and had hated that enough to marry a man she didn't love in order to leave it. She'd miss the advantages she now had of theaters, stores, posh restaurants, wouldn't she?

And she'd blame him eventually for isolating her. She'd allowed him to love her out of loneliness, but once she'd returned to her element, she'd probably regretted it. Negative thinking was unhealthy, Steen reminded himself as he grabbed the ax handle and heaved it upward.

He'd split half a dozen more logs before stopping to watch Red come racing through the trees toward him. The playful Irish setter loped over and looked up at Steen, seemingly happy to be back home again. Steen set the ax aside and leaned down to rub his head. Gratefully Red held still while his chin was scratched.

Frankie would probably enjoy Red. But she'd left the day before Steen had picked him up. He glanced toward the clearing between the trees where they'd walked together that last day. He could easily picture her wearing that brown suede jacket, her golden hair flying loose in the breeze, the red setter running alongside her. *Frankie, Frankie. Life could be so good here. Why didn't you give us a chance?*

Straightening, Steen narrowed his eyes and mentally reviewed for perhaps the hundredth time the many conversations they'd had. She'd told him about her lonely childhood, about why the Christmas holidays depressed her, about her parents who never should have married each other, and about the circumstances of her own marriage.

That last afternoon walking in the woods, Frankie had been more upset than usual. She'd confessed that she hadn't loved Matt when she'd married him. She'd been talking freely, talking truthfully, spurred on by emotion, of never loving Matt, only Sara. He frowned, trying to remember what she'd said next, her exact words. *I've never loved a man, no man, not until . . .*

Something significant there, Steen decided, if only he could get a handle on it. She'd looked up at him with stricken eyes and not finished the thought. Until who? By her own confession, Steen had been the only other man in her life, in her bed, since Matt. It had to be him. Never loved a man until him.

Steen kicked at the tree stump and let out a shout that echoed in the snowy hills. He stood looking at the surprised expression on Red's face, and he grinned like a fool. That was it. She loved him and she'd almost said it out loud. That was all he needed to know.

Yes, she'd left, but only because she was afraid. Afraid to face her feelings, afraid to risk loving, probably afraid of losing someone she cared for again. He should have realized that it was fear, not stubborness that had caused her to return to the safety of the familiar. She'd chosen to live alone and uninvolved rather than gamble on a future together that she felt was uncertain. Hadn't she told him early on that she didn't like to gamble, that she hated losing?

Moving inside the house, Steen stopped to wash his hands at the kitchen sink. She loved him, he was certain. All he'd have to do would be to convince her, somehow, that loving was the only risk worth taking. Fight? Hell, yes, he'd fight, for his own. And she *was* his, had been from the first moment he'd seen her, back when even he hadn't known it. But he knew it now. Life was too short not to have it all, once you knew what you wanted.

Grabbing his keys, he walked to the Jeep. He'd go over to Hannah's and use her phone to call Frankie. His first instinct was to go to San Francisco, knowing he could be far more persuasive in person. But he'd discarded that thought almost immediately. Frankie hated being pushed. He could make his feelings known on the phone, then give her time to let his words sink in, to let her decide. He wanted her to return willingly, joyfully, of her own volition.

The ride over to Hannah's seemed longer than usual, and his neighbor's chatter almost annoying today. Steen listened politely to the news about Hannah's new grandson, for the first time regretting not having his own phone. But he hadn't wanted to take the time to drive into town to a booth. At last, Hannah went back to her needlepoint in the living room and Steen picked up the phone.

She was listed with Information, as he'd suspected, because of her business. Impatiently, he waited as the phone rang for the third time. Finally, he heard the receiver being picked up.

Securing the towel around her wet body, Frankie held the phone to her ear. "Hello?"

"Hello, Frankie," Steen said, feeling his heart lurch at the sound of her voice.

Frankie let out a deep breath, feeling as if the wind had been knocked out of her. She'd known, deep inside, that she'd hear from him again, hadn't she? "How are you, Steen?"

"I've been better. How are you?"

"Keeping busy." Frankie clenched her fingers into a fist. Is this what they'd come to, this maddeningly polite conversation? "Did you call to yell at me for walking out on you like that?"

"I don't believe I could ever yell at you, Frankie," he said honestly. "It jarred me, I admit, but I understand why you left the way you did."

"Do you?" She ran a shaky hand through her damp hair. "Perhaps you can explain it to me."

"Oh, I think you know." Steen shifted, turning his back to the open doorway where Hannah sat rocking in her chair. "You love me and it scares you."

"No, I don't." Frankie felt the knot form in her stomach. Anger. If she could muster up some anger, she could get through this. He would hang up then, leave her alone so she could lick her wounds in peace.

"I know you won't admit it, even to yourself, but I believe you do. And I love you, very much."

Closing her eyes, Frankie leaned against the door frame. "I told you I don't want to talk about love."

"You taught me to love, Frankie, so much that I feel pain, real pain, when you're not with me."

"I can't believe that." *Why was she saying that when she, too, had been in pain away from him?*

"I'm willing to make changes, if necessary, to compromise, if you are."

She felt the anger leave her, replaced by a yearning so strong she felt her whole body tremble. "I don't know, Steen, I want to, but . . . but . . ."

He caught the change in tone and felt his spirits lift. He'd been right to call. "You're afraid, I know. Trust me, please. You've trusted me with your body. Trust me all the way.''

She wanted to. God, how she wanted to. "I do, when I'm with you. You make me forget all my fears, for a short while. But there's always the morning.''

Steen gripped the phone, his voice intense. "Come stay with me, Frankie, and let me show you I can make your mornings shiny and new and free of pain. We'll tear down all the old memories and build new ones.''

She felt herself withdrawing, even as she wished she could believe him. "I have a life here, Steen. One I like." One that had been enough, until recently.

Slowly, Steen reminded himself. He needed to go slowly with her, to count the minor victories. She was no longer angry; she was bending a little. "I'm not asking you to give up your life. Let's see what happens. Come to the cabin over New Year's. Give us a few days together. Come tonight, or early tomorrow.''

"I can't. I'm having dinner with Corbett tonight and I have an appointment tomorrow at a bank in Santa Barbara. I don't know how long the job will take.''

"Is that the last job scheduled for this year?" At her soft yes, he smiled. "Then come whenever you're finished. Please, Frankie. I honestly need you.''

Tempting. So very tempting, especially since she needed him, too. She remembered the warmth of his home, the joy she'd found in his arms. The tug of memories drew her in. "How's Emily's kitten?''

"Thriving. We'll go see her while you're here and she can tell you all about her new baby brother.''

A boy. So Hannah had been right. "Is Red back yet?''

"Yes, and anxious to meet you." He waited, while the silence lengthened. What more could he say? Suddenly, a thought occurred to him. "Would you rather we fly to Maui for a few days together? You could show me that house you're so crazy about."

If she told him she'd turned the house down a mere hour ago, he'd make too much of it. "No. I like your cabin."

"I like it, too. But much better when you're in it."

Frankie sighed, feeling the indecision weighing heavily on her. "You're very persuasive, but I still don't know if I'll come. I can't handle pressure right now, or expansive plans for a future I'm not sure we'll be sharing. We've known each other less than two weeks. I've never been comfortable being impulsive."

He'd done the best he could, Steen told himself. The rest would have to be up to her. "All right, Frankie. If you show up, I promise you no pressure. You know where I live. I want you with me, but you have to want that, too. I'll be there. I hope you decide to come."

"Let me think about it, okay?"

Did he have a choice? "Fine."

"Goodbye, Steen." She heard him echo her words, then slowly replaced the phone in its cradle. Gazing out the window at the darkening sky, Frankie wondered if she had the courage to go, to spend time with Steen, and then leave him again.

Glancing at the clock, she hurried toward the bathroom. She'd think about all that later, she decided as she took a deep, calming breath. Right now, she'd have to get ready or she'd be late. She wasn't in the mood to go, but she'd promised Corbett and he frowned on tardiness.

At precisely seven, Frankie pressed the doorbell to Corbett's apartment. His building, high up a hillside, was old, quaint and very expensive. The moment he opened the door wearing a dark green smoking jacket and a white scarf tied at his throat as only he could, she felt his warmth reach out to her. Smiling a welcome, he hugged her to his tall frame while she inhaled the lush scent of his extravagant cologne.

"I thought the holidays were over," she teased as she touched the soft velvet of his lapel.

"Far from it," Corbett said as he ushered her inside. "The new year is nearly upon us." Helping her with her coat, he looked her over. "You don't look any the worse for your ordeal in the backwoods. Matter of fact, you look wonderful. I'm glad to see you finally took my advice and started wearing your hair down."

Yes, she had, but not for him. Someone else had admired her hair down and... Frankie cleared her throat. "I brought you something," she said, handing him the book on sailing she'd had wrapped in Tahoe the day of her shopping spree. Sailing was one of Corbett's passions. "Happy belated Christmas."

"How lovely of you. Sit down by the fire and I'll get us some wine." Corbett turned toward the kitchen. "What do you think, a Beaujolais on this chilly night, or a nice Riesling I've got on ice?"

Frankie chose the red wine as she moved to her favorite wing chair by the fire. She hugged her arms, gathering her silk jacket around her, feeling slightly chilled, though it was warm in the apartment. As always, looking about Corbett's stylish living room with its antiques and collectibles from his travels, made her feel comfortable. She'd lost track of the hours she'd spent here, chatting with him, learning from him, listening to his advice and encouraging words about her fledgling business. Other than her own apartment,

Corbett's place was as close to another home as she had. She leaned back with a sigh and closed her eyes.

"What's this," Corbett admonished as he returned and extended a silver tray toward her, "napping already and the evening's just beginning?"

With an apologetic smile, Frankie reached for the crystal Waterford goblet. "Sorry. It's been hectic catching up since returning."

Corbett sat back in the matching wing chair at an angle to hers, his dark eyes measuring. "It's a bit early, I know, but shall we toast the new year?"

The new year stretched before her, vaguely disturbing, with new decisions to face, something to get through rather than look forward to. Frankie gave herself a mental shake. Her attitude needed a little work. And Corbett deserved better for his efforts. Putting on a smile, she touched her glass to his. "To the new year."

"Did you miss going to Maui this year?"

Setting her glass down on the small table between them, Frankie shrugged. "I can always go later. I...I'm not as keen on Maui as I once was."

She didn't see the quick look of surprise on Corbett's face as he stroked his chin while he studied her. "Is that a fact? Any particular reason? I thought there was a certain house there that you were intent on owning."

"Yes, well, people change their minds. Real estate in Hawaii is ridiculously overpriced, as you know. It's not wise to overextend yourself. Isn't that what you've always told me?"

"Yes, it is. Perhaps later, another house."

"Perhaps." This ambivalence, this evasiveness was not like her, especially not with Corbett. Any moment now, he'd start firing questions at her. She gazed about the room, groping for a new topic. "You've put away all the Christmas decorations already. You don't usually this early, do you?"

"When I invited you over for this evening, I took the tree down. I thought by now that you'd had your fill of Christmas, knowing how you feel about the season."

Had she been so obvious, so depressingly self-indulgent, that the few friends she had had walked on eggs around her during the holidays? She sent him a contrite smile. "That was sweet of you, Corbett, but unnecessary. Christmas is... not so bad." Her mind drifted to the four of them gathered around Hannah's tree, and the arrival of the skinny Santa named Ben. And sitting on the couch in front of the fire wrapped in Steen's arms while carols played; and later, walking in the snow holding his hand. "I think I've come to grips with Christmas."

He took his time lighting one of his gold-tipped cigarettes. "So where did you spend Christmas Day, at the casino?"

She could lie, or change the subject. It seemed too much effort. "I rented a car and drove back to Steen Olson's cabin." She raised her eyes to his, almost a challenge. When he didn't speak, she went on. "His sister was there, on holiday break from college. And we had dinner at Hannah's, Steen's neighbor, the one I mentioned on the phone to you."

"The motherly lady who makes cookies."

"Yes. And her granddaughter, Emily, was visiting. She's eight and she'd lost her kitten. So I took her a replacement." Babbling. She was babbling and she couldn't seem to stop. "We took a walk in the woods. It's so peaceful there, so quiet."

"And a deer ate from your hand?"

"No, from Steen's hand. He has a way with animals." And children. And women with broken wings. "I know it sounds country hokey, but it wasn't. It was a wonderful day." She'd run out of steam. Lowering her gaze, she took a sip of her wine.

Corbett inhaled the bouquet of the wine, then took a swallow before setting down his glass. "You're a little subdued, Francesca." He leaned closer to her. "Is anything the matter?"

Getting a hold of herself, Frankie shook her head. "No, I'm fine." She flashed him a quick smile meant to reassure. "Really. Now, tell me about your party. I want to hear everything."

She hadn't fooled Corbett, she knew, but she needed the ten minutes it took him to go on about his annual Christmas party to compose herself. Trying hard to follow his conversation, she kept a smile on and nodded in what she hoped were the right places. She must have lost track somewhere though, for suddenly, he was standing in front of her.

"Come to the kitchen and keep me company while I make sure our dinner's going well."

Grateful for the break, Frankie followed him, standing in the arch to watch. "What delectable dish are we having?" Corbett was a fantastic cook and she'd been looking forward to his menu.

"Bouillabaisse. A new recipe I recently obtained from this wonderful French woman who lived for years in New Orleans." With the ease of long practice, Corbett assembled basil, thyme and savory along with minced garlic. "She's too young for me, of course, only forty, and though she says our age difference doesn't matter to her, it most assuredly does to me." With a flourish, he tossed the spices into the big black pot and reached to stir the contents. "But I do love to have her over to teach me her secrets, cooking and otherwise." Corbett sent her a devilish wink.

"Why, you old fox! Don't tell me you're taken with this French lady?" Since she'd known him, he'd had many women float in and out of his life, but none remained for long. Still, she loved to tease him about them, and he'd almost come to expect her inquiries.

Corbett angled the lid over the pot. "Very taken with her. But you know me, Francesca. Love 'em and let 'em go, that's my philosophy."

She'd never asked him before, but suddenly she needed to know. "Why have you never married, Corbett?"

He took a moment to place foil-wrapped French bread into the warmer oven before turning to her. "There now, we'll just let everything simmer and heat a bit while we talk some more." Arm around her waist, he led her back to the coziness of the fireside. "The answer to your question is simple. I'm too selfish to marry."

"You, selfish?" Frankie shook her head in disbelief. "You're one of the most generous people I know. You're kind, considerate, even extravagant, with your time, your money."

"Oh, certainly, with my friends. Friends go home, Francesca, and you see them again next week, or the following. It's the day-to-day living that makes marriage difficult." He crossed his legs, obviously searching for the right words. "I don't want to give up my ways. I like to eat certain foods, and that's what I cook. I don't want a woman, or anyone, to tell me how to decorate my apartment, how to dress, where to go on trips, what to buy or not buy. I readily admit that's selfish and I don't apologize for it. Now, who'd want to live with a man like that?''

"I think you're too hard on yourself. And I believe there are quite a few women out there who could add significantly to your life, and you to theirs.''

He gave her an exaggerated frown. "An advocate of marriage, you?''

"No, not especially. I just don't buy the reasons you list for *not* marrying.''

"Really? Let me ask you a few questions then. Would you give up the apartment you've slowly and beautifully decorated to your own taste and move in with someone else, live with his selection?''

Frankie considered his question. She'd worked hard to make her place into a home, at last having the means to make it reflect her needs, surrounding herself with things she'd chosen with great care. Yet, to pick a random place, for instance, she could be happy in Steen's house. She'd come to love that isolated cabin with its wonderful fireplace and cozy kitchen. "Yes, I think I could. Besides when two grown people marry, they combine their things, don't they?''

"I suppose they can. Would you learn to eat a different way then, let's say plain meat and potatoes fare when you love gourmet choices and rich sauces?''

Steen had made her steak, baked potato and a salad and she'd loved it. And what could beat Hannah's pot roast? "I'm very adaptable when it comes to food. I can be happy with your bouillabaisse or with canned soup.''

"All right, would you be happy with camping when you love traveling first-class? Would you leave this beautiful cosmopolitan city and go live in some backwoods cottage? Would what you get be worth all you gave up?''

Frankie took a sip of her wine, her hand none to steady as his words sank in. She knew exactly what Corbett was doing. He'd played devil's advocate often enough with her when she'd been planning to start her own business and had had so many doubts. "We've somehow switched the focus of our conversation, haven't we?"

"Have we?" Corbett moved his chair closer and took her hand in his. Noticing the ring she wore, he ran a finger over the smooth surface. "Something new?"

She nodded, realizing he would probably find out anyhow. "Yes. Steen carved it, from an acorn."

"From an acorn, imagine." He touched her chin, drawing her eyes to his. "Francesca, I don't meddle in your personal life, as a rule, do I?"

She felt a lecture coming on and was desperate to avoid it. Her emotions, so close to the surface lately, just might spill over and embarrass her. "I haven't known you to. Is it your New Year's resolution?"

Corbett sighed. "Perhaps. Dear girl, you're like the daughter I never had, you know. And I don't want you to get hurt."

She squeezed his hand. "I know."

"You're in love with him."

It wasn't a question. There was no point in denying the obvious, not to Corbett. "Yes. But I walked away. You must know how I feel. All those questions you asked just now, about food, and where to live, where to travel— I could compromise on all that, and Steen certainly would. It's the loving I can't handle, the pain if something goes wrong. Like you, I'm better off alone. If you don't care, you can't be hurt."

"But you already care."

"I'll get over it. Out of sight, out of mind." Maybe if she was flip, she could convince him.

Corbett leaned back, taking another tack. "Tell me about this Steen Olson who has you in such knots. What's he like?"

"Just a man."

"Oh, come now, Francesca. You didn't fall in love with 'just a man.'"

Relentless. The man was relentless. She felt a quick flash of temper. "Why do you want to know?"

"Do you love him as much as you loved Matt?"

Frankie felt the breath shudder from her. "I never loved Matt. I liked him, I depended on him, but I never loved him. Perhaps I should have mentioned that."

"You didn't have to." She looked at him, her green eyes wide with surprise. Corbett nodded. "When you told me about the accident, your agonies were over your child. You said that Matt had been good to you, that he never should have died. But you never once mentioned loving him, missing him. Only Sara."

Frankie gripped her hands tightly in her lap. "I guess I'm more transparent than I thought."

He placed his hands over hers. "Only to me, my dear. So now that you are in love, how does it feel?"

"Rotten, thank you."

"Ah, now do you see why I have flings, even affairs, but never lasting ones?" Corbett finished his wine, then returned his dark gaze to her. "But you're different than me, Francesca. Since I've known you, I've felt you had so much to offer, so much stored up to give, to the right man. I don't know if this Steen Olson is the right man, but in the six years I've known you, he's the only one who's made you this miserable, so I have to assume he's more than a passing fancy. That's why I broke my own rule of not meddling. I'd hate to see you make a mistake. I don't know if this man's good enough for you."

She gave a short, mirthless laugh. "It's the other way around. Steen deserves better than me."

"Nonsense! I won't listen to that."

In her need to make him see, she leaned forward. "He's so kind—to his neighbor, walking two miles in snowshoes to chop down a Christmas tree for her, then decorate it. And generous. He made a sled for Emily, and he gives her expensive carvings like they were flowers he'd picked in the field." Her voice grew stronger in her anxiety to convince him. "And gentle. You should have seen the doe, Corbett. She actually strolled right up to us, unafraid, trusting. And responsible. He raised his sister after their parents died. He was only twenty. He even uprooted himself to move her to the country when she got in with the wrong crowd. How many young men would have . . . Why are you smiling like that?"

Corbett sat back, his hands folded across his middle, a pleased grin on his face. "Listen to yourself. Would any woman in her right mind run from a man with all those sterling qualities?"

Frankie let out a deep breath as she sank down into the protection of the chair. "You think you're smart, don't you? All right. He's not 'just a man.' He's a very special man. *I'm* the one who's all wrong. Steen needs a carefree woman, not one who's hauling around enough emotional baggage to sink the *Titanic*."

"Nonsense. He needs exactly what all men need. A woman who loves him unconditionally, who accepts him as he is, his virtues and his faults. Do you qualify?"

She hesitated, then finally looked up. "Put that way, I suppose. But love isn't enough."

"It'll do, for starters. You know, Francesca, I've always believed that the heart recognizes its own. I recognized you as someone I would love forever as a daughter immediately upon meeting you. I've never married because, though I'm attracted to a variety of women constantly, my heart remains my own. If I ever lose it, I'll go down on bended knee to her."

She smiled at the mental picture of that. "And she'll be one lucky lady." Reaching over, she laced her fingers with his. "You should have been a philosopher, you know."

"I thought I was." Corbett stood, drawing her to her feet, embracing her for a long moment. "Let's go eat my wonderful bouillabaisse now, and you think later about what we've talked about. All right?"

"Yes. And thank you for caring." Frankie followed him to the dining room, wondering if she'd be able to swallow a simple spoonful with her thoughts in such a jumble.

She did, however—several spoonfuls—along with a delectable salad, hot buttered bread and more wine. The dinner conversation centered around computers and her business and sleazy characters like Eric Hanley. Frankie was surprised to find herself enjoying the evening.

"And now for dessert," Corbett announced as he cleared the table, insisting she remain seated. "I had to scour the city for this, so you'd best appreciate my efforts."

"I always appreciate your efforts. If it's half as good as the main course, I . . ." She stared down at the dish he'd placed in front of her. Raspberries in whipped cream. Despite her best effort, her eyes filled.

"What's the matter? I thought you'd be pleased? Do you know that raspberries in December are scarcer than hen's teeth?"

Blinking, Frankie nodded. "I know." She dipped her spoon in, memories flooding her mind as she tasted them. "Delicious." Would it always be this way, every reminder of Steen sending her into a turmoil?

Somehow, she made it through coffee, then finally stood, telling Corbett she was tired and needed to get home.

"But we haven't opened our gifts. Just a moment longer." Like an excited kid, he led her back to the living room where he ripped the paper from his package. He smiled as he thumbed through the book on sailing. "This is wonderful. Look at these pictures. Lovely." He kissed her forehead. "Thank you."

Corbett turned to the alcove and came back holding a glazed terra-cotta pot. "And this is for you. I couldn't wrap it."

Frankie stared into the pot. Only black dirt. She raised questioning eyes to his, looking skeptical "You're giving me a pot of black dirt?"

"Not exactly. In the soil are several crocus bulbs. Soon now, they'll come up and bloom. If you had a house, you could even plant them outside. During the winter, they're dormant and in the spring, they're the very first flower to make an appearance. A tiny, fragile green leaf pushing through frozen ground. Imagine that." He shifted his eyes from the pot to Frankie who was watching him with an ever sobering expression. "Do you know why I'm giving you crocuses, Francesca?"

"No. Tell me."

"Because they're survivors. Like you are. Survivors are to be admired because they epitomize the very best in all of us."

Moved, Frankie leaned to hug him. This man, this kind, loving man, had given her a great deal this evening. "I love you, Corbett," she whispered. Taking her gift, she hurried out the door.

The cab ride home was short. As the vehicle climbed the hill to her apartment, Frankie sat staring at the mound of dirt in her pot, Corbett's words echoing in her head all the while. Much to digest. When the driver pulled up, she paid him and got out, then stood looking up at the building she'd chosen with such care to be her home.

Why, suddenly didn't it look as inviting as a small cabin tucked away in the Sierra Nevada Mountains where a soft-spoken man wearing a Bugs Bunny sweatshirt and furry slippers was probably sitting gazing into the fireplace?

Chapter Twelve

She was dreaming, a soft, warm dream. She and Steen were walking in the snow through the woods near the cabin. A reddish blur of a dog flashed by and they laughed for no reason except that it felt good to be alive, to be out in the clean fresh air, to be together.

Suddenly Steen scooped up a mound of snow and tossed it her way. Ducking, she scrambled out of the snowball's path, then bent to retaliate. Only her weapon hit its mark and snow trickled down Steen's dark hair, onto his red cheeks. Contrite, she went to him and brushed it off, then kissed away all traces. Pulling her close, he touched his lips to hers. As always, Frankie forgot everything, her mouth opening to him, her arms going around him.

Safe. She felt so safe wrapped in Steen's arms, in Steen's love. Warmth spread through her as the kiss went on and on. From a distance, she heard a buzzing, but she ignored it, not wanting to break the kiss. Finally, Steen drew back and she looked into his eyes. They were smiling at her. Frankie smiled back.

The buzzing persisted. Frankie opened her eyes and saw that she was in her own bed in her own apartment. Flipping over, she hit the alarm button and there was silence. She lay back, remembering the dream, and realized she was still smiling.

Stretching, she gazed out the window at the early sunshine. *Let me make your mornings shiny and new and free of pain,* Steen had said. She'd gone to sleep last night, still worrying and fretting over what to do—to go or stay. But she'd awakened wrapped in a warm dream, happy and excited, ready to face the day with enthusiasm. Her excitement didn't revolve around flying to Santa Barbara to set up a more efficient computer system for the bank. It had its basis in the anticipation of possibly seeing Steen again.

It was the same way she'd felt the morning she'd awakened in Steen's arms at his cabin and had lain contentedly watching him sleep awhile. Then she'd gone to the kitchen to make coffee and water his plants. No regrets, no overpowering fears, no lingering guilt. Could it be that merely being with him, her fears and guilt would disappear?

Tossing the covers back, Frankie got out of bed. She'd have more time to ponder this later. Right now, she needed to get ready for her appointment in Santa Barbara.

She was in the shower when she heard the phone ringing. For a moment, Frankie considered letting it ring. But years of discipline had her turning off the water. Grabbing a towel and wrapping it around herself, she hurried to answer the phone.

Minutes later, she hung up, smiling. A cancellation. The bank manager had called, changing their appointment to the following week when the head of their computer programming would be available. It would seem he was currently out with the flu. Usually, cancellations didn't make her smile. Today was an exception. She had four days without a commitment. Frankie returned to the shower.

Later, as she dried off, she had a sudden flash of insight and realized that she was doing exactly what her mother had talked her into doing when she'd been too young to know better. She was taking the easy way out. Then, with a little persuasion, she'd used Matt to get out of an unpleasant life. Now, she was turning her back on Steen, choosing a safe existence without confrontations and entanglements. Living alone, she wouldn't have to experience compromise or tough decisions or risk losing someone she loved. She also wouldn't experience the joy of sharing, the wonder of love, the possibility of children.

Her first mistake could be chalked up to youth and a certain gullibility. But she was no longer young nor gullible. True, she was frightened of facing the risk of loving. Yet without Steen's love, she was only half-alive. A survivor; Corbett who knew her so well had called her that. Was she?

Draping the towel over the rack, Frankie wiped off the steamy bathroom mirror and peered closely at her image. A woman in the prime of health gazed back at her. Her hair was shiny, her skin glowing, her eyes bright and alert. Despite the restless night, she looked rested, vibrant, alive. Was it because, deep down inside, she'd believed Steen's words yesterday, believed that he loved her?

Slowly, thoughtfully, she picked up her comb and pulled it through the wet strands of her hair, watching her reflected image. She looked happier, as if she'd let hope trickle into her life again. Hope for a future she'd spent years denying herself. And Steen had given her that hope.

She loved him. A fact, she admitted, not merely a tenuous thought. Dare she dream of a future with him, of a life with him and perhaps—dear God—children? Frankie dropped the comb.

She hadn't allowed herself to think along those lines, afraid to even experience the dream. He was so good, so patient. If from time to time, she'd sink into re-membered despair, she knew he'd help her get through the bad moments. And life with Steen would be so good, so healing. He wanted to share his life with a woman and he wanted children, she could tell. Could she be that woman? Could she make him happy?

This time for love, she told the woman in the mirror. No guilt, no excuses, only love leading the way. *Love is all there is,* Steen had said. *It doesn't get any better than this.* Maybe, if she tried, it would work.

Leaning closer, she saw her diamond earrings wink-ing in the glass. Slowly she removed them from her ears and studied them for long moments. Symbols of her independence, she'd always thought. Only in a few short days, she'd discovered that independence could be carried to an extreme. She had no doubt that Steen would not stifle her need for freedom, or her work. But through him, she'd learned that interdependence could be appealing, and personal sharing with a loved one could be equally exciting.

Closing her fingers around the earrings, Frankie reached a decision. She'd take them to Steen and tell him what she'd discovered. She'd have the diamonds made into cuff links for him, or whatever. She no longer needed them, or the symbol.

Picking up her hair dryer, she turned it on. She'd get dressed, call the airline and fly to Steen. She'd surprise him, for when they'd hung up, he hadn't sounded very hopeful that she'd show.

Blow-drying her hair, she recalled his words to her on the phone yesterday. *I want you with me, but you have to want that, too.* Oh, but she did. Smiling foolishly, Frankie began to hum.

By late afternoon, Frankie was at the Tahoe airport signing the papers for a rental car. Thanking the girl behind the counter, she took the keys and walked outside into a weak sunshine. The air was crisp and cold and not much of the snow had melted, but at least no new storms were predicted. Not that she'd really mind, Frankie thought.

In short order, she was humming along with the radio as she drove down the now-familiar highway toward Steen's cabin. Even if he had a phone, she wouldn't have called, but she did wonder what he was doing. The possibility that he might be out shopping or whatever had occurred to her and she'd decided she could always wait for his return at Hannah's. Taking a deep breath of the fresh mountain air, she pushed down on the accelerator, anxious to get to her destination.

She was singing along with Willie Nelson as she turned off the highway and onto the road leading to the house. Suddenly the song died in her throat as the scene through the windshield came into focus. Flames shooting toward the sky, huge snaking arms of fire racing along the trees and black billowing smoke. Dear God, no!

Hardly aware of what she was doing, Frankie pressed on the pedal and shot along the snowy, rutted road. Vapors of steam surrounded the cabin as it came into view, the accumulated snow evaporating rapidly in the heat and forming hazy clouds. Steen. Where was Steen? She could make out his Jeep, barely visible alongside the house, parked at a crazy angle. The darker smoke was pouring from the backyard. Screeching to a halt, Frankie slammed the car into park and yanked open her door.

Heart thudding, she ran onto the porch yelling his name, but found the door securely locked. In frustration, she pounded but heard nothing except her own shrill voice. *Please, God, not again,* she prayed as she hurried down the steps, nearly falling on the slippery boards.

Rushing around back, she thought she heard a dog barking above the crackle of flames, but the mist combined with smoke was so thick that she couldn't see clearly. Running closer, she felt the heat now as the fire whipped at the old wood of the storage shed and along the dog run. The shed. It was only the shed. But where was Steen?

Then she saw it, several yards from the shed, a single hand-tooled boot wedged in the snow, its sole charred and still smoking. She recognized it as Steen's and she let out a cry that was swallowed by the roar of the fire.

Was Steen trapped in the toolshed? She saw the dog then, the Irish setter, barking while he circled the shed. Fingers of flames enveloped the door as the entire structure raged like an inferno. Frankie sank to her knees in the snow, frozen with a mindless fear, unable to move.

With the wisdom of hindsight, she saw how foolish she'd been, and how right Hannah was. She should have grabbed every moment with Steen. She should have reached out with both hands and squeezed happiness from each separate minute spent with him. She should have told him how much she loved him.

But she hadn't. She'd lost another chance, her last one. She'd given him mere crumbs of hope that one day she might come around. She'd walked away and now, he might very well be gone.

The dog left his post and came running toward her as she lifted her head. She reached out her hand, but he ignored her and ran past. Through the mist, she could just barely make out his red coat as he stood barking at the back door to the cabin. If the dog could breathe there, she could, too. She had to get inside, to see if Steen was in there, perhaps hurt. *Please, God, let him be in the house.* Crawling toward Red, she was perhaps a dozen feet from the door when it swung open and she heard a stream of ripe curses fill the thick air.

Steen!

The man raced past her in a swirl of thick smoke, not noticing her on the ground as he tugged a tangled hose behind him. Stopping close to the shed, he turned the nozzle and water spurted forth, spraying the wood, the ground and the man who held the hose.

Rising clumsily to her feet, Frankie ran to him, recognizing his jacket, but still needing to reassure herself. "Steen!" she yelled as she grabbed his arm.

He swung about, his face soot marked and reddened, his hair singed and his clothes soaked. He'd never looked more beautiful to her. His mouth shot open in surprise as Frankie flung herself into his arms, nearly knocking him over and almost sending the hose flying.

"Frankie! What are you doing here? Get back, you'll get hurt." Steen steadied himself in the slippery snow. It was then he noticed her tear-stained face. "What's the matter?" He tried to keep the hose on the blaze while his eyes searched her face. "It's only a shed." Where was the damn fire truck?

"I came like you asked me to," she said through gulps of smoky air. "I saw the fire and I thought . . . I was afraid that . . ." She couldn't complete the sentence. Tears streamed down her cheeks as she just stared at him, her fingers still gripping his arm. She knew she'd overreacted, but she couldn't help herself.

Steen understood immediately. She was seeing not this blaze, but another fire. He'd thought she'd overreacted to a burning shed, but, of course, she would. Fire meant death to her, and untold pain. Switching the hose to his other hand, he slipped his arm around her and pulled her close.

Her face in his neck, she choked out a sob. "I thought I'd lost you." She shook with the force of her fear. "I can't lose you, not now." Her small hands clutched the material of his jacket, clenching and unclenching.

From a distance, he heard the sirens coming closer. He dropped the hose, realizing it was doing precious little good anyway. Besides, he didn't care if the whole damn cabin burned down if that's what it took for Frankie to face her feelings. He drew back from her, holding her at arm's length from him, gazing into her tear-drenched eyes. "Why, Frankie? Why not now?"

She gave a shudder, then took a shaky breath. "Because now I know that I love you. I was coming to tell you." With that, Frankie took a step, the longest of her life, closing the gap between them. Safe in the haven of his arms, she tilted her head up to his. "I love you so very much, Steen."

He didn't have to say a word. The look on his face said it all, he knew. Soot, singes and all, he lowered his mouth to hers and kissed her, long and hard. He tasted smoke, he tasted relief, he tasted love. Finally, as the fire engines drew to a stop and he could hear the men leaping from the truck, he lifted his head. "Don't go away. We'll finish this later."

She staggered a step backward. Go away? Hardly. She'd just come home.

In his stocking feet, Steen walked to meet the first fireman who was marching toward him, a huge fire hose in his hand. "About time, fellas," he said, wiping his blackened brow.

Exhausted in more ways than one, Frankie headed for the back door as Red stood beside Steen, barking at each fireman in turn. For long minutes, she stayed at the screen, watching through the smoke the tall man who stood talking with the fire marshall. He was alive, he was well, and he was hers.

She was soaking wet, dirty and in dire need of a shower. But more than a shower, she needed to keep Steen in her line of vision. When it was all over and the men left, when he was safe inside with her, there'd be time enough to bathe. A smile forming, Frankie thought that since the fire had used up so much of his reserve, she might have a suggestion or two on how they could conserve water.

* * *

Steen tugged Frankie's damp slacks down her slender legs and dropped them onto the growing pile of smelly clothes. He began unbuttoning her blouse as she stood still, simply watching him. "Never shared a shower before? Can't believe it."

"Believe it. Another first. I find my education sorely lacking in many areas. Fortunately, I've found someone willing to fill in the gaps."

He planted a quick kiss on the end of her nose, then peeled off her blouse. "Lucky you."

Her eyes softened, filled. "Yes, lucky me. Damn lucky."

In another moment, she was as naked as he and he brought her tight up against him. "I know I smell terrible, but I can't wait another minute to feel you."

"Don't wait." And she hugged him fiercely, her mouth finding his. Would she ever get enough of him now that she'd found him, really found him? Frankie seriously doubted it.

Quickly, Steen adjusted the water temperature and helped her under the spray. He insisted on lathering her, every sweet inch and delicious curve, so the washing took awhile, with time out for kisses and lingering touches. Then he handed her the soap and she returned the favor, taking great care to wash away all the soot and grime, her lips kissing to heal each cut and scratch. When the sluicing water had rinsed them both free of soap and shampoo, he stepped out and grabbed a towel. Wrapping her in it, he carried her to his bedroom.

"You're going to get the bedclothes wet," she warned as he placed her onto the mattress.

"We have others. I want to dry you myself." And so he did, patting the fluffy towel all over her satiny skin.

Only halfway through his chore, he lost sight of his goal as his mouth settled on the peak of one breast while his hand moved to caress the other.

With hungry mouths and familiar hands, they pleasured each other. Their coming together had always been exciting, Steen thought, but there was something extra now, something more. Each wanted to give more than to receive, murmuring the sweet words that touched the soul and healed all wounds. And when at last he was inside her, with her arms and legs wrapped about him, he thought his heart was filled to overflowing.

She watched his grey eyes smile into hers as he began the climb, taking her up.

"Tell me again," he whispered.

"I love you."

"Again."

"I love you, love you, love you." She felt the explosions begin. "Oh, Steen."

He let go then, and flew with her, higher and higher, over the precipice and onto a golden shore. And when it was over, she was still with him, safe in his arms.

Holding him close to her heart, Frankie ran her hands over his back slowly, lovingly. She'd never been wanted like that, had never thought she could inspire a strong man to be weak with need for her. Before Steen, she'd never experienced passion uncontrolled nor known she would willingly run to meet it head-on. She'd never known loving could be frantic and exciting or slow and tender. Now she knew, and felt the incredible power of love.

"I never thought it could be like that," she whispered.

"It isn't with everyone, is it?"

"No."

"Think we may have latched on to something here?"

Frankie shifted to look at him, her eyes serious. "I didn't realize that it would be important to me to know I can make you want like that, to make you forget everything, where you are, who you are."

"Now you know."

"Yes, now I know." She shifted, pulling the sheet up to cover them. "I might get crazy with this new power."

Steen smiled and kissed her lightly. "I'll risk it."

Sighing contentedly, Frankie settled her head more comfortably on the pillow. "I still don't understand why you were outside in your stocking feet."

"I didn't start out that way. Red and I were returning from delivering some firewood to Hannah. When I pulled the Jeep into the side yard, I thought I heard a popping sound coming from the direction of the shed. I ran around back just as the roof of the shed blew, boards and shingles flying in every direction." He shook his head. "What a mess."

Frankie drew her knees up, listening intently. "What did you do then?"

"I knew I couldn't put the fire out with just a simple hose, so Red and I hopped back into the Jeep and I raced back to Hannah's. I asked her to call the fire department and then we rushed back to try to prevent the blaze from reaching the house."

"That still doesn't explain why you were barefoot."

Stretching the sheet across his middle, he angled his body toward her. "I'm getting to that. I had one hose against the back of the house nearest the shed. It was wedged in this enclosure and when I moved closer to pry it loose, I stepped on some burning boards. The leather soles caught fire and I had to wrestle the boots off in a hurry. Got my hair singed, my face blackened. Then I went inside to find my other hose. That's where I was when you arrived, searching around in the damn utility closet."

Frankie laced her fingers with his. "I never want to live through another few minutes like that again."

Steen shook his head disgustedly. "My own damn fault. I've been meaning to build some shelves for those paints. I should have known better than to keep them next to the hot water heater out there. But I had plenty of ventilation and it was winter so I figured they wouldn't heat up and explode. Wrong."

"Let's just be grateful that it blew *before* you opened the shed door. And also that it didn't spread to the house." She glanced around the bedroom. "I've grown pretty fond of this cabin."

He inhaled the wonderful scent of her hair. "I've grown pretty fond of you, have I told you that lately?"

"Mmm, not in the last ten minutes or so." She smiled at him, then remembered something and jumped up. "Hold on a minute." She rummaged through her purse, returned with a small envelope and handed it to him. "A little surprise for you."

Steen peered inside and carefully removed her diamond earrings. Holding them in his hand, he looked at her questioningly. "Does this mean I have to get my ears pierced?"

"No, silly. But they're yours. Have them made into cuff links or something else, or throw them away. I don't need them anymore."

He remembered then. She'd bought them herself, she'd told him proudly. Was she giving up that hard line of independence? "Are you sure?"

"Yes, very. I think it's great to be able to stand alone, and I've proven to myself that I can. But it's also great when two people who are able to stand alone, choose not to. They choose to combine forces and together are stronger because of that."

He set the earrings on the nightstand and took her hand again. "Any particular two people we're talking about here?"

"Are you going to make *me* ask *you*?"

He gave her an innocent look. "Ask me what?"

If she hadn't seen his eyes take on that teasing glint, she might have stopped in her tracks. All right, two could play that game. Frankie shrugged, affecting nonchalance. "Never mind."

"No, no, finish what you were saying."

"It's not important." She examined the nails of one hand as if they fascinated her.

"I see." Pushing aside the sheet, he rubbed his hand in slow, gentle circles over her belly, watching his own movements.

"What are you doing?"

"Checking things out." He shifted his gaze to her face.

"I'm not pregnant, if that's what you're thinking. I've been on the Pill for years."

"Would you like to be?"

"I . . ." No blasé answer on this one. He was asking about children before he asked her to be his wife. He had every right to know how she felt on such an important matter. "Yes. Yes, I want your baby."

"*Our* baby. Maybe several." He kissed her then, slowly, thoroughly.

Raising her right hand, Frankie held up her acorn ring. "But not until I move this to my left hand."

Gently he rubbed the ring. "I think we can manage something a little more appropriate. We can consider that an engagement ring though."

She removed the ring and held it out to him.

"What?"

"Ask me."

"From this position or should I get down on one knee?"

She squirmed closer, tossing the sheet aside and throwing one leg over his. "Mmm, I rather like you in this position."

"All right. Francesca Taelor, will you marry me?"

"Yes, Steen Olson, I will." Green eyes shining, she watched him slide the ring on the correct finger, then touched her mouth to his. The kiss was filled with promise.

"You're sure some kisser, Mrs. Olson-to-be," Steen murmured in her ear. "I predict lots of babies in our house, lots of animals for them to play with, lots of noise and confusion. How does that suit you?"

It sounded wonderful, if a little frightening. But Steen would be there, to help her adjust. "Let's take it one at a time. I also have a job, remember?"

"I have no problem with your work. Maybe you could even find time to paint some of my carvings."

She'd been thinking the same thing. "A distinct possibility. If you trust me with them."

"I trust you." He sighed then, looking around the room. "Looks like we'll have to find a bigger house, or maybe I should just build on a few more rooms."

"I vote for the latter. And perhaps get a phone and move into the twentieth century. Besides, the doe would be disappointed if you left her. And so would Hannah."

"Want to stop over there tomorrow and tell Hannah our good news?"

"That would be nice. And maybe we could call Corbett."

"Right. And, of course, Hank."

"Hank? Who's Hank?"

"How soon we forget. The bus driver who brought us together. If it weren't for good old Hank..."

Frankie laughed, feeling giddy. She rubbed his lightly bearded chin, loving the rough texture. "You're crazy."

He moved nose to nose with her. "Yeah. Crazy in love with you. Wanna fool around?"

"I thought you'd never ask." And she reached for him.

"Happy New Year," Steen sang out as he led Frankie into Hannah's ever fragrant kitchen. He gave her a hug and planted a kiss on her brow. "You smell almost as good as your oven, Hannah."

Hannah smiled. "Well, it's about time you made it over here. You could have come back and let me know how you made out from the fire, you know." Her words scolded, but her firm arm around him told of her concern.

"Sorry, Hannah," he said with a wink. "I got sidetracked."

Hannah nodded knowingly as she reached to welcome Frankie. "You're back, I see. And a welcome sight you are. Emily's been wondering if we'd see you again before she leaves for home tomorrow."

As Emily came around the corner carrying her calico cat, Frankie smiled a greeting. "Then I'm glad we decided to come tonight. How's Rascal?"

"Good," Emily answered. "But he sleeps a lot."

Slipping her arm around the child's shoulders, Frankie walked to the living room with her. "All young things sleep a lot. That's when they grow. Your new baby brother will be sleeping a lot too. Are you anxious to go home and see him?"

"Yes, but...but I'll miss Grandma. And Mittens. He's not back yet, you know."

In the kitchen, Steen raised his brow. "She's still waiting for that lost kitten?"

"Yes. No one believes stronger than a child." She squinted up at him. "Except perhaps you." She nodded toward the living room and Frankie. "I see a different look about Frankie tonight. Is she back for good this time?"

Steen couldn't keep the smile from breaking free. "We're going to be married, Hannah."

"You don't say. So you made a believer out of her. I'm glad for both of you." Hannah reached up into her cupboard for her special glasses. "That calls for a bit of brandy."

"Now we go to work on finding someone for you, Hannah. You already cook enough for two. Might as well move someone in here to eat the surplus."

Hannah laughed heartily. "Not me. Some of us prefer the single life." As Frankie walked back in to join them, Hannah handed her a glass, then held up her own. "Here's to your happiness, in the New Year and always."

"And to yours, Hannah," Steen said. "And to your new grandson."

Steen drank the toast and soon it was time to sit down to Hannah's dinner. They ate and drank tea and told stories and laughed while the sky darkened and the moon came out.

Leaning back in his chair, Steen glanced at his watch and saw that it was nearly nine. Early for a New Year's Eve, but he wanted to ring in the new year alone with Frankie. Watching the two women finish the dishes, he thought of the champagne he had chilling, the fire he'd laid, the night ahead of them. Had he ever been this happy? he wondered. The answer was no.

Emily poured milk into Rascal's dish and stifled a yawn. Walking over to Steen, she climbed on his lap.

"I think you're getting sleepy, young lady."

"No, I'm not."

"How about one quick bedtime story before I go?" Frankie asked as she dried her hands.

Emily jumped up. "Okay. I'll get in my pajamas and get my book." But as she walked past the back door, she paused, listening to a sound. "I think there's someone outside."

Hannah frowned in her direction. "At this hour? I doubt it."

"Really," Emily insisted. "Listen." She leaned closer, then suddenly, her face lit up. "It's Mittens. He's scratching and meowing at the door." She began to tug at the knob.

"Wait, Emily." Steen went to help her.

"Of course, it can't be the cat," Frankie said, following Steen.

Behind her, Hannah moved closer. "Of course not."

As soon as Steen had the door open, Emily bent down. They watched as she scooped up something, then turned toward them. In her arms was a small white kitten with four black paws, its pink tongue licking Emily's beaming face. Around his neck was a plaid collar with a small bell attached.

"I knew you'd come back, Mittens," Emily crooned as she walked into the kitchen. "I knew you would." She nuzzled the kitten to her neck. "Steen said if I believed, you'd come back, and you did. I never stopped believing." She bent to place the kitten alongside Rascal. "You can share Rascal's milk. There's plenty."

"I don't believe it," Hannah said.

"It's not possible," Frankie added.

Steen closed the door and joined the women, placing an arm around each of them as they watched Emily with her two kittens. "A Good Samaritan maybe, who returned the kitten?" he suggested.

"Santa Claus on a late mission?" Hannah offered.

"Or maybe just something we'll never be able to analyze or explain." He looked into Frankie's eyes.

She smiled up at him. Mittens was another survivor, like she and Steen. "Or like believing strongly enough that things will turn out all right?" she whispered, and squeezed his hand.

"Yes, like that."

AUTHOR'S NOTE: If you're wondering how Mittens could possibly have survived all that time outdoors in the winter, there is no logical explanation. Just like there is no logical explanation for the magic and wonder of Christmas. Or of love.

* * * * *

Take 4 bestselling love stories FREE

Plus get a FREE surprise gift!

PASSPORT TO ROMANCE
SWEEPSTAKES RULES

1. **HOW TO ENTER:** To enter, you must be the age of majority and complete the official entry form, or print your name, address, telephone number and age on a plain piece of paper and mail to: Passport to Romance, P.O. Box 9056, Buffalo, NY 14269-9056. No mechanically reproduced entries accepted.

2. All entries must be received by the CONTEST CLOSING DATE, DECEMBER 31, 1990 TO BE ELIGIBLE.

3. **THE PRIZES:** There will be ten (10) Grand Prizes awarded, each consisting of a choice of a trip for two people from the following list:
   i) London, England (approximate retail value $5,050 U.S.)
   ii) England, Wales and Scotland (approximate retail value $6,400 U.S.)
   iii) Carribean Cruise (approximate retail value $7,300 U.S.)
   iv) Hawaii (approximate retail value $9,550 U.S.)
   v) Greek Island Cruise in the Mediterranean (approximate retail value $12,250 U.S.)
   vi) France (approximate retail value $7,300 U.S.)

4. Any winner may choose to receive any trip or a cash alternative prize of $5,000.00 U.S. in lieu of the trip.

5. **GENERAL RULES:** Odds of winning depend on number of entries received.

6. A random draw will be made by Nielsen Promotion Services, an independent judging organization, on January 29, 1991, in Buffalo, NY, at 11:30 a.m. from all eligible entries received on or before the Contest Closing Date.

7. Any Canadian entrants who are selected must correctly answer a time-limited, mathematical skill-testing question in order to win.

8. Full contest rules may be obtained by sending a stamped, self-addressed envelope to: "Passport to Romance Rules Request", P.O. Box 9998, Saint John, New Brunswick, Canada E2L 4N4.

9. Quebec residents may submit any litigation respecting the conduct and awarding of a prize in this contest to the Régie des loteries et courses du Québec.

10. Payment of taxes other than air and hotel taxes is the sole responsibility of the winner.

11. Void where prohibited by law.

COUPON BOOKLET OFFER TERMS

To receive your Free travel-savings coupon booklets, complete the mail-in Offer Certificate on the preceeding page, including the necessary number of proofs-of-purchase, and mail to: Passport to Romance, P.O. Box 9057, Buffalo, NY 14269-9057. The coupon booklets include savings on travel-related products such as car rentals, hotels, cruises, flowers and restaurants. Some restrictions apply. The offer is available in the United States and Canada. Requests must be postmarked by January 25, 1991. Only proofs-of-purchase from specially marked "Passport to Romance" Harlequin® or Silhouette® books will be accepted. The offer certificate must accompany your request and may not be reproduced in any manner. Offer void where prohibited or restricted by law. LIMIT FOUR COUPON BOOKLETS PER NAME, FAMILY, GROUP, ORGANIZATION OR ADDRESS. Please allow up to 8 weeks after receipt of order for shipment. Enter quickly as quantities are limited. Unfulfilled mail-in offer requests will receive free Harlequin® or Silhouette® books (not previously available in retail stores), in quantities equal to the number of proofs-of-purchase required for Levels One to Four, as applicable.

PR-SWPS

OFFICIAL SWEEPSTAKES
ENTRY FORM

Complete and return this Entry Form immediately—the more Entry Forms you submit, the better your chances of winning!
- Entry Forms must be received by **December 31, 1990**
- A random draw will take place on **January 29, 1991**
- Trip must be taken by **December 31, 1991**

3-SSE-3-SW

YES, I want to win a PASSPORT TO ROMANCE vacation for two! I understand the prize includes round-trip air fare, accommodation and a daily spending allowance.

Name_____

Address_____

City_____ State_____ Zip_____

Telephone Number_____ Age_____

Return entries to: **PASSPORT TO ROMANCE**, P.O. Box 9056, Buffalo, NY 14269-9056

© 1990 Harlequin Enterprises Limited

COUPON BOOKLET/OFFER CERTIFICATE

Item	LEVEL ONE Booklet 1	LEVEL TWO Booklet 1 & 2	LEVEL THREE Booklet 1, 2 & 3	LEVEL FOUR Booklet 1, 2, 3 & 4
Booklet 1 = $100+	$100+	$100+	$100+	$100+
Booklet 2 = $200+		$200+	$200+	$200+
Booklet 3 = $300+			$300+	$300+
Booklet 4 = $400+	____	____	____	$400+
Approximate Total Value of Savings	$100+	$300+	$600+	$1,000+
# of Proofs of Purchase Required	4	6	12	18
Check One	____	____	____	____

Name_____

Address_____

City_____ State_____ Zip_____

Return Offer Certificates to: **PASSPORT TO ROMANCE**, P.O. Box 9057, Buffalo, NY 14269-9057

Requests must be postmarked by **January 25, 1991**

✂- -

ONE PROOF OF PURCHASE

3-SSE-3

To collect your free coupon booklet you must include the necessary number of proofs-of-purchase with a properly completed Offer Certificate

© 1990 Harlequin Enterprises Limited

See previous page for details